MY KIND OF GUY

MY KIND OF GUY

SARINA BOWEN

Tuxbury Publishing LLC

ONE

Hockey Fans are Special

FOREST

December

HOCKEY FANS ARE SPECIAL. For example, they believe that yelling at a TV screen helps their team score more goals. After five years of serving drinks on game nights, it's a miracle I don't have permanent hearing loss.

And yet I wouldn't want to be anywhere else tonight. As a bartender, I appreciate fans' energy, their loyalty to the Colorado Cougars, and their lofty bar tabs. Not necessarily in that order.

Unfortunately, tonight's contest against the New York Legends isn't going so well.

"Holy hell! We should trade Stoneman!" one of our regulars yells as the boys fail on another turnover.

"Dude, you don't mean that," I argue, because Stoney is a rainmaker, and I know this fan pretty well. His name is Fred, and since he's in here all the time, we call him *Fregular*. Also, he'd *lose his ever-loving mind* if the Cougars' management ever traded Stoney.

Fregular burps. "Maybe. But they should get him some skating lessons! Can I have another beer?"

1

"Sure, pal." Although, every beer I serve him makes him a little more certain he could do a better job than Clay Powers, the best coaching talent Colorado has ever seen.

"Need two more margaritas, boss." Izzy, our cocktail server, approaches the bar a second later.

"On it."

Suddenly, I'm hustling again as more drink orders roll in. That's how it goes on game night at Sportsballs. I'm a co-owner of the queerest, least pretentious sports bar in North Denver. If the Friday night crowd wants to get loud and sloppy, I'm here for it.

I open a row of beer bottles, slide one to Fregular, and then shake up those margaritas. Scully—the other co-owner—works the opposite end of the bar, making drinks and talking smack and tapping credit cards. The Cougars are down by two goals at the second intermission, which means everyone's drinking faster than usual.

When the order queue is finally empty, I wipe down the bar, and Scully checks his phone. "Ah, shit," he says, looking like someone just kicked him.

"Donny drunk texting you again?" I ask. His ex-boyfriend just doesn't know when to quit.

"No, it's worse. Chen has a problem making one of our games."

Oh shit. Scully and I are co-captains of a beer league hockey team. "Which game?"

His shoulders droop. "Tuesday after next."

"*Fuck.* Is he going to be late again?" We almost had to forfeit a game when he got held up at work.

"Worse." Scully rubs his chin. "His boss is sending him on a business trip."

The glass I'm bussing stops halfway to the dish bin. "No way. We have no goalie?"

"Not unless his dickhead boss changes his mind. There's some client dinner in Chicago."

I'm just processing this when I notice Quiet Kid, who's seated right in front of me at the bar. He comes in once a week, always alone. He orders a single beer and then tips like he's trying to make up for something. Tonight, he's wearing a faded Cougars hoodie that looks soft enough to sleep in.

And he's listening in on my conversation with Scully with unusual interest. Like he's trying to catch every word.

"Next Tuesday?" Fregular bellows from his end of the bar. "That's your game against the Plague, right?"

Quiet Kid drains his beer. Without asking, I pour him a diet soda, which is all he ever drinks after his beer is gone.

"We could put Marcus in the net," Scully suggests, not sounding convinced.

"Seriously?" I snort. "Last time he played goal in street hockey, he got scored on by an eight-year-old."

"The boy was talented."

"The boy was wearing Crocs."

Quiet Kid grins, and it lights up his incredible face. But Scully groans. He grabs a towel to wipe down the taps. "So what, we forfeit to those assholes? After all their bullshit?"

I make a grunt of dismay just thinking about it. During our last game against the Plague—which we lost 8-1—our opponents spent the whole game making homophobic comments, always out of earshot of the ref. The thought of forfeiting to them makes my teeth hurt.

"We'll ask around and find a sub for Chen." But we both know it's a long shot. Nobody will want to sub in against the Plague. They play like they're trying to make up for having tiny penises. Lots of sharp elbows and obnoxious chirps.

Fregular slams down his empty bottle. "Hey! Forest! You seeing this shit? Third line's a disaster!"

As I turn to deal with him, I catch something odd cross Quiet Kid's face, like he's gathering courage to say something. But when I glance his way a minute later, he's focused on the game again, watching with a studied intensity.

A moment later, the Cougars score, and the whole bar erupts. Fregular actually hugs the stranger next to him. When the noise dies down, I hear a voice that's become familiar despite how rarely I hear it.

"When's this game?"

Scully and I both turn to look at Quiet Kid.

"Sorry?" I ask. "You need another soda?"

He shakes his head. "Not what I asked. What time is your game next Tuesday? I could do it."

"Do what?" Scully asks.

"Tend goal. Unless I'm..." He seems to catch himself. "...at work."

Scully and I exchange a look. The kid has an athletic build. He's all lean, angular muscle and square shoulders, but that doesn't mean he can stop a puck.

"Can you play?" I ask.

"Dude, does it even matter?" Scully laughs. "We're desperate. The game is at nine p.m.," he tells the kid. "Even if you have to call in sick at work, let's make this happen. We could all chip in to compensate you for your time, maybe. Just this once."

"I can't call in sick," Quiet Kid says, shifting his gaze to Scully. "But nine o'clock is no problem."

"Slow down," I tell Scully. "Do you have your own equipment?" I ask the kid.

A flash of humor lights the kid's blue eyes. He's super attractive, with a square jaw and hair the color of a wheat field. His nose has a bump in the middle, like maybe it was broken once.

Maybe he really is a goalie.

"I play," he says. "Here, I'll show you my high school highlights reel. One sec." He pulls out his phone and starts scrolling.

Scully gives me a meaningful glare that says, *Be nice. We need this guy*.

He's probably right, but Scully is the kind of charmer who says yes to anything, and I'm the asshole who says, "Wait a minute while I overthink this."

Someone has to be the grownup around here.

The kid holds out his phone, and Scully and I lean in to watch a video. It's high school hockey, sure, but after watching for just a few seconds, it's obvious the goalie is a stud. He moves like water. A breakaway shot deflects off his blocker like he knew where it was going before the shooter did. In the next highlight, he's down in a butterfly, kicking out his right pad to deny what should have been a goal.

The third clip shows him tracking through traffic, somehow finding a slapshot that I can barely see through the mass of bodies. He makes each save look easy, like he's casually swatting flies. Even in shaky phone footage, the talent is obvious. The kid has that sixth sense that all great goalies have, like he can read the puck's mind.

"You'll do," I say drily, trying not to sound too impressed.

"Yeah, but I have one condition," he says, his voice gathering strength.

"Name it," Scully says. "Anything."

The kid points at me. "I win this game, and he takes me home after."

I blink. "You need a ride? Where do you live?"

"No, man." He sighs and shakes his attractive head. "I mean for *sex*."

Oh shiiiiit. I'm actually speechless at this request. And not in a good way.

Beside me, Scully puts his head in his hands. "Oh God, really? *With Forest*? And here I thought we had a chance against the Plague."

TWO

My Fantasy in Flannel

BECK

MY FACE IS BURNING. I can't believe I finally did it—I propositioned Forest. The hot bartender. My long-time crush. I've spent so many hours on this barstool watching him make drinks, admiring his tattooed forearms, trying to gather my courage.

Sportsballs is my happy place. He can't possibly understand what it means for me to be sitting here. It took all my courage to walk through the door. I wasn't quite sure what I was hoping for. Just a chance to acknowledge myself, I guess. I was actually shaking a little the first time I walked across the battered wooden floor toward the bar.

And there he was—my fantasy in flannel, a tattoo peeking out of the V of his collar, his sleeves rolled up. I've been stuck on him ever since, and it's taken *months* to actually do this—to tell him what I want from him besides a light beer.

When I heard his beer league team lost their goalie? I knew I had to speak up. They need me so badly. So after all this time, I'm finally shooting my shot.

Yay me. Except Forest isn't having the reaction I'd hoped for, which was, "Sure, dawg, let's roll." Or whatever you're supposed to say when you agree to sex. I wouldn't really know.

Instead, he looks tortured. He sticks out one strong arm and pushes Scully away. Then he leans his elbows against the bar and studies me. I get the feeling it's the first time he's really noticed me, in spite of all the attention I've given him for months.

A feeling of doom descends. I'm not good with people, but even I can tell he's about to shoot me down. At least I'm getting a closeup view of his muscled arms. Forest is the reason my search history includes the term "lumberjack porn."

"Kid, look, I'm sorry," he says in his growly voice. "I can't promise you something like that."

"Why?" I demand. "I'm not ugly. And I know I'm awkward, but I promise to shut up while you fuck me. You can even use a gag. If you want. I bet you're into that. I hear you and Scully joking sometimes. He teases you like you're into bondage."

His eyes widen, and he swallows roughly. "Okay, slow down."

"Or wait... Do you need me to win the game first? Because that won't be a problem."

Maybe I should just come clean about who I am. I play for the Ice Cats, which is a minor league affiliate team in Loveland, about an hour from here. I'm not out to my team, so I always keep my trap shut when I'm in Sportsballs.

I don't know, though. If Forest checks my stats for the Ice Cats right now, it might not help my case. I'm in a slump. A bad one.

He looks down at his rough hands, and for the hundredth time I wonder what they'd feel like on my body. "Shut up and listen a sec, okay?"

My body quiets down immediately. I don't mind being told to shut up. Not by Forest.

"You're cute as hell," he says, "but you're too young for me.

Even if you weren't, I don't really do hookups anymore. Not to mention that trading sexual favors isn't my style. I'm trying to be an upstanding citizen, here."

"See, I appreciate that. But it's unnecessary, because I'm literally *upstanding* in bed every night after I watch you work a shift."

The stranger on the barstool next to mine laughs loudly.

Fuck. This is turning into the most embarrassing night of my life. It's even worse than the interview I gave after my first college game, when I told the reporter that my pregame ritual involved talking to my pads in French, which I don't even speak. They played that clip for weeks.

I pocket my phone and grab a pen off someone's order pad on the bar. I scribble my number on a paper coaster. "Here's my phone number. Text me if you decide it's worth it. I'll be a great goalie for you guys, and I promise not to speak French."

I slide the coaster in Forest's direction, and he looks at it the way he might look at a cockroach scurrying across the bar.

Scully, though. He reaches around Forest, picks up my coaster, and pockets it, grinning like he just won the lottery. "I'm keeping this safe. For the team." He winks.

I drain my soda and stand up. My face is still burning, but at least I tried. My coach always reminds us that you miss all the shots you don't take.

Propositioning bearded bartenders isn't really his milieu, though.

"Thanks for the soda," I mumble, pulling my wallet out to leave a fat tip. Tipping well is one of my rules. That, and never eating gas-station sushi, no matter how fresh it looks.

As I push back my barstool, I realize several people are staring at me. *Oh man.* Let's just pray none of them are Ice Cats fans. Maybe I just ruined my sexual fantasies, but it would really suck if I managed to wreck my privacy, too.

I head straight for the door, stepping out into the freezing cold in just my sweater. All my jackets say Ice Cats on them, so I never wear a coat to Sportsballs. I jog to my Jeep and climb inside to start the engine.

My playlist starts right up, blasting a song by the Smiths called, "Last Night I Dreamt That Somebody Loved Me."

"Shut up," I growl, advancing to the next track. "That's way too on the nose."

Most of this album is depressing, though, and the engine takes ages to warm up, so I have plenty of time to stare gloomily at the exterior wall of the bar, wondering why everything having to do with other humans is so difficult for me.

I mean—Forest is attracted to men. I know this because I hang on every damn word he says. *I don't really do hookups,* he'd said, but that's gotta be a lie. The way Scully teases him, I know Forest has had plenty of sex.

My self-esteem slides down another several notches as I put the Jeep in gear and head for home. But the self-recriminations keep on coming. Because—why not *me*? Every time I go to Sportsballs, I see guys picking up. Sometimes they barely exchange more than a few words before they leave together. *You down? Let's bounce.*

It gives me life to see that. Dudes hitting on other dudes. Living their best lives. Like maybe I will someday. But today is not that day for me, and given the streak I'm on, tomorrow doesn't look good either.

Maybe I *am* ugly, as well as awkward. And maybe defeat has an odor, and the bartender gets a whiff of it every time I sit down at the bar.

It's an hour's drive home, which is plenty of time to question my whole existence. I let in four goals last night, and we lost to a team near the bottom of the division. If I don't turn things around, I'll get sent down to an even more minor league. Or worse, I won't get renewed at all.

These are the things I should really be focusing on. Not hot, grumpy bartenders with big, brown eyes.

My phone rings, and it's my mom. Against my better judgment, I accept the call, if only for a pause in the doom cycle of my thoughts. "Hey, Mom. How are you?"

"*Great!*" she practically yells. "We just finished putting all the ornaments on the tree!"

"Cool. What's the theme this year?"

"Lobsters! Ron Junior chose it."

Five years ago, my mother married Ron. He has two adult sons—Junior and Trevor—and the four of them live on Ron's family compound and run a few small businesses in a beach town about a half hour from where I grew up. I get a lot of updates about their lives but very few questions about my own.

"There!" she announces. "I just sent you a photo."

"Cool. I'll look at it later, Mom. I'm driving."

"Did you have a game tonight? How are the Wildcats doing?"

My team is called the Ice Cats, not the Wildcats. But whatever. "The team is doing fine," I say, not wanting to discuss it.

But I must sound low, because she pounces. "If things aren't working, Becker, you can always come home and work for Ron. He's adding a hot-dog stand next to the mini golf this spring. You could manage it. We're always hiring."

Managing a hot dog stand. My mother honestly believes that to be a step up from professional hockey. "I'll keep it in mind." *Especially when I'm lying awake at four a.m., feeling tortured over my stat sheet.*

"Are you coming home for Christmas this year?"

I hold back a sigh. "No, sorry. Our schedule doesn't break for long enough." I've explained this several times already, but she doesn't seem to believe me.

"That's criminal," she says gravely. "Everyone needs time off to be with their family at the holidays."

Do they, though? The last time I had Christmas with Ron and his sons, they watched the ice fishing championships on TV. Is there a dumber sport? Perfectly good ice just sitting there, and nobody wears skates. They *drill holes in it* instead.

I don't even want to go "home" for Christmas. I don't even know what home means anymore. My mom has moved on to babbling about entering her gingerbread whoopie pie in a cooking contest, and I'm suddenly exhausted.

"Hey, Mom? I should let you go. Practice is early tomorrow."

"Okay, sweetie! Just let me know if your plans change, and you have time to come home! We all miss you!"

Sure you do. "Thanks, Mom. Later."

After we hang up, I take a slow breath. I don't want to go home to Maine, anyway. My life is here. I have hockey, and...

I think of Sportsballs and my favorite barstool. Forest's stern face, and his solid forearms. And the truth hits me in the chest like a slap shot—I can't *ever* go back to Sportsballs again. Not after what happened tonight.

Fuckity fuck.

How did this happen?

THREE

Unknown Caller

I SPEND the next night on the bench, watching Henderson, our starting goalie, save forty pucks and seal our team's 3-2 victory over Ontario. What am I even doing? I'm twenty-five years old, and I've become one of those players who never lived up to his potential.

It wasn't always like this. At eighteen, I was a high-draft pick for Columbus. In college, I was a Frozen Four winner and All-American my junior year. I thought I'd pay my dues in the minors for a couple years and then trade up to a starting spot on an original six team.

Nothing went according to plan, even in the minors. First, Columbus sent me to their AHL team, where I promptly got my ass kicked. For three years. Then, they finally got sick of me and failed to renew my contract.

But my stats had improved a little by the end, and Colorado picked me up. It felt like a fresh start, and last season I did some good work, only to slump again this year.

Seven years after getting my draft photo in *Sports Illustrated*, my agent barely remembers my name. I make seventy thousand dollars a year, but my rent is high, my gear costs about six grand a year, and I eat enough organic groceries a week to feed a family of four.

And I don't have a backup plan. Or, well, a life. I spend a lot of time on this bench watching our other goalie play. Then I go home alone.

The buzzer finally sounds, ending the game, and I let out a cheer as a reflex. *Go team.*

Showering is sort of pointless, but I do it anyway. I'm throwing clothes onto my still-damp body when my roommate, Beau "Big Rig" Riggins, asks me if I'm going to the pub with the rest of them.

"Nah, Rigsy, kinda tired," I grumble.

"Dude. Laaaaame."

"Yeah, yeah." At least he didn't say, "That's gay," which I've heard him say before. Only once, but still.

On my way across the frozen parking lot, my phone rings. I take it from my pocket and give it a look. *Unknown caller.*

Forest?

Hell. I want to kick myself for that thought. Everybody knows that unknown callers are always a scam.

The phone rings again, and I'm not that strong, I guess, because I answer the damn thing. "Yeah? Is this about one of those extended warranties? I don't buy those. But I would if you insured goalie sticks. You ever see how fast a composite stick snaps? Like it's made of spaghetti."

"Hello?" says a male voice. "Is this the kid from the bar last night?"

My heart detonates. "Um, maybe? Depends on who this is."

A chuckle. "This is Scully, I'm friends with—"

"Forest," I grunt.

"Right," he says brightly. "You gave us this number."

Do not get excited. If Forest really wanted to see me again, he'd call himself. "I recall. Didn't go so well."

Another chuckle. "I know. That's why I wanted to talk to you for a second. We still need a goalie to help us defeat the worst team in the beer league."

I lean against the Jeep and look up into the dark sky. "I dunno, man. If you need my help to defeat the worst team in the beer league, maybe they're not the worst team in the beer league? And it can't be me. Sorry. Too embarrassed now."

"Okay, let me clarify. I meant the worst *people*, not the worst players. But we'll get to that in a second. First you need to know that the rejection wasn't about you. When Forest said he doesn't do hookups, he really wasn't lying."

"Oh," I say heavily. "Cool. Thanks." But I don't see how that makes things better for either of us. Because that doesn't sound fun for Forest, and I'd also like to have sex before I die.

"And you put him in a spot, kid. He turns you down, and his team forfeits to a bunch of assholes."

"Yeah, that sucks." And yet, it's not my problem. It shouldn't be anyway. The Ice Cats wouldn't be thrilled about me volunteering for a beer league game. It's probably against the rules. Hockey loves rules.

"This team is called the Plague. They chose that name. It tells you a lot."

I snort. Not sure why I'm still on the phone with this guy, but I hear myself ask a question. "What's your team called?"

"It's a queer-friendly team. We're called the Stickhandlers."

I bark out a laugh before I can help myself.

"The Plague, though. You know what they pulled during our last matchup? Their D-man made AIDS jokes the whole game. Their goalie called us the 'Sugar Plum Fairies' and asked why our jerseys aren't pink. Real original stuff." Scully's voice drips with sarcasm. "But the worst part was when they started in on Forest's kid. Asked if he was gonna grow up to be a—" Scully cuts himself off. "Well. You can imagine."

I grip my phone tighter. "Shit."

"So now you know what we're up against. Don't you want to give us a shot at stopping them?"

Damn it. I kinda do.

"We're having a practice Monday."

"Monday when? I've got... I'm busy until at least noon."

"Practice is at nine p.m. And it's in Boulder, which is a haul. But it's in a fantastic facility. You'd love it."

I don't give a crap about the facility. I just want to stop some pucks, shut down some assholes, and impress Forest. Maybe not in that exact order.

"If Boulder is an issue, I could pick you up..."

"That's not the issue. But what does Forest think about this? Is he gonna run the other way when I show up at practice?"

"No way," Scully says quickly. "He's totally onboard. He thinks you're great. He just..."

"Doesn't want to tie me up and fuck me. Got it."

Scully makes a half-laughing, half-choking sound. "I'm not sure that's even accurate. But Forest is a stubborn bastard, so there's no point in discussing it."

"Whatever," I grumble. "Text me the address. I'll see you Monday."

Scully lets out a whoop of joy. "Hero! Thank you!"

He ends the call, and I get into my Jeep, feeling upbeat, which is kind of pathetic. I'm no closer to getting out of my slump, or getting Forest naked, but at least I made one dude happy.

I drive home to our quiet little house on the outskirts of Loveland and go inside. When my phone lights up with a text, it's Scully again, with a mapped address.

After I tap on it, I say, "Oh shit."

FOUR

Like a Sloth Doing Tai Chi

FOREST

"I'LL DRIVE," Scully announces after I greet him outside my house before practice on Monday night. "It's no fun riding in your truck when it makes that death rattle. When are you finally going to replace that pile of shit?"

"Soon," I grunt, cramming my hockey bag into the back seat of his Frontier. "I'm still saving up for the down payment. And for our expansion." He has no idea what kind of a financial hole I'm in. And I hate it. We have big plans to build an addition onto the bar, and I don't have my half of the capital. I'm not even close.

Scully gives me a sideways glance, but doesn't press it. "But I can drive, right?"

"Sure. Whatever it takes. I want us to have a chance against the Plague."

Another sideways glance. We settle into his car, and Scully puts on some tunes, humming along with the Eagles.

"Did you figure out next few month's promotions yet? I need to put in some orders before the weekend."

"Sure did," he says brightly. "We're having a Superbowl party, so I'd like to get a couple food trucks for that night."

"Sounds fun."

"This will all be so much easier once we have our own kitchen," he says. "What if we just took out a bigger bank loan?"

I flinch. "The interest rates they show me suck."

"I think it will pay for itself," Scully insists.

"Yeah, but will it pay for itself before or after we go bankrupt?" I've spent a lot of time with the spreadsheets, trying to figure this out. "Besides, we have a fifteen-year-old boiler and a leaky roof. It's not smart to commit to the expansion when we're vulnerable like this."

"I hear you," Scully says, because he trusts me. "Just let me know if there's anything I can do to move the process along."

My gut churns. "Will do."

We're almost to the facility in Boulder when Scully turns the radio off and glances over at me. "So, uh, speaking of practice. I asked the kid to come tonight."

My chin snaps toward him. "Which kid?"

"You know exactly which one. The cute one who offered to tend goal."

"Jesus Christ, Scully." Heat rises in my chest. "Are you pimping me out so we can win this game?"

"Wouldn't dream of it." He holds up one hand in defense. "But since you put it like that, I have questions. I know you had a bad night last year, so staying off the apps made sense for a while. But *come on*. It's been months, and that guy is just your type."

My jaw clenches as soon as he says *a bad night*. Scully doesn't know the half of it. I only told him the bare bones—that a hookup I'd brought home had run off with a lot of my cash and electronics, including my son's gaming console.

But it was much worse than that. I'm still trying to come back from that experience, emotionally and financially.

And my son? The poor kid doesn't even ask about the gaming system anymore.

Now I want to punch Scully for making me think about this. And for sticking his head in where it doesn't belong. "You shouldn't have invited him. What does he think is gonna happen?"

Scully shrugs, maddeningly. "I gave him a little background on the Plague. I think he just wants to beat them fair and square and maybe show off for you a little bit. If he even comes tonight. Maybe he won't. He said he was embarrassed."

I let out a sigh. Then I ice out Scully for the rest of the ride. He turns up the radio again and ignores me.

Dickhead.

Before I'm ready, the Colorado Cougars' training facility rises before us, all clean lines and modern architecture. The team plays their home games in a Denver arena, but they built this cathedral to hockey in Boulder, with floor-to-ceiling windows showing off the gleaming rink inside. Under the LED lights, the blue cougar at center ice appears to prowl beneath the shimmering surface. The place is glorious.

The only reason the Stickhandlers are allowed to train here is that a few of my teammates are employees of the Cougars organization. Walt and Javier work in the ticket office, and Nicky is in the travel department. They worked out a deal to get ice time a few evenings a month, when the team doesn't need it.

Scully parks in the lot and I grudgingly follow him inside. I scan the lobby warily, but I don't spot the ridiculously attractive blond goalie. It figures he wouldn't show. Probably his way of saying *fuck you* after I shot him down.

We suit up on the bench, because we're not allowed in the locker facilities. I scan the big room again, but there's no sign of the kid.

And what is this weird feeling in my gut? It's actually disappointment. Which is just strange. Hell, I don't even know his name.

I'm just finishing lacing up my skates when movement catches my eye. Someone's trudging along the walkway toward the bench, a hockey bag over his shoulder. Wait... is that him? It's hard to tell because the guy has a baseball hat pulled low over his face and a hoodie pulled up over the hat.

But as soon as he reaches the bench, he throws down the bag and whips off both the head gear and the hoodie. My chest fizzes weirdly when I get a glimpse of the shape of his pecs under his compression shirt.

He is, as Scully pointed out, exactly my type. Tall. Lean body. Blue eyes.

Ignoring all our stares, he starts pulling on pads.

"Who's this?" asks Javier, our center. "Got a name, kid?"

"It's, um, James." He pulls on his goalie mask—light blue with the Ice Cats logo on the side. Interesting. Kid must be a Cats fan. I've never been to an Ice Cats game, but I hear it's a good time.

"Good of you to come, James," Scully says, grinning. "Thanks for practicing with us. If it goes well, you think you can make it to the game Tuesday?"

"Yeah. Sure. It's not *here*, is it?"

"Unfortunately, no. It's at a high school rink in North Denver."

"Oh, awesome," he says. "Let's kill those fuckers." He rises off the bench, all six-foot-several inches of him.

And what follows is the most surreal practice of my life. James is easily the best goalie we've ever had on the ice. Not only does he stop every shot, but his chirpy feedback during the scrimmage is both weird and perfect.

"Your release is too slow," he tells Javier after a save. "Like a sloth doing tai chi. Try moving your lower hand down the stick."

To Randy, our defenseman: "You're screening me worse than my roommate watching porn with the volume up. Two steps to your left and we're golden."

And to me, after I try to go five-hole: "That was predictable. Like ordering vanilla ice cream at Baskin Robbins. They have thirty-one flavors for a reason, Forest."

I can't decide if I want to strangle him or kiss him.

But the hour flies by, and when Scully blows the whistle to end our practice, I have the weirdest feeling in my chest. It's *optimism*.

We might actually have a chance against the Plague.

Like an Ad for Cheap Menswear

I WOULDN'T SAY the Stickhandlers are a *good* team. They couldn't score on the Ice Cats even on their best day.

But they try hard. And they have *fun*. Seems like a weird thing to notice, but it's true. These guys laugh after every play. They're taking it seriously, but only up to a point.

I'd honestly forgotten what that's like.

It shouldn't really come as any surprise that Forest is their best skater. He's a defenseman, which totally fits his personality. And he plays hockey the same way he tends bar—with this quiet intensity that makes everything around him run smoother. He's not flashy, but he's always exactly where he needs to be. He uses his size to his advantage, and watching him use that big body to protect the puck, all controlled power and solid muscle, makes my stomach do things that have nothing to do with hockey.

I just want to strip him down and show my appreciation in some highly specific ways. Is that really too much to ask?

Apparently, it is.

Practice ends before I'm ready, and as soon as my ass hits the bench, I start shucking off my sweaty pads. I need to get out of this building before anyone sees me. It's not like I know everyone in the Cougars organization, but I've been to goalie clinics and training camps here.

My whole goal in life is to get back into this building for good. But that can only happen if I play some better hockey.

It takes a while to pack up goalie gear, and by the time I've put on my hoodie and my cap again, some of the guys are already streaming toward the lobby. Sadly, Forest isn't one of them. I feel him waiting for me, so I hustle away from the bench area.

Unfortunately, he's hot on my heels. "James, hold up a second."

"No can do. I gotta..." My brain glitches as I try to think of an obligation I might have on a weeknight after ten p.m. "Wash my car." Even I wince after that comes out of my mouth.

Forest catches up to me easily, because the guy is fit. He steps in front of me, blocking my path. "You can do that in a minute. I just wanted to say I appreciate what you're doing, but..."

"Yeah, I got the message already," I grumble. "Don't worry."

"Kid, it's not you."

"Sure. I totally believe you. Maybe you could stop calling me *kid*, though. 'Too young for me' is a dumb excuse, by the way. Like, penguins mate for life and nobody tells them they're too young. They just waddle around being all committed and stuff." Oh God, why did I say that? Why do I always say things?

"Ki—" He catches himself. "James, it's *really* not you."

"Sure. Right." I sidestep him and accelerate toward the lobby. And, fuck, as I step through the doors, I remember there's a poster on the wall with my face on it. Not just my face—it's a promotional flyer for the Ice Cats, and four of us are featured in our game-day suits. It looks like an ad for cheap menswear. I'm careful not to make eye contact with it as I enter the lobby.

The exterior doors are in sight, and I lengthen my stride. But then the impossible happens—Clay Powers, head coach of the Colorado Cougars, struts into the lobby from an adjacent hallway, wearing Cougars workout gear, a puffer vest, and a duffel bag over his shoulder. There's a beautiful gym in this building, and he probably got a workout in before heading home for the night.

I keep my head down, but it doesn't work, because Forest draws an audible breath. "*Coach Powers*," he stage whispers.

Of fucking course, Forest recognizes him. Powers is something of a legend at Sportsballs for the way he supported his player Hudson Newgate when he came out last year. Besides, the guy's handsome face shines out in HD from every screen in the bar on game nights.

I've only spent snippets of time with Powers, but he's always been a gentleman and far better at peopleing than I ever will be. Which is why he stops to acknowledge Forest. "Hey, you're the bartender from Sportsballs. I remember you. Good practice?"

"The best!" Forest booms. When he smiles, it totally changes his face. "Thanks again for letting us use your ice."

Powers smiles back at him. "Our pleasure." Then his polite gaze shifts to me, and he does a double take. "Beck? Is that you under there?"

Fuck! "Hello, Coach. I'm just, um... It's a little volunteer work. Before I wash my car." Oh God. That was fumbly, even for me.

Coach gives me a quizzical smile. "Nice. So generous. How are things going for you this season?"

"Great!" I say, in spite of mountains of evidence to the contrary. "Getting my legs under me. Gonna have a strong January."

"Happy to hear that," he says, slapping my shoulder. Then he gives us both a wave and heads outside.

I sag. "Shit."

Scully skids to a stop beside us. "Something wrong, boys? That was a great practice."

"Yeah, it was." Forest points at me. "Until Coach Powers stopped by to say hi to this guy. What are you not telling us? Who's *Beck*?"

"I am," I mumble.

"Then who's *James*?"

"Also me." I sigh. "Becker James."

"Becker James," Sully says slowly. "I've heard that name before. You're the backup goalie for the Ice Cats in Loveland? That must be why your face is on that wall." He points at the poster, and I sigh again.

"No shit?" Forest says, dropping his hockey bag. "Really, kid? What the hell have you been doing in my bar?"

"Dunno, man. The same thing as everyone else in your bar?"

He squints at me like it doesn't quite compute. "Then what are you doing here *tonight*? Is this a joke to you?"

"*No*, asshole," I snap. "Just playing some hockey and shutting down some idiots. You're the one who's making it weird."

Scully chuckles. "Kinda true."

Forest turns on his friend. "Is it even legal for him to play for us?"

Scully rubs his chin. "Pretty sure there aren't hockey police, Forrester."

"Forrester?" I squint at my favorite bartender. "You have two names, too? Alert the media."

Scully claps him on the shoulder. "Seth Forrester. Forest is just a nickname."

Seth Forrester. I like it. I like everything about him, even though he never misses an opportunity to shut me down.

Is there such a thing as having a kink for hot bartenders who hate me? Must be.

"Now that we know who everyone is," Scully says patiently.

"Why don't you stop making that angry face, Forest? Jesus. We're going to give the Plague the smackdown they deserve. Everything is right with the world."

He sighs. "All right. Sorry." He picks up his bag. "You're not going to get in trouble with your team?" he asks me.

"Not if we don't tell them," I say. "Nobody has to know. Unless the Plague all have Ice Cats season tickets, and also a special fan club for goalies who don't get a lot of playing time."

Forest's expression softens just a little. "They're mostly based in Centennial, so you're probably in the clear."

"Good to know." I head for the doors and out into the night.

"See you next Tuesday!" Scully yells after me. But I don't even turn around.

SIX

Why Don't You Make Yourself at Home

FOREST

SCULLY DRIVES ME HOME, parking his truck in my driveway even though I haven't asked him in. Still, he pulls a six-pack out of the back seat and follows me inside.

It's good beer too. Almost like he knew I'd be a grumpy idiot after he recruited Becker James to our practice.

"Why don't you make yourself at home?" I ask, after he's already plonked on my couch, put his feet on my coffee table, and opened two beers.

"I think I will. Cheers." He hands me a can, then picks up my TV remote and starts flipping channels.

I pull out my phone and do the only obvious thing, which is to search the Ice Cats, specifically a certain hot goalie. And there he is, his blue eyes staring out at me from their roster page. He wasn't lying when he said his save percentage was a little shaky this season.

Some more browsing provides a few extra details. Becker James—all six feet three, hundred-ninety-five pounds of him— has been banging around in the AHL for a few years. That's got to be a hard life. His schedule is brutal. This weekend his team is

27

playing back-to-back games in Abbotsford. I don't even know where that is, but the internet thinks it's in British Columbia.

Then I google "Ice Cats gay player" and come up empty. The team hosts a Pride Night once a year, but as far as I can tell, Becker James isn't out. At least not to the media. And maybe not at all. When I picture him at my bar, nursing his one beer, I see a lonely guy.

I mean—once a week the guy drives an hour to drink a single beer in front of me, before driving home alone again. I've never seen him pick up at my bar.

Scully glances at me. "Whatcha doing."

"Never mind, you nosy bastard."

My best friend and business partner laughs. "You looked up the kid, right?"

"Fuck off."

He howls.

"He's twenty-five years old," I say. "Almost twenty-six."

Scully nods. "Old enough to know what he wants. Which is you."

I sigh.

He says, "Just...thank the guy for coming out tonight, would you? He didn't have to. It would be the friendly thing to do."

"Since when have I been friendly?"

"Not lately, that's for damn sure."

"I have my reasons," I grumble.

"Do you, though?" he asks. "Seeing as I'm your best bud, and I don't know what those reasons are, it's kinda hard to take it on faith."

This lands, and I feel a stab of guilt. Scully is always there for me. "Some things just aren't easy to share."

He shakes his head. "Okay. Just don't take your pain out on Becker James. He doesn't deserve your rage."

I finger the edges of my phone. "What's his damn number?"

Scully chuckles and reaches for his phone.

FOREST

Hey, it's Seth Forrester. Got your number from
Scully. Sorry if I was short with you after
practice. Thanks for coming out tonight in the
cold.

BECK

NP. It's not even that cold. Winter is objectively
the best season because you can always put on
more layers but there's a legal and moral limit to
how many clothes you can take off in summer.

Are you always like this?

Pretty much. I get weird when I'm nervous.
When I'm super nervous I start ranking
breakfast cereals by structural integrity.

I make you nervous?

You know you do. But it's fine. I'm used to
being the weird goalie.

You're not weird. You're entertaining.

Still planning to make the game next week?

Probably. Unless I get called up. Or traded. Or
hit by a meteorite.

Hope it's not that last one. We need you.

The team, I mean.

The team needs my goaltending. What do YOU
need?

I'd like to see you stop some more pucks.
You're pretty amazing in net.

Cop-out, dude. I can be amazing in other
places too. Or I could be. If this one hot
bearded guy would let me prove it. Kinda need
to see what's under those flannel shirts.

Kid... Sorry. Beck...

Right. Too young. Even though I'm old enough
to have a 401k and strong opinions about the
proper way to load a dishwasher.

Just come to the game. Please?

Since you said please. And since I want to
crush those homophobic assholes.

Also I like your beard.

Pretend I didn't send that last text.

No, fuck it. I sent it. I'll own it. And please
consider changing your mind about rewarding
me for my service. I have an objectively good
body, unless you hate muscles. If you don't like
my face, you don't have to look at it. There's
always doggy style.

...

...

I have a way of stunning people into
speechlessness. I'll show myself out.

But just consider it.

Okay.

SEVEN

A Master's Degree in Overthinking

BECK

"OKAY," I say to myself during practice the next day.

"Okay," I repeat while showering afterwards.

"Okay. *Okay.* Okay?"

That's what Forest had said before ending our text conversation. The problem is, I have no idea what it means. So I stare at that damn text message a thousand times over the next few days, until the word itself ceases to have meaning.

What *kind* of okay was it? Like, *okay-I-give-up-you-can-suck-my-dick*?

Or, more likely, *okay-I-agree-to-pretend-to-think-about-it.*

A whole week of my life is spent in deep speculation. So, on the evening of the game against the Plague, I try one more trick. I ask a chatbot what "okay" means in this context.

This is the answer I receive:

Based on extensive linguistic analysis, "okay" in this context could mean:

1. Acceptance of your sexual proposal.

2. A panic-induced typo.

3. A subtle rejection.

4. An emotionally repressed yes. Or no. Possibly a maybe.

5. An agreement to engage in further discourse at a later date.

6. A glitch in the matrix.

7. A sign he's been replaced by an alien pod person who doesn't understand flirting but is trying to blend in.

8. A cry for help in Morse code. But just the "K."

Given how unhelpful this response is, you'd think I'd chuck my phone out the window of my Jeep. But I need my phone to navigate to the rink where we're playing the Plague.

And also, I need it to play my pump-up song, which is "Just Can't Get Enough," by Depeche Mode.

On the way, I remind myself to focus on goaltending instead of dissecting Forest's intentions. As if my brain even worked that way—I've got a master's degree in overthinking.

So I sing along to Depeche Mode and hope for the best.

The Red Mountain High School looks like most high schools—a cross between a hospital and a prison. A severely pissed-off mountain goat is pictured on a sign over the rink's entrance. I assume it's Red Mountain's mascot.

After yanking my hoodie over my cap in the parking lot, I walk inside. Their rink is an echoey, low-slung barn with flickering fluorescent lights, just like so many others. But the ice looks smooth, and I feel the familiar itch.

Which dressing room is ours, though?

That becomes obvious a moment later when I find that one of the doors has the enemy's sweater taped onto it. It's a generic black jersey with "PLAGUE" spelled out in a dripping red font. Real subtle.

I find the other dressing room and heft my gear bag a little higher on my shoulder. For this game, I dug out my old juniors gear. No Ice Cats logos anywhere. The last thing I need is someone recognizing me and asking why a pro player is slumming it in the beer league.

For a team called the Stickhandlers.

"You made it!" Scully's voice booms as soon as I open the door. He and Forest are pulling on their gear, and just seeing Forest makes my stomach do that fizzy thing. He's removing a flannel shirt, because of course he is. So I get a glimpse of a broad chest with exactly the right amount of fur on it.

Oh man. If this is as close as I get to Forest's naked body, it's almost enough.

I give them an awkward wave with my stick. "Hope that mountain goat outside isn't an omen. They're actually pretty aggressive animals. Did you know they can climb trees? Which seems like showing off, honestly. Like, pick a lane—are you a goat or a squirrel?"

Forest just stares at me for a moment, then shakes his head and grabs his compression shirt.

Right. Shutting up now.

The locker room smells like every other locker room I've been in—that unique blend of equipment funk and determination. The Stickhandlers are joking around as they dress. They're a mix of ages and builds that somehow works together.

"Boys, tonight changes everything," Scully crows. "Barkley's ankle is healed up, and we found ourselves a goalie who can actually stop a puck."

"Unlike Marcus," someone adds.

"Hey, that child had skills!"

"That child was wearing Crocs!"

Javier tosses me a red Stickhandlers jersey. "Here, buddy. Make us proud."

"On it." These guys feel right, somehow. Like maybe I could belong here, if I wasn't...well, me.

As I strap on my gear, I sneak a glance at Forest. His arm muscles bunch beneath his compression shirt as he tugs up his socks, and my heart starts beating wildly with a singular question: do I have a chance with him tonight?

Probably not. But a guy can dream.

When we take the ice for warmups, I hear the chirping start immediately from the other bench. Real creative stuff about rainbows and fairies. I tune most of it out—five seasons in the minors teaches you that much.

But then one of them skates by our bench and calls out, "Hey, Sugar Plum! Nice pads. They come in men's sizes?"

I can't help myself. "Oh, you're chirping me? That's cute. Like a bunny growling."

The guy actually stops skating, probably trying to figure out if he's been insulted or not. His teammate skates into him from behind, and they both go down.

Forest, gliding by, actually cracks a smile, and it feels like a win.

I stretch carefully during warmups, because I can't afford to pull something. God knows how I'd explain that to management.

Soon enough, the puck drops, and I'm in my happy place. Between the pipes, everything makes more sense. The world narrows down to angles and trajectories. I concentrate on reading players' intentions via their shoulders and their stick blades.

Unlike my usual competition, none of these guys are very good at disguising their intentions. Regardless, they're not afraid to shoot, or to crash the net.

Five minutes in, their captain tries to deke me on a breakaway, but I've seen better moves in juniors, and my glove is there to snag it. He swears—real creative stuff about my mother and a moose.

"Sorry," I call after him. "But your stick handling is giving me secondhand embarrassment. It's like watching someone try to eat soup with a fork."

His face turns purple, and now I'm really enjoying myself. The first period ends scoreless, which seems to really piss them off.

"Looking solid out there, Beck," Forest says during the break.

I light up inside like a Star Wars droid. "Thanks. I'd say I'm trying to impress you, but that would be desperate. And I'm saving my desperation for later." I wink at him, then immediately regret it because I probably look like I have something in my eye.

But he laughs, soft and low, and the sound goes straight through all these pads and right to my dick.

We head out for the second period. Unfortunately, the Plague scores early—a garbage goal off a scramble in front. I should have had it, but there were three guys in my crease, and I couldn't find the puck.

Those assholes celebrate like they just won the Stanley Cup.

"That all you got?" their center sneers as he skates by.

"Nah, I'm just getting warmed up. Like your mom at a truck stop."

"What did you say?"

"Sorry, was that too complicated? I can draw you a picture. Though you'd probably eat the crayons."

His friend hauls him away, which is probably for the best. If I blacken some chump's eye, I'd have to explain *that* to management.

Besides, our fortunes have turned. A minute later, Scully draws blood with the first goal for our side.

"There it is!" Forest yells.

Both teams seem to draw energy off the goals, and the game becomes a blur of saves and chirps. The Plague play dirty, but they're not as good as they think they are. I make save after save. It's like I'm back in high school, except everyone has better facial hair. I feel completely competent for the first time in months.

And our skaters? They're playing like they've got something to prove. With two minutes left, we're up 3-1, and the Plague is getting desperate. Their captain takes a run at Forest, boarding him hard. He goes down, and I'm halfway out of my crease before I remember I'm supposed to be anonymous here.

Forest gets up slowly, shaking it off, and I force myself to stay put. But when the same guy comes in on a breakaway ten seconds later, I'm ready. He tries to go five-hole, but my pads are already there, and the rebound rockets into the corner.

"Sorry," I call after him. "This goal is closed for business. Try us tomorrow between the hours of nine and five. Or leave a message after the beep."

The buzzer sounds, and just like that, it's over. We won. The Plague players slam their sticks against the boards as they leave, but the Stickhandlers don't even notice. They're all at center ice, slapping backs and exchanging high-fives. Like they've never been happier.

It's the most useful I've been to anyone in months.

Afterward, I hurry to the showers. I need to be clean, just in case lightning strikes and Forest lets me follow him home.

By the time I'm dressed, guys are headed for the doors. I would have thought that "beer league" involved actual beer after a win, but our game started at nine, and it's already eleven. They make plans to celebrate tomorrow night.

But I'll be on the road, which sucks.

The parking lot is almost empty, just a few cars under lights that flicker like they're beaming messages into space.

"Great win, boys!" Scully calls out, jangling his keys with way too much enthusiasm. "Oh shoot, Forest—I forgot to mention. I promised Javier a ride home. His car's in the shop." He turns to me with a broad grin. "Beck, you wouldn't mind giving Forest a lift, would you? He's out in Erie. It's on your way."

My heart does that thing where it forgets how to beat normally. "No! I mean, not at all. That would be... if you want?" I glance at Forest, trying not to look desperate. But also trying to look reliable. And attractive.

Forest could totally call an Uber. He's probably going to call an Uber. But then he nods, just slightly. "Yeah, thanks. If it's not too much trouble."

"Trouble? No way. I mean, Erie's on my way home." I fumble my keys like I've never held keys before.

Scully gives Forest some kind of meaningful look before heading to his truck. Like, super meaningful. The kind of look that should come with subtitles.

I show Forest to my Jeep. "It's kinda rough. Sorry." The inside probably smells like hockey gear and desperation.

"My truck is a POS, Beck. I don't think you need to apologize." He tosses his bag in the backseat and climbs into the passenger side, looking relaxed.

As soon as I start the engine, my playlist starts up again. This time the song is "Obsession" by Animotion and I quickly shut it off.

Oops. "Your address?" I ask, as if that didn't happen.

He tells me, and I tap it into my phone before easing out of my parking spot. "So that was fun, right? I mean, watching those guys lose their minds when we scored that last goal? That winger looked like he might spontaneously combust. Which would have been interesting to watch, actually. Like a hockey-themed superhero origin story. The Human Torch, but make it winter sports."

His chuckle is low. "Yeah, it was a blast. You were amazing tonight."

"Yeah?" I glance at him quickly, then back at the road because a car accident would really ruin this moment. "I mean, it wasn't anything special. Just some basic positioning and..."

"Beck. Take the compliment."

"Yessir."

He takes a slow breath.

I drum my fingers on the steering wheel. "So... your place? I mean..."

The question feels huge. Like, planet-sized huge. The kind of huge that makes you wonder if Pluto got demoted from being a planet just to make room for this moment.

Forest is quiet for so long that I start composing my own rejection in my head. *Thanks for the ride, kid, but dream on. See you at the bar, if you're even brave enough to show up again.*

But then he speaks, his voice low and a little rough. "I want you to know that if I hadn't sworn off hookups, you're exactly my type."

My heart actually stops. I'm technically dead for like two seconds. "Really?" I blurt eventually. "That's just mean. I finally met a guy who likes awkward blonds with a lot of dental work, and you're like, nah. I decided blowjobs are overrated."

He laughs.

I clamp my mouth shut and think about what he said, though, and realize I'm probably missing something important. "Why did you swear off hookups? Because I really doubt blowjobs are overrated."

He sighs. "It's complicated."

"Try me."

EIGHT

Like the 4th of July in My Body

FOREST

I'D BEEN ATTEMPTING to reassure Beck that all my fear and bullshit doesn't have a thing to do with him, but it's not working.

"Look, I don't talk about it. But I had a bad experience last year, and I don't bring guys home anymore."

He glances over at me. "So it's like a trust thing?"

"Well, yeah. But it's bigger than that. It was the kind of thing that made me realign my priorities. I've got an ex-wife, and a kid..."

"No shit?" He shoots me a glance that's full of curiosity. "How old?"

"Thirteen. He's with his mom most of the time. But when I invite someone into my life, it affects more people than me, you know what I'm saying?"

His handsome profile nods thoughtfully. I wasn't joking when I told him he was my type. I like 'em pretty and willing, and he's the whole package. And that was *before* I watched him demolish the Plague. So sexy.

"So, you're...bi?" he asks.

"Yup. Married too young. Water under the bridge, though. My wife and I are still friends." *Most of the time anyway.*

"You are full of surprises." He shoots me a smile, and, fuck, that dimple might be my undoing.

"Not lately," I mumble. "Being responsible is really boring. But that's where I'm at."

Another thoughtful nod. "Well, let me tell you where I'm at —besides getting tailgated by this mofo on 25." He lifts a finger to flip off another driver. "I'm a closeted gay athlete in a big slump, with like, zero friends and a roommate whose entire personality is just vaping and *Fortnite*."

I bark out a laugh.

"So, I hear you about trust. Because I'm really bad at talking to people, so mostly I just don't try. Then I found this bar called Sportsballs. I didn't even know such a thing could exist—a queer sports bar. The first time I drove there I was too afraid to even get out of my car. I just sat there watching other guys go inside. Like it was so easy."

Oh, kid. I swallow roughly, because so many of us have been there.

"A week later I tried again. My balls were sweating, because I'd cranked up the heat and I had on some tight jeans that make my ass look fantastic..."

"That's all of your jeans," I murmur. "But do go on."

He shoots me a grateful look. "You know how this story ends, though. I opened the door, and I might actually have been shaking. I don't know what I was so afraid of—a lightning strike, maybe. Or just someone looking at me too close.

"But I walked in anyway, and there you were behind the bar, looking like every fantasy I'd never let myself have. Big guy. Deep voice. Nice eyes. And you treated me like I belonged there. Just put the coaster down and said, 'What can I pour you, kid?'"

Oh, Beck.

"And then you and Scully started talking smack about the playoffs. You said you didn't think L.A.'s second line could mop up the floor together, let alone make any scoring opportunities. And I'd had that exact same thought the night before. Their coach should put down his clipboard and yeet himself directly into the sun."

"He should," I agree.

"Right. Of course. But here's my walking wet dream giving great hockey commentary like it's no big deal. Like you can sit at a gay bar and love all the same things I do. Like hockey and beer, but also cocks. I spent my whole life thinking I was some kind of frankendude who didn't belong anywhere. But I'm not, because you exist."

I swallow roughly. "Wow. Not sure what to say. I'm honored."

"You should be. But I swear it's not like I imprinted on you like a baby duck." He shrugs. "After that, I spent months watching you make drinks and break up fights and take care of everyone in the bar. Sportsballs is my safe place because of *you*."

Okay. Weird. My eyes are stinging all of a sudden.

"So, yeah, that's why I trust you. You're not a stranger to me. And I'm sorry some fuckface ruined hookups for you. I'd like to crosscheck his ass into next Tuesday. Because you should have all the fun, Seth Forrester. You *deserve* it."

I take a slow breath in through my nose as the GPS tells Beck to exit the highway.

Beck focuses on the next few turns, while I try to regroup. I've heard Beck claim that he's terrible with people, but it doesn't seem to be true, because I'm over here in the passenger seat with my soul turned inside out.

You deserve it, he'd said. But I've been living like a hermit. I've been living scared. My sex drive has been zero.

Well, until right now. I'm all too aware of his lean body, and how close together we are, and of the way his long fingers wrap around the steering wheel.

I take a breath, and my body remembers, suddenly, what

wanting feels like. There's this hum low in my gut, like someone flipped a breaker I didn't know was shut off. It's like waking from a long winter. I feel alive in my own skin again.

Come on, Forrester, I coach myself. *He's the least creepy guy you've ever met. Maybe it's time to get back on the horse.* "Beck?"

"Hmm?" He's focusing on the street numbers.

"It's that one. With the ugly truck in the driveway." He pulls up in front of my house, and I take a breath. "And I think maybe you should come inside."

His hands grip the steering wheel. "Like..." He swallows. "*Inside,* inside? I'm not great with contextual cues."

"Yeah, you win, okay? You're right. I don't want you to go home just yet."

He lets out a shocked breath, and it's almost unbearable— this guy who just schooled an entire hockey team, now completely undone by a simple yes. "Wow. Okay. Let's round some bases. Kinda annoyed that's a baseball metaphor, when hockey's the better sport, you know?"

I chuckle. "You don't think we can do sex metaphors in hockey? And here I thought you wanted me to score in your crease."

He opens the door of the Jeep and somehow leaps out in one fluid motion. "Yes. Yes. Do that."

I don't rush. I climb out of the vehicle and retrieve my gear from the back. "Let's go through the garage."

Beck follows me like a puppy. A tall, strapping puppy with a sexy gleam in his eye.

I discard my hockey bag in the garage and fit my key into the lock. He doesn't have any idea how huge this is for me. Because the last time I opened the door to a hookup, I lost so much. Money. Electronics. My faith in humanity.

Tonight, though, I'm not going to think about any of that.

Instead, I herd Beck into my kitchen. "You want…" the words "a drink" snag in my throat. "…anything?"

He shakes his head. "Unless it involves your naked body, I'm really not interested."

"Good to know." Then I add, "You've done this before, right?"

Beck leans against the kitchen counter and frowns at me. "Barely. But that shouldn't matter, right? I know what I want."

Record scratch.

"Wait, you're a…?" The word gets stuck on the tip of my tongue. Because it can't be true.

He squints at me. "A virgin. Like, it isn't obvious? Do I strike you as someone with a lot of seduction experience? Or, like, any?"

My cock shouts, *Noooo.*

Okay, so maybe this was a truly bad idea. Or a bad joke—did you hear the one about the ex-party boy with PTSD and the virgin?

I must be telegraphing my discomfort on my face, because Beck actually rolls his pretty eyes. "What, like that's scary to you?" He takes two steps forward and is suddenly right in front of me. "Everyone is a rookie at some point, right? You must have been, too."

"I suppose," I murmur. But it's hard to remember any of that with Beck advancing on me, a determined look in his bright eyes.

"Maybe you're worried that I'll be terrible in bed," he says as he unzips his coat and tosses it on a chair. "But I know you're attracted to me, Forest."

He's right, and I'm not about to lie. But that misses the point. "Beck, I…" Whatever I'm about to say gets lost as he lifts the waffle-knit shirt he's wearing over his head and tosses that onto the chair, too.

His abs ripple into view, and I can't look away from washboard bumps that I'd like to test with my tongue, and a dusting of sandy-blond hair gathering above his navel and disappearing into his track pants.

"Maybe I'm not that good at reading people," he says, a smirk in his voice. "But you might literally be drooling right now. Besides..." He takes a step closer again, and I feel my breath hitch.

There's a pause. His intelligent eyes measure my reaction, and I see the moment he decides to go for it. Two warm hands land on my chest, and he licks his lips. "I'm shit at talking," he says quietly. "But I've always been good with my hands."

Before I've even digested this announcement, he leans in and drops a kiss on my shoulder, and it feels like a fucking lightning strike. My whole body tenses—not from discomfort, not even close—but from the sheer *jolt* of sensation. His palms are curious, reverent, like I'm something worth exploring. And maybe I forgot what that felt like.

Heat surges low in my belly. My cock stirs in a way that's sudden and inconvenient, because *God*, I want to let him. Want to close my eyes and let those hands keep going and to go wherever they want.

But that's not how this works. Not for me. Not tonight. If I'm going to survive this experience, I need to be in control.

I reach up, gently but firmly, and cover his wrists. "I'll take it from here, rookie."

He blinks, a little breathless, maybe a little proud of himself.

A second later I've got him pinned against the cabinet, my body crowding his. Not to intimidate—just to assert who's in charge here.

He exhales like he's been waiting for this exact moment.

I lean in, lips grazing the curve of his neck. His breath hitches as I tongue the spot below his ear and then a little lower. He smells like shower soap and heat. It knocks me flat.

When I bite the tendon between his neck and shoulder, he moans.

"You like that? Unbutton my shirt," I order, and it comes out sounding a little rude.

Beck seems fine with it. His fingers fly to the buttons on my flannel, and he gets to work. He is good with his hands. My shirt is on the floor a moment later, and he groans as all my ink comes into view.

And I love the hungry gleam in his eye. It sends an unfamiliar zing down my spine. Like someone reconnected a broken wire, and suddenly my blood's running south.

"You see something you like?" I ask, like I'm starring in the world's most clichéd porn film.

The answer must be yes, because he's bending slightly to run his tongue over the ink on my pecs. Sparks of joy shoot through my veins. My body flares, and my brain shuts up, and now my hand is cuffing the back of Beck's solid neck as I lead him out of the kitchen.

"Let's save time and move this into the bedroom."

"Hallelujah," he mutters. "I literally thought you'd never ask."

You and me both.

I usher him into my darkened room, haul the comforter off the bed, and flick on the lamp. The light creates golden shadows on Beck's rippling chest as he lets out a happy sigh.

"You ready to round those bases?" I rumble.

"Yeah, go on. Wreck me." He grabs the waistband of his track pants and shoves them down. "I just stopped forty-seven pucks and took the most thorough shower of my life. So let's see how this is done."

"All right," I say, but I don't move. I just take a moment to appreciate the view. Standing here, with Beck looking at me like I'm everything he's ever wanted, my own desire feels painful in its intensity, like blood rushing back into a limb that's fallen asleep.

Finally, I step into his personal space and run my hands down his pecs. The animal heat of him is like medicine.

"Fuck." Beck tilts his face toward the ceiling and gasps. "Again."

I do even better. Clasping his trim waist, I lean in and kiss his throat.

"Nnng," he says as his hands join the party. Eager fingers skim around my back and then down to my ass, which is still clad in sweats. And just that simple touch gives me goosebumps.

It's been so, so long.

Taking a slow breath, I run my hands over his abs, my thumbs sweeping down to the waistband of his boxer briefs. I use one thumb to lower them by a single inch.

"Yeah, yeah," he begs. "Do it."

So naturally, I make him wait. I kiss his collar bone and then his nipple before slowly sinking to my knees. Along the way, I run my mouth over the bumps of his abs and across the tight skin just above his waistband.

He sucks in a breath as my knees meet the carpet. And then I finally get a look at his very hard cock, trapped inside those briefs. It's long and strong, like the rest of him. Slowly, teasingly, I lean in and run my lips along the tightly stretched cotton covering his shaft.

"Oh wow, oh wow, oh wow," Beck chants, shoving down his briefs and stepping out of them. A porn-star-worthy cock flops up to stand proudly beside my face.

"Christ, Beck," I murmur. "You're beautiful." I nuzzle his cock, inhaling the clean scents of soap and salt.

Above me, Beck gulps for air.

We probably walked into the house less than five minutes ago, and I'm already wrapping my hand around his girth and taking the fat head of him against my tongue. Like it's easy, like I do this every day.

"Just so you know, if I pass out, it's a compliment. Like the highest form of compliment. Five stars. Would recommend."

"Aw, brace yourself, honey. I'm just getting started." I run a hand up his lightly furred thigh, feeling his muscles twitch with anticipation. Then I open my mouth and take as much of his cock as I can manage.

With a groan, Beck curls his hands into my hair. And when I glance up at him, he looks wrecked, his mouth a sexy grimace.

I feel triumphant as I suck him down. Beck told me he needed this, but what if I needed it even more? I'd forgotten how this works—the way that getting on your knees is both vulnerable and powerful. The push and pull. The tension and the glory.

And who knew it would take the most socially awkward man in Colorado to shove me out of my rut? I'm pleasuring him with everything I've got, and we're both loving it.

His legs start shaking, and I can tell he's trying so hard not to come. I release him with a wet pop. "Be a good boy for me and don't blow yet, okay?"

"Trying," he pants. "But the inside of my brain right now is just your name on repeat with exclamation points—like a really aggressive text message. I'm not ready to finish, though. Let's switch it up."

"Yeah?" My dick throbs at the very idea. "Sit on the bed," I order. Then I shove down my pants and step out of my underwear, and we both kick off our socks.

This really isn't where I thought I'd end my night. But now we're both naked, with Beck seated on my bed, his legs spread wantonly. I'm standing over him, and he's staring up at me like he just won the lottery.

I grip the back of his neck and step between his legs. "Go on, then. Let's see how you use that mouth."

He lets out a little moan as I guide his face to my groin. He kisses my abs, as his long fingers wrap around my shaft. "God, you feel good."

He strokes me slowly, and I hiss.

"Okay, I'm going in." He dips his head and takes my cock-head into his mouth, still moving slowly, almost experimentally.

"There it is," I say. Or I try to say it, anyway. The second his tongue meets my cock, my body bursts into flames, and I'm pretty sure what comes out of my mouth is more of a mumbled groan.

Blue eyes flick upwards to mine as Beck clocks my reaction. Then he actually smiles around my cock.

It's smug, but I like it. My body thrums with an intensity that shocks me. He experiments with a lick and then a suck.

"You're..." I try. "So..."

He tilts his head to a new angle, and talking's impossible again. There's only sensation—the slam of my heart into my ribs and the erotic assault of Beck learning the ins and outs of a blowjob.

He's a quick study. As one hand curls around my shaft and the other one cups my balls, his tongue tries out wicked, wicked tricks.

Breathe. I lift my gaze and try to center myself in the moment, but all I can do is gasp and spin out of control in the best possible way. Winding my fingers more tightly into Beck's hair, I experiment with a couple of shallow thrusts.

He moans. God. I look down and see that he's freed one of his hands to jerk himself.

"Hey, none of that," I rumble. "Don't get yourself off. That's *my* job."

He makes a horny noise of protest but then releases himself.

He also releases me, though. I'm about to ask why, when he gives my hand a sharp tug. The result is that I end up on the bed sprawled alongside him.

"Fuck yes," he says, hauling me up on the mattress, rolling toward me. "I want your skin on mine."

I open my mouth, but anything I might've said is lost when he cups my chin and plants a hot, hungry kiss on me.

Okay, wow. Beck is new at this, and also, he can't know I never kiss my hookups on the mouth. I guess that policy has changed, because a few seconds later I'm chasing his tongue with mine.

And who's the virgin here? It's like I've never been kissed before. Beck's tongue slides against mine, and I moan loudly.

What is *happening*?

NINE

Like I Know What I'm Doing

BECK

WHEN I FIRST KISSED HIM, Forest made a grunt of pure surprise, and my heart stuttered like maybe I'd fucked something up already.

But now he's rolled on top of me, and he's diving back into my mouth like he's reenacting a scene from *Finding Nemo*. I almost pass out from excitement. I tug on his hair like I own him, like I know what I'm doing. Which I absolutely do not.

Miraculously, he moans, and the sound vibrates through my entire body as we merge into another blistering kiss.

Honestly, all those hours I've spent daydreaming about blowjobs were off base. It turns out that kissing feels even better —like blocking an overtime goal while simultaneously being hit by lightning.

It gets even more intense when he settles over me, pushing me down into the bed like I'm a panini in a press. And the scrape of his dick against mine gets me so hot that I'm shamelessly rolling my hips beneath his. I should probably be embarrassed about how desperate I am, but I crossed the line of dignity about three exits back on the highway.

Forest jerks his mouth away, grabs my wrists, and lifts them over my head. "Ease up. Didn't I warn you not to get off without me?"

My balls throb in protest. "Is it gonna happen, like, soon, though?" I pant. "Team bus leaves for the airport at six a.m., so I've got a full itinerary planned for tonight—at least two orgasms, awkward post-sex small talk, find my pants, drive home..."

He smashes his mouth against mine again, so it's hard to know what he thinks of my plans. I lose myself in deep, slow kisses and faster, rougher ones. He sets the pace. And the whole time, the beard that's starred in approximately ninety-four percent of my dreams tickles my neck, giving me fresh goose-bumps each time he changes the angle.

When we come up for air, I blink up at him, wondering how I got so lucky.

But he has other things on his mind, like pressing one of his palms across my mouth. "Lick this," he commands.

There's a brand-new moment for my spank bank as I lick his palm, and then he swans his thumb into my mouth and commands me to suck that, too.

I'm unclear on the point of this, unless it's just to raise my body temperature another few degrees with the bossy tone of his voice. But then he drops that slicked hand between our bodies, taking both our cocks in hand at the same time.

Oh.

Oh.

"Fuck," I whine. "I need to—"

"I know what you need," he growls. "Because I need it too. Come all over me, and you'll take me with you."

It happens so fast that I gasp. The first wave of pleasure barrels through me, and I'm flying. Hot seed coats Forest's hand and both our cocks a half second later.

"Fuck," he says through a clenched jaw, and then I feel him

shudder. I grab his head and fuse his mouth to mine, and we ride out the orgasm, groaning in stereo into each other's mouths.

When Forest finally breaks our kiss a minute later, my head is full of peace and static. I've become one with the universe, and also with his hot body. Which is why I'm startled a moment later when he rolls off of me.

"One sec," he says, and I'm too blissed out to reply.

I hear water running somewhere before he returns with something warm and damp that is gently mopped across my body. It feels nice, but I don't comment on it. Instead, I focus on the more important information. "I just need a minute," I slur. "I have, like, no refractory period."

"Yeah, that makes one of us," he says with a chuckle.

"Hmm," I say thoughtfully. "We'll see."

"Will we?"

"I need you to fuck me," I insist.

"If you say so."

"Oh, I do. It's honestly unfair the way you kept all that talent hidden under your grumpy bartender persona. We could have been doing this the whole time."

He snorts. "I'd argue, but I don't enjoy sounding like a hypocrite."

I grin, but my eyelids are heavy. "Just give me a minute," I mumble.

And then I fall asleep like a dead man.

TEN

Like a Damn Rookie

FOREST

AT FIRST, I notice the sunlight against my eyelids, like I've forgotten to close the drapes. And then I clock how heavy my body feels. How pleasantly worn out, from a blissful night of...

I jolt awake, panic surging through me like an electrical current.

I invited a guy into my house. I *fell asleep* when he was still here.

In my *bed*.

I sit up so fast my vision blurs at the edges. The sheets beside me are rumpled but empty. The clock reads 10:14 a.m. Images from last night flood my brain—Beck's lean body, his ravenous kisses.

My heart hammers against my ribs as I scan the room. Nothing seems out of place. But that's how it started last time. Everything looked normal until it wasn't.

I swing my legs over the side of the bed. The silence in the house feels oppressive, threatening. I strain to listen for any sound that doesn't belong—footsteps, breathing, anything.

"Beck?" I call out, my voice rougher than I expect.

No answer.

I snatch up my sweatpants from the floor, hands trembling slightly as I pat the pockets. My wallet is still there. I pull it out, count the cash. Same as it was last night, and my credit cards are in place.

But wait. Where's my phone? My heart punches my ribcage when I don't spot it.

On that shitty night that I try not to think about, the guy drugged me and then used my phone to transfer money out of my accounts, before he stole everything of value in the house.

I need my damn phone.

Moving quickly through the hallway, I glance into Charlie's empty room. It's untouched. The bathroom is exactly as I left it.

In the living room, nothing has been moved. The shitty replacement TV is still on the wall. But where the hell is my phone?

I practically sprint to the kitchen, relief washing over me when I see it on the counter, right where I left it. I grab it, punching in my code with an unsteady finger. My banking app opens without asking for additional verification. The balance is unchanged.

I let out a long, shaky breath, sinking into a kitchen chair.

My eyes land on something I missed in my frantic inventory —a plate on the counter with breadcrumbs scattered across its surface. Beside it, there's a folded paper towel with scrawled handwriting that says, *Stole a PB&J. Sorry!*

I drop my head into my hands, and the breath I let out is almost a sob.

Jesus Christ, what's wrong with me? Beck isn't some rando off the internet. Rationally, I know he wasn't running some kind of long con to clean me out again.

The shame hits me, thick and suffocating. I'm not okay. I've spent the last ten minutes freaking out over a guy who was kind enough to leave a note about a peanut butter sandwich.

My phone buzzes on the counter—a text from Scully.

> So? How'd it go with goalie boy? Don't spare
> the details.

I stare at the message, not sure how to respond. How do I explain that the sex was incredible, that Beck was hot and eager, that I slept better with him than I have in months—and that I just spent ten minutes in a full-blown panic attack because of it?

FOREST

> He fell asleep in my bed like a damn rookie.

Three dots appear immediately.

> Bastard. Call the cops.

Despite everything, I feel a smile tugging at my lips. I set the phone down and pick up the plate, rinsing off the crumbs. The countertop still has a smear of peanut butter on it, and there's a knife in the sink that wasn't there before.

Evidence of Beck. Proof he was here.

Proof that I survived it.

I lean against the counter, trying to steady my breathing. I'm not sure what scares me more—that I let someone into my space again after swearing I never would, or that part of me wants to do it again.

That would be a terrible idea.

Wouldn't it?

A new notification pings my phone, only this time it's about the weather. There's a snowstorm coming tonight.

Hell.

I open my bank account and check the balance again. It's just south of fifteen thousand dollars. I need at least eighteen to put money down on a high-end used truck and also buy a plow for it. You can't finance the plow, which sucks.

But with a plow, I can do the snow removal from the Sportsballs parking lot myself, then we can keep saving money we'd pay a plow guy, and use the savings to invest in shit we really want like the kitchen and screening room. And probably a new boiler.

Also, it's almost Christmas, and I want to get Charlie a killer present.

This is what you need to be thinking about, I remind myself. *Adulting. Not sex.*

If Beck wants a rematch, I'm going to gently turn him down. He's fun, sweet, and young. He deserves someone who's free, who can give him undivided attention. I can't be that guy right now.

ELEVEN

Bus to Hell

BECK

BY MIDDAY, I'm at a hockey practice in Abbotsford, which is somewhere in Canada.

It wasn't easy getting here. Hours ago, I'd jolted awake in Forest's bed, my phone screaming at me. My game day alarm is labeled *BUS TO HELL IS LEAVING DUMMY*.

My heart nearly exploded when I saw the time: 5:17 a.m.

I'd done my best to get out of there quietly. Forest is a sound sleeper, though, because he didn't move as I thumped around his room like a nervous elephant, grabbing my stuff before sneaking out.

In his kitchen, I'd made myself a sandwich and called my roommate.

It rang five times before a groggy voice answered. "Somebody better be dead."

"Rigsy! Thank God. I need a massive favor."

"It's not even five thirty, Becks. What the actual—"

"I'm not at home and I need to make the bus." I'd shoved my feet into my shoes and let myself out of Forest's house, sandwich in one hand, keys in the other. "Can you pack my travel bag? Just throw in whatever. Three days of clothes. My passport's in the—"

"Hold the fuck up. You're not home? Where are you?"

I'd hesitated. "A friend's place."

"A friend." I could practically hear him grinning through the phone. "Becks, did you finally get laid?"

"Just pack the bag, man." The car had started with a growl, and I'd swerved onto the main road, pushing my poor Jeep as fast as it'll go.

"Holy shit, you did! Who is she? Anyone I know?"

The "she" made my stomach clench. "No one you know. And I'm driving, so—"

"Was it that chick from the smoothie place? The one with the nose ring?"

"No! Jesus, Rigsy, just help me out here. My passport's in the desk drawer. And grab my lucky socks—the blue ones with the penguins on them."

He'd finally agreed, but not without more commentary. "Fine, fine. But you're telling me everything later. Can't believe you're finally getting some. Was starting to think you were, like..."

My blood had stopped circulating.

"...broken."

God. "Rigsy."

"Yeah?"

"If I make the bus, I'll buy you breakfast for a week." That message had finally gotten through, and we'd both made the bus on time.

Even though I'd saved myself from getting reprimanded and fined, the danger isn't over, because I'm finding it hard to concentrate on hockey. My body might be in Canada, but my brain is doing its best impression of that new concert venue in Vegas—the spherical one. There's video on every surface, and it's super loud.

But instead of rock music, I'm tuned into the sex channel. All I can think about is Forest—his beard against my skin, his hands gripping my hips, the way his voice got deeper and rougher when he... Yeah. That happened. It actually happened.

And when I picture the face he made when he climaxed, I skate the wrong direction around a cone. Luckily, the coach is looking at someone else.

We take a water break, and I flip my phone over for the hundredth time, weighing the pros and cons of texting Forest. Too soon? Too needy? I've never experienced the "after" part of hooking up. So I open up my favorite AI chatbot and ask it another question: *I'm a socially awkward loser who just had his first hookup with another dude. How much time should I wait to text him, and what should I say?*

The little dots pulse as the AI thinks. Then:

Hi there! Congratulations on your new connection! There's no strict timeline—text when it feels right. Be authentic and express genuine interest without overwhelming. Perhaps a simple "Had a great time last night" with a specific detail you enjoyed about your conversation.

Conversation? We barely spoke. Most of what came out of my mouth were sex noises. I probably sounded like a drowning seal.

I try again: *No, you don't understand. This is a hot, bearded bartender who reluctantly agreed to have sex with me after I helped his hockey team. The specific detail I most enjoyed was when he growled into my mouth and came hard all over my chest.*

The bot recalibrates.

In that case, consider keeping your text a little more subtle. To encourage a continued relationship, perhaps invite him to an event that will demonstrate the full breadth of your personality. Like an art exhibit, or an interesting concert.

I lock my useless phone and go back to practice.

During the scrimmage, Coach has me splitting time with Hennie, our starter, which means I might actually get to play tonight. Or I might spend another game watching from the bench, getting colder than day-old coffee.

"James!" Coach bellows. "Heads up!"

Right. Focus. On hockey. Not on Forest's killer tattoos, or on the perfect amount of chest hair that gathers into a happy trail on his abs.

I shake my head and drop into my stance. And it's weird, but my body knows what to do even when my brain is elsewhere. I'm loose. Calm. Making saves I didn't make last week.

"Looking sharp, Becks," Rigsy says after practice, punching my shoulder. "You still owe me details about last night."

I nearly trip over my own feet. "What? No. I mean—no way. I'm a gentleman."

He raises an eyebrow. "Dude, you got on the bus smelling like bad decisions and someone else's shampoo."

"Shut up."

"Nope. Not until you give me details. Who's got you sneaking around like a teenager missing curfew?"

I focus on refilling my water bottle, pretending the question isn't making my palms sweat. "Just a hookup, man. Not a big deal."

Rigsy stares at me. "Bullshit. You've never hooked up with

anyone since I've known you. You don't even go out except to that one bar you're obsessed with."

My heart stutters. It hadn't occurred to me that he'd noticed my weekly disappearances. "I'm not obsessed with anything."

"You go there every week like it's church."

I guzzle my water, mind racing for a believable lie. Nothing comes.

"Who is it?" Rigsy's voice drops to a dramatic whisper. "A bartender?"

This is it—the perfect moment to come out. To just say, "Actually, it's a him, and his name is Forest, and he has a beard that makes me want to cry with happiness."

But I don't do it. "Maybe," I say. Anyone can tend bar, so it's a safe cover. "And there's a reason I go to the bar alone. I don't want the rest of you cutting in on my action."

As if.

He hoots with laughter. "I see how it is. Must be something special if you're willing to almost miss the bus."

I swallow hard. "Yeah. Special."

"So let's talk about my prize," he says, smacking his gloves together and mercifully changing the subject. "Breakfast for two weeks. I want those fancy egg sandwiches from that place by the rink. Not gas-station crap."

"Whatever you want, Rigsy."

We board the bus to go to lunch, and I check my phone again.

Nothing. Forest is probably working, or buying groceries, or doing a hundred other things that hot, interesting guys do the day after a hookup. He's not obsessing like me.

Fuck it. I have to say something. I have to shoot my shot. I pull up our texts.

BECK

> Hey, I'm in Abbotsford BC, which is the
> raspberry capital of Canada!

> Just a random fact I thought you should have in
> your bartender arsenal. For trivia night.

Then I immediately add:

> This is Beck btw. The goalie who stole your
> peanut butter. Not a random berry enthusiast.

God, I'm bad at this.

> I just wanted to say hi, and to tell you I can't
> stop thinking about last night. It's not hurting my
> game for some reason. Made like 40 saves in
> practice today. Coach only yelled at me twice.
> Personal best.

And, yup, my whole screen is full of text. Ugh. I lock my phone and put it in the bottom of my gym bag, so I won't be tempted to keep staring at it.

The next morning, there's still no response. And then Coach confirms it—I'm starting in goal tonight. My first start in four games.

So I add something to the text chain.

> Starting in net tonight. Thinking about changing
> my pregame ritual from listening to Depeche
> Mode to thinking about you tying me up. For
> scientific purposes. To see if it improves my
> save percentage.

I send it and immediately regret it. Too much? Definitely too much.

But then I think, *screw it.* If he's already pulling away, what do I have to lose?

The arena fills up slowly during warmups. I'm tracking pucks, feeling the ice under my skates. My phone is locked away in my stall, probably still showing zero notifications.

Right before the puck drops, I close my eyes in the crease. *Just pretend you're back at that high school rink. Playing for the Stickhandlers. Playing for Forest. He needs you to shut the Plague down again.*

Our opponent has black jerseys, actually. Just like the Plague did. *See? It's the same.*

And somehow, this bit of trickery works. When the game starts, I feel a little calmer than I have lately. These are just a bunch of assholes, and I'm here to teach them a lesson.

Three minutes in, when Abbotsford's first line crashes the net, I track the shot through traffic and snag it with my glove, almost like it's in slow motion.

Then, when their power-play unit tries to thread a cross-crease pass, my pad is already there.

"Fucking right, Becker!" Rigsy shouts after I stop their captain on a breakaway.

That's when I make a deal with myself—If we don't win, I can't check my phone at all tonight.

And it works, too! For two more periods, I'm untouchable. We win 3-0, my first shutout of the season. The guys are slapping my helmet, shouting in my ear.

It's not until I'm back in the locker room, peeling off my sweaty gear, that I finally look. Ten hours after I'd sent my last text, there's a reply.

FOREST

Great to hear you're starting. Good luck tonight.
Hope it goes well for you.

That's it. No innuendo. No hint that he's thinking about me the way I've been thinking about him. Just... polite. Like he's responding to his dentist's appointment reminder.

The shutout doesn't feel as good anymore.

No, wait, it does. I needed that shutout bad. I reply to his tepid message, because fuck it.

> We won 3-0. I didn't let in a single puck. Kept picturing those homophobic Plague assholes every time I made a save.

I wait a few minutes, then add:

> Also was thinking about your beard on my balls.

I don't expect a reply tonight. Or maybe ever. But apparently, I'm a glutton for punishment.

He doesn't reply. And I'm kinda bummed out, but I'm also kinda busy, because we're playing Abbotsford again the next night, and Coach starts me *again*. "You seem to have 'em dialed in, so go for it," he says.

This catches me totally off guard, but I don't get much of a chance to worry about it. Warmups rush past, and suddenly it's game time again.

The second night in Abbotsford starts differently. They know I'm coming now. Their coach has shown them video of my glove side, and their players are chirping before the puck even drops.

"Nice shutout, pretty boy, but you won't do it twice."

But I'm still coasting on the high of yesterday's game, still channeling that weird calm I found when I pictured the Plague game, with the Stickhandlers supercharged to vanquish their opponent, and Forest there on the ice, watching me, needing my help.

Yeah, okay. Let's just do it again. I tap my posts—left, right, center—and settle in.

First period, I'm a wall. Nothing gets through. Not their top line's tic-tac-toe passing play. Not their defenseman's booming slapshot. Nothing.

Second period, they get desperate. Their captain—Holmgren, a thick-necked guy with three missing teeth—crashes my crease on every play. On their power play, he plants himself right in front of me, his ass basically in my face.

"How's the view down there?" he jeers.

"Better than looking at your face," I answer. "Maybe fire your dentist."

He's so annoyed that he doesn't see his teammate's shot coming. It hits him in the leg and ricochets in. Just like that, my shutout streak is over.

I slam my stick against the post, furious with myself. But then I remember two things: One, sticks are expensive. Two, my high school coach always said, "The only save that matters is the next one."

Right. Reset. Focus. When Holmgren comes in alone five minutes later, I read his move before he even makes it. Glove save, clean as they come.

"Fuck you," he spits.

"You're not my type." I toss the puck to the ref.

Our guys feed off my energy. Rigsy scores on a breakaway. Martinez adds another on the power play. Our captain gets an empty-netter when they pull their goalie in desperation.

Final score: 3-1. Back-to-back wins. Sixty-six saves on sixty-seven shots for the weekend.

Coach claps me on the shoulder. "Whatever you've changed, Becker, keep doing it."

In the locker room, I check my phone again. Nothing from Forest.

I open the chatbot. *How do I convince the hot bartender to bring me home again and fuck me? He had a really good time the other night. I don't know why he's ghosting me now.*

The AI thinks for a moment:

Perhaps he's not ghosting you but simply busy. Or perhaps he's a one-and-done kind of guy. Or perhaps he'd like to text you, but he's trapped under something heavy.

Even AI is punking me now. Still, when I cram my long legs into a coach seat for the three-hour flight back to Denver, I pay for the WiFi like a loser and keep my phone in my lap on the way home.

Which is why I notice right away when I get a new text from a strange number.

> Hi Beck, this is Coach Powers from the Cougars. Congratulations on your two wins this weekend.

I almost drop my phone. This can't be a real text. In fact... I hike myself up a few inches and look around the plane at my teammates. Someone must be playing a trick. But nobody seems to be looking at me. Everyone is asleep. Rigsy is legit drooling on Martinez's shoulder.

Huh.

I sit back down again and stare at the text. I guess it won't hurt to reply.

> Thank you, Coach! Happy to put up some great
> stats.

I read it twice before hitting send. But for once I didn't include any obscure trivia or awkward bits and bobs.

POWERS

A little bird told me that the worst beer league
team in Colorado got their ass whooped a
couple nights ago, with the help of an unfamiliar
goalie.

Oh God! This might even *be* Coach Powers. He *knows*. But how? He's like the Eye of Sauron.

Oh wait, some of the Cougars staff are on the Stickhandlers. Okay, think fast. For once in my life, I actually play it cool.

BECK

> Did they now? I wouldn't know anything about
> that. Must have been a one-off.

POWERS

That's what I was thinking. It would have to be a
one-off, because a pro player can't really step
out on his team like that.

> He would never.

> Well not usually.

I cringe, and consider adding, *please don't fire me, sir.* But I don't have to, because the next message from the coach isn't what I'm expecting.

POWERS

Let's have lunch sometime soon. Right after
New Years? Maybe Jan 3. We'll just have a
check in, you and me.

My stomach does a weird, swirly thing. Lunch doesn't sound like a firing squad, exactly. But since I'm me, I'll probably fuck it up somehow. Yet I can't exactly turn him down.

BECK

Sounds great. Just tell me when and where.

I hit send and then check my thread with Forest.
Still nothing.
I squeeze my eyes shut and sigh.

TWELVE

Free Seats are Free Seats

FOREST

JANUARY

IT TURNS out there are only so many back-to-back days of watching his son play video games that a man can endure before losing his mind. And on New Year's Day, I've officially hit my limit.

"Charlie, maybe we could do something else?" I suggest from the kitchen, where I'm staring into the refrigerator, wondering what to make for dinner. Teenage boys really burn through the groceries.

"Like what?" Charlie asks without looking away from the TV. His thumbs move at superhuman speed across the controller. "Everything's closed tonight."

Unfortunately, true. We're also in the middle of a cold snap, so the skiing I'd planned to do with him during our week together was nixed when we both decided that the icy wind was too much.

So here I am at hour eleventy billion of watching Charlie master *Reavers of the Void* on the PlayStation 5 that I bought him for Christmas.

69

On one hand, I hated to buy him a gift that reminded him of what was stolen from him. On the other hand, he hasn't stopped playing with it since he opened it the day after Christmas. "Why don't we…?" I trail off. What could we do? It's fifteen degrees outside. "I don't know. Play a board game? Go for a drive?"

Charlie snorts. "Dad, I'm about to level up my Voidlord to Tier 4. That's like, impossible to do in one week."

I give up. "Right. Of course. Very important."

Just as I'm considering whether day drinking is an acceptable parenting choice, a sharp knock sounds at the front door.

On New Year's Day? It can't be Scully, because he's busy covering all my shifts since I took the week off to spend time with Charlie.

I go to the door and peer through the peephole. Then my heart stutters in my chest.

Beck. He's standing on my doorstep, cheeks flushed from the cold, looking unfairly attractive in a wool beanie and parka.

Uh-oh. I haven't responded to his last several texts. But what was I supposed to say? *Thanks for the great sex, but I have too much baggage to deal with your hotness right now?*

And now here he is, at a not-ideal moment.

"You planning to open that door, or just stare through the peephole all day?" Charlie calls from the couch.

I take a deep breath and open the door. "Hey, Beck. This, uh, isn't a great time."

Beck's blue eyes roll. "Dude, I know you've been avoiding me, and I get it. Message received. But I'm not here for sex. I came here for advice." Even before I can process that sentence, Beck is pushing past me into the entryway. "Let me in. My balls are going to shrivel up, and the wings are getting cold."

"The what?" I yelp, but it's too late. Charlie is swiveling around, eyebrows raised in amusement as Beck stomps snow off his boots in the entryway.

"Hi," my son says, his eyes darting between me and the stranger. "I'm Charlie."

"Oh! You're the kid," Beck says, seemingly unfazed. He pushes a plastic bag into my hands. Then he shrugs off his parka and hangs it on the coat rack like he's been here a hundred times. "Look at that sweet console. Are you playing *Reavers of the Void*?"

Charlie's face lights up. "Yeah! Do you play?"

"Do I play?" Beck scoffs, heading straight for the couch. "I've got a max-level Shadowblade with the Deathwhisper armor set."

"No way!" Charlie's so impressed that he forgets to do that weird, fake smile. The one that's supposed to conceal his braces. "You want to play? I've already unlocked the Void Gate to the Nether Realm."

"Seriously? That's supposed to take like a month!" Beck drops onto the couch beside Charlie, who's already handing him the second controller. "Let's see this."

"Um," I say loudly, holding the plastic bag at arm's length. "And this would be...?"

"Wings," Beck says, as if it's obvious. "Glad I brought a few dozen. I didn't know if you like 'em hot or whatever."

I stand by the door for another beat, utterly flummoxed. What the hell is happening here?

"Dad, aren't you letting the heat out?" Charlie says without looking away from the screen, where he and Beck are already battling...something. "Man, those wings smell good."

I close the door with a thud. This is... not how I expected this day to go. I'd never in a million years introduce a hookup to my kid. That's a line I've never crossed, not even before The Incident. But it's out of my hands. Charlie and Beck are already laughing about something in that ridiculous game.

I don't know how to feel about this. Should I be mad at Beck for barging into my house, uninvited? As I listen to his goofball gaming commentary and my kid's appreciative chuckles, I gotta admit that I'm not even close to feeling mad. In fact, the gloomy day suddenly feels as bright as Beck's blond hair in the lamplight.

Is this progress? Or am I just an idiot?

Shaking my head, I carry the plastic bag into the kitchen and set it on the counter. There's a *reason* I don't date anymore. It's too confusing. I've lost my faith in people, but I'm not sure I want it back.

Yet the smell of chicken wings is making my stomach rumble, and I peer into the bag—hot wings, mild wings, BBQ wings, plus six buttermilk biscuits and a container of blue cheese dressing. So I pull out some plates, napkins, and find some carrots and celery sticks from the fridge. And I pour everyone a glass of water.

When I return to the living room, Beck is showing Charlie some kind of combo move that involves a lot of button-mashing and exaggerated sound effects. "So then you hit R2 and L1 at the same time while jumping, and BOOM!" Beck demonstrates, his character on screen executing a spinning attack that decimates a group of enemies. "Shadow Vortex. It's basically cheating."

Charlie is laughing, his eyes bright with excitement. "That's wild! How do you even know this stuff?"

"My roommate plays like eighteen hours a day," Beck explains. "He's basically fused to our couch at this point."

Charlie cackles and pauses the game. "Are we eating now, Dad?"

I guess we are. I carry the tray in, and I try not to feel too weird about it when the two of them make room for me on my own couch.

After dinner, plus another hour of on-screen decimation, I finally convince Charlie to shut it off for the night. "You need to shower and call your mother. You told her you would."

"All right," he says with a sigh. He puts his games away. "That was fun, Beck. We can do it again, right?"

Beck shoots me an uncertain glance, proving he's more attentive to my hesitation than he'd let on. "Maybe? We'll have to see."

When Charlie's footsteps fade upstairs and the bathroom door shuts and the shower starts running, Beck puts his elbows on his knees. "So, um, thanks for not kicking me out. Your kid is cool."

"He is," I agree, still trying to process the surreal experience of seeing Beck and Charlie bonding over digital carnage. "So what's this advice you supposedly came for? Because it seemed like you had gaming tips to spare."

Beck's face transforms into an expression of pure panic. "Oh shit, that part was real. I mean, not that the other parts weren't real too. I actually do need advice. And I don't know who to ask."

I raise an eyebrow. "About?"

"Clay Powers found out that I was actually playing goalie that night for your team. And now he wants to have lunch with me." His fingers tap nervously on his knee. "In two days. Like, a one-on-one lunch with the head coach of the Cougars."

"Lunch... That's good, right?" I ask, still not seeing the problem.

"No! I mean yes, but also no." Beck's hands flutter in distress. "What if he's mad? What if he asks me something important, and I start talking about how cereal is really a soup? Because I do that when I'm nervous."

I can't help the smile that cracks my face in two. "Soup. Really?"

"Yes!" Beck hisses. "But that's not my issue right now. What do I wear? What if he wants to talk about my future, and all I can think about is you naked?"

"Beck—"

"Is there a way to practice not being weird for three hours?" He's truly spiraling now. "Should I take notes? Is note-taking weird? Is it weirder to be weird or to try too hard not to be weird?"

I reach out and put a hand on his knee, stopping the frantic bouncing. "Beck. Breathe."

He inhales sharply, looking at me with those impossibly blue eyes.

"Powers isn't going to fire you for helping out a beer league team," I say calmly. "And if you want my advice? Just be yourself."

Beck looks horrified. "That's the worst advice I've ever heard. Have you met me?"

I can't help it—I laugh. "Yeah, I've met you. And Powers must see something in you too, or he wouldn't be inviting you for lunch."

Beck groans, flopping back against the couch. "Would it be weird if you went with me? You could sit at another table and hold up signs when I'm being too Beck-like."

"Very weird," I confirm. "Look, you want my actual advice? Powers sees something in your game. You had back-to-back wins, right? He wants to talk about hockey, not test your social skills."

Beck considers this. "But what if—"

"No what-ifs," I interrupt. "Just go, be respectful, talk hockey, and don't overthink it."

"Don't overthink it," Beck repeats skeptically, as if I've suggested he sprout wings and fly. "Right. Sure. Do I apologize for ruining the Plague's night?"

That's trickier. "You can apologize, if he seems really put out by it. But just be honest—tell him you wanted to help out, and you didn't think it through. But now that you understand how much management objects, you won't do it again."

"Okay," he says heavily.

Looking at him sitting there on my couch, all twisted up about a lunch meeting, I feel something unfamiliar stirring in my chest. It might be affection. And that terrifies me. "Where did you get the idea that people don't like you?"

"Because they don't," he says simply. "It's always been this way. I'm a weirdo. Terrible conversationalist. Even my music is weird."

It is, but I don't point that out. I let my bartender instincts kick in instead. "But what if that's your superpower? A goalie has to have a unique perspective. He has to look at the world his own way so he can figure out what the opponent is up to."

Beck lifts his head from his hands. "Huh. I like this idea, but I think you're just bullshitting me."

"No, I'm really not. And Clay Powers has been around for a while. He probably understands it better than I do. Maybe you're worrying for nothing."

"Maybe," he says slowly.

The water shuts off in the bathroom, and I glance toward the stairs, where Charlie is probably heading to his room.

"I know I have to leave," Beck says quietly. "I'm sorry I didn't call first, but I didn't think you'd answer."

My face heats, because he's probably right. "It's not you," I whisper. "My life is messy, Beck."

He gives me a sideways glance. "I really enjoy making it even messier. Especially when you put your tongue..."

I hold up two hands. "Don't finish that sentence."

He winces. "Okay. Yeah. Sorry."

I walk him to the door, keeping a careful distance between us. When we reach the entryway, I cross my arms over my chest and lean against the wall—a deliberate maneuver to keep myself from touching him. Because I want to. Even though I shouldn't.

"Thanks for the wings," I say, my voice sounding stiff even to my own ears. "And for entertaining Charlie. He really enjoyed it."

Beck's eyes track the movement of my arms, a knowing smile playing at the corners of his mouth. "You're doing that thing."

"What thing?"

"The thing where you physically restrain yourself." He gestures to my crossed arms. "Like you're afraid you might forget you've been trying to ghost me."

I feel heat creep down my neck. "I'm just standing here."

"Uh-huh," he says, stepping closer. "I know you had fun that night, Forest. You probably want to do it again, but you don't want to lead me on."

That's exactly right, and the accuracy of his assessment makes me shift uncomfortably.

"I'm not as clueless as you think," Beck continues, his voice dropping lower. "Well, not about you. I see through your tough-guy routine."

"Beck—"

"Oh, shit, I almost forgot," he interrupts, digging into his pocket. He pulls out a small envelope and hands it to me. "Ice Cats game on Sunday afternoon. Four tickets. In case you want to bring Charlie or some friends. I promise not to read anything into it. Free seats are free seats."

I take the tickets, careful not to let our fingers touch. "That's... actually really nice. We've been trapped at home this week."

"It's okay," he says with a shrug. "Your life is complicated. But just so you know, I'm not fooled by the crossed arms and the ghosted texts. You're totally down for a repeat."

Before I can formulate an argument, he leans forward and

grabs my sweatshirt in one hand. Then he presses his lips to mine.

My brain shorts out at the first brush of his scruff against my face. The kiss is slow but insistent, and confident in a way that seems utterly at odds with his earlier panic. My arms unfold of their own accord, hands hovering uncertainly for a moment before one traitorously finds its way to the back of his neck.

And, fuck it. Since we're here already, I slide my tongue into his mouth. He tastes like hot wings and hotter times. I forget for a long, achy minute why I'm not supposed to do this.

When he finally pulls away, I'm embarrassingly breathless. "Good luck with your lunch," I manage to say, trying to regain some composure.

Beck grins, looking entirely pleased with himself. "See? Not such a tough nut to crack after all. Although most nuts aren't. Except Brazil nuts. Those are cast iron." He opens the door and steps out into the cold. "Happy New Year, Forest. Tell Charlie I'll show him that secret dungeon next time."

Next time. As if it's already decided.

I close the door behind him and lean my forehead against it, feeling the cold seep through from the other side. The worst part is, I'm already looking forward to it.

THIRTEEN

Even the Backup Goalie

BECK

COACH POWERS LIVES in a kickass house at the top of a hill. Not that I expected anything less from an uber-successful coach who also dominated the ice during his years in the big leagues.

Yesterday, he'd texted to say that he'd rather make lunch for us both than eat out. Cue a fresh wave of panic over what to bring, because my mom taught me to never show up empty handed. I hope the box of bakery cookies I picked up doesn't seem too random, in spite of the hour I spent in front of the counter picking them out.

Now here I am, parking my old Jeep on the meticulous gravel driveway to the side of a half-timbered garage. Inside is a gleaming Mercedes, as well as a sporty SUV.

I pat my Jeep on the fender as I leave it behind. "Someday you'll be a racehorse, too."

If only. I'm still not sure why I'm here, except to bow down and kiss the ring. And maybe absorb an ounce or two of big-league wisdom.

Oh, and to make a good impression on Coach Powers. If at all possible. Just in case he has a strange desire to promote a socially awkward goalie whose stats have sucked donkey balls for most of the season.

I clearly need a pep talk. Or at least a hug from my favorite bartender. I'm still thinking about that moment in Forest's entryway...

Focus, James. I knock on a front door so massive that it could be used for an airplane hangar.

A few moments later, the door swings open to reveal Coach Powers. He's wearing a Cougars track suit and an apron that says *I'll Feed All You Fuckers.*

Huh. I guess I didn't have to sweat over my clothing choices.

"Hey, Beck!" he says with a big grin. "Sorry to drag you all the way up this hill, but I'm doing some meal prep, and I thought we could eat well at the same time I set myself up for a busy week."

"No problem, Coach. I brought cookies," I blurt, thrusting the box toward him like I'm passing a live grenade. "It's a weird mix, because I couldn't decide between chocolate chip and those maple ones, and then they had these pistachio things that looked like alien eyeballs, so I just got some of everything."

Powers takes the box with a raised eyebrow. "Thanks. Sounds fun. Come on in."

I follow him through a foyer with ceilings high enough for a giraffe, past framed jerseys and photos that probably tell the story of his career, but I'm too nervous to really look. The house smells amazing—garlic, herbs, something roasting.

"Good drive up?" he asks, leading me into a kitchen that's roughly the size of my entire house.

"Yeah, fine. My Jeep doesn't love hills, though. It's more of a flat-road enthusiast." Shut up, Beck. "I mean, yes. Good drive."

Powers laughs, which seems like a positive sign. "Have a seat," he says, gesturing to a stool at the massive kitchen island. "Beer? Water?"

"Water's great, thanks." Last thing I need is to get buzzed and point out that hockey sticks are basically just permission for hockey players to carry weapons in public as long as they're wearing matching outfits.

He slides a glass of water my way, then returns to chopping vegetables. There's already something simmering on the stove that looks like sauce, and a pan of what might be lasagna cooling on a rack.

"So, Beck," he says casually, "first, I want to say congratulations on those back-to-back wins. Sixty-six saves on sixty-seven shots is impressive at any level."

My stomach flips. "Thanks, Coach."

"You know why I wanted to meet with you?" He doesn't look up from his chopping.

"To tell me to stay out of the beer league?" I venture.

He chuckles. "Well, there's that. Though, I'm more impressed than angry that you shut down the Plague. Those guys have a reputation."

I relax slightly. "They weren't nice people."

"Nope." Powers stops chopping to look at me. "They're notorious assholes. And helping out the Stickhandlers was a standup thing to do. It shows character. Not that I want you to do it again."

"Okay," I say, genuinely surprised. "Got it."

Powers moves to the stove and starts stirring something. "But that's not why you're here. You're here because I saw something in your game recently that I didn't see earlier in the season."

I blink. "You review Ice Cats games?"

"When I can. You guys are our farm team. Part of my job is tracking who might be ready to move up." He gives me a pointed look.

My heart rate kicks up. "Even the backup goalie?"

"Especially goalies." He turns and leans against the counter.

"Look, I'm going to be straight with you. Your numbers at the start of the season were concerning. Your confidence seemed shot. But something changed."

I swallow hard, thinking about a certain bearded bartender who scrambled my brain right around the time my game improved. "I, um, found my footing."

"Good. Because the Beck James I scouted in college was fearless. He played his own style, didn't care what anyone thought. That's the goalie the organization wants to develop."

I'm temporarily speechless, which might be a first in my life.

"Two things changed last week," Powers says as he plates up some kind of amazing pasta dish with grilled chicken. "First, your technical game improved. Your angles, your rebound control—it all tightened up." He slides the plate in front of me. "But more importantly, you started playing like you were having fun again."

I stare at him, stunned.

"Hockey's a job, sure," he continues, serving himself. "But the best players, they never lose that joy. That's what I saw in your last few games—a guy who remembered why he loves stopping pucks."

My throat tightens, because he's right. Something did change. And it wasn't just Forest, though he definitely had a part in it. It was remembering what it felt like to stop pucks for a team that appreciated it. To feel like I belonged somewhere.

"Now," Powers says, sitting across from me at the counter. "Eat up and tell me what you think about Desjardins' high glove side. I've been trying to get him to fix that release all season."

"The thing about Desjardins," I say, relaxing even more, "is that he telegraphs that shot by opening his shoulders too early. It's like he's wearing a billboard that says, *I'm Going Glove Side*, in neon letters."

Powers laughs and points his fork at me. "That's exactly what I keep telling him!"

Just like that, we're talking hockey—real hockey, coach to player. And it hits me that Forest was right. Powers doesn't care if I'm awkward or weird. He cares if I can stop pucks.

For the next hour, we talk goalies and shooters, systems and strategies. I manage not to say anything about cereal versus soup, or how hockey pads are really just marshmallow armor. I even make Coach Powers laugh a few times on purpose.

"So let's talk about you for a sec," Coach says eventually, and my stomach drops.

"Me," I grunt. "We've already been over my stats. What else is there to say?"

He gives me a friendly grin. "Not your stats. *You*. We need a strategy to even out your performance for the rest of the season. Where do we start?"

Le sigh. "It's not a matter of discipline. Or will," I say slowly.

He shakes his head. "I never thought it was. In a young goalie like you, there are two other critical factors—experience and belief in yourself."

"Experience we can fix," I mutter under my breath.

He grins again. "Certainly. And there's a reason why goalies are often the oldest players on the ice. It takes time to internalize the game at its most elite level. Every shot adds data to your supercomputer."

I nod along, because it's true. "Every time you level up, there's work to do."

"Right, and you've already shown us that you're capable of that. You just need to do it more consistently. Which brings us to our second potential issue—belief in your own success. That can be harder. You have to be able to visualize the game."

"I can do that," I insist. "My last goalie coach was great at teaching this, and now I visualize the shot like a champ."

"I don't doubt it," he says. "But you have to visualize *yourself*, not just the puck. You have to see yourself becoming a seamless part of the game play. And that means being a seamless part of the team."

Oof. Well good luck with that.

My face must tell a story, because he leans forward. "Beck, I have to ask—is there something going on in the Ice Cats locker room that I should know? Some reason you don't feel a part of the team?"

I play that question back a couple of times, trying to grasp whatever he's alluding to. Coach Tanner is great. Everybody knows that. And the locker room is fine, I guess, if you like bad jokes and loud music. That can't be what Coach is asking me.

And then it clicks. "Are you asking if I'm an outcast because I like both hockey and dick?"

Goddamn it. I need to stop blurting shit, because now he's laughing. "Maybe. But I might have put it differently."

"No. Yeah," I say quickly. "That's not the issue. The locker room is fine." *Except for that one thing Rigsy said...* But no. "I'm the problem. I'm a weirdo."

He shakes his head, still grinning. "But all goalies are weirdos. I should know. I live with one."

"Really?" That's news to me. I flip through my mental Wikipedia entry for Coach Powers and come up empty. I didn't know he had a wife, although the size of this house sort of suggests that he might.

"Yeah, in fact..." He swivels his head toward the sound of a door closing somewhere nearby. "We're in the kitchen! Want a plate? I cooked."

Nobody answers for a few beats, and then I get the shock of my life as Jethro Hale, the winningest goalie in hockey history, strides into the room in athletic shorts and a threadbare T-shirt.

He's red-faced and drenched in sweat. "Hey," he says, his voice breathy.

"Hey, yourself." Coach gives him a fond smile. "This is Becker James, puck eater for the Ice Cats. You may have met him before at one of our preseason clinics."

The legend spares me a glance that registers only a glimmer of familiarity. "Nice to see you again. Oh—cookies!" His attention turns to the counter and the box I brought. He opens it and makes a noise of approval.

"Don't you want lunch?" Coach asks.

"Sure I do," he says. "This cookie is my shower snack. Nuts have protein, right?" He grabs a pistachio cookie and winks at Coach Powers. "Back in fifteen. Save me a plate." He ruffles Coach's hair and then strides out of the room.

Then he's gone, and I realize I haven't taken a breath in, like, a full minute. So I gulp some air. I'm also staring at Clay Powers with amazement. "He's your..."

Nope. I can't even say it aloud in case I'm way off base.

"Boyfriend," Clay says, shrugging. "Or, if we're talking about kitchen detail, he's my freeloader."

"Don't believe him!" Hale yells from somewhere distant. "Who washes the dishes around here?"

Clay snorts. "Coffee, Beck? I'm having some with one of your cookies."

"Thank you," I manage, still recovering from my surprise. The fact that the Stickhandlers have ice time at the Cougars' practice rink makes more sense to me now, I guess.

Coach Powers gets up to make coffee. "As I was saying..." He grabs two cups off a shelf. "Whatever it is in your life that's standing between you and more of that greatness you've shown us the last couple weeks, let's figure out what it is. I need a deep bench in Colorado, Beck. Don't let us down."

Reeling, I realize that some response is called for. "I'll try not to," I murmur, trying not to get distracted by the mental image of Jethro Hale and Clay Powers sharing a house.

And a shower. Possibly at the same time...

Mind. Blown.

FOURTEEN

The Shirtless Men Section

FOREST

THE NEXT COUPLE of days are spent wrestling with myself over whether or not I'll use the hockey tickets Beck gave me. They're burning a hole in my consciousness from their spot on top of my dresser.

I'd love to go to the game, and I'd love to watch him in action. But if I don't intend to see him again, I shouldn't use the tickets. It's not cool to string the guy along.

Beck wasn't wrong the other night when he called me on my bullshit. I still want him, even though I know I shouldn't. He's the cute, sexy, weirdo goalie I never knew I needed.

Okay, *need* is the wrong word. What I really need is to work double overtime next week, so I can keep rebuilding my savings account and buy a vehicle that isn't on the brink of death. And hire two more employees, and switch our bookkeeping system over to a better one and...

And a million other things that demand my attention.

The problem is that I can't stop thinking about him. His calm confidence in the net as he helped us shut down the Plague. His sly smile in the Jeep that night before I invited him in. I've already memorized the dimple on his left cheek, and the way he and Charlie bumped fists after they...whatever it was they were up to in that game.

I just like him, and I can't turn it off. So when the day of his lunch with Coach Powers arrives, I open up our text thread and send him a message.

> How did lunch go? I'm pulling for you.

Unsurprisingly, he responds about a minute later with a long word vomit.

> It went okay! I wasn't too weird. But it was hard keeping my shit together because I learned a lot about Coach Powers. First: he cooks like a badass. Also his salt and pepper shakers are Cougars themed. Even though everyone knows salt shakers should always be shaped like a goalie because we're the ones preserving everything. Pepper can be whatever.

I crack up. But he's not even done.

> And OMG did you know Powers lives with Jethro Hale???? I'm not sure I'm supposed to talk about it. Lives with him. Not as roommates. Like THEY HAVE SEX I THINK.

I tap his avatar and call. "Hello?" he answers immediately. "I didn't hallucinate that. They share a house, and Hale touched Powers's hair."

"They come into Sportsballs, Beck," I say as soon as I can get a word in edgewise. "So yeah, I knew that."

There's at least a half second of blessed silence before he says, "Fuck, really?"

"Sure. We have these ping pong tournaments, and they've shown up once or twice with Newgate and his guy."

Another half beat of silence and then, "*My God.* Do you know what this *means?*"

"Um...?"

"I *have* to fix my game, Forest. I have to play for the Cougars at least once before I die. They're, like, the perfect team."

"That's a lot of pressure to put on yourself." Even as the words come out of my mouth, I know I sound like someone's dad.

"Nah," Beck scoffs. "It's motivation. He thinks I've improved by studying video or something, but really I'm just manifesting the beer league vibes. It's like I tuned myself to a different channel."

"That's good?" I try. But I don't really understand goalie energy, so I should probably just shut up.

"Not gonna lie, it would be so valid if you came to watch me play this weekend. The tickets are actually fire. And they serve those boujee soft pretzels with the cheese sauce that's literally just melted Velveeta but slaps harder because it costs eleven dollars. Absolute emotional damage to your wallet, but worth it."

I snort, because he's right. I love that shit. "I'll consider it."

"Cool. Cool cool cool. No pressure. You should know that goalies perform sixteen percent better when hot bearded guys are in the crowd. It's literally science."

I can almost hear the smile in his voice, that nervous energy that makes him ramble. Part of me wants to shut this down. But another part—one that's getting harder to ignore—wants to see him standing in the crease, making impossible saves. "Beck? I've gotta run. Charlie's waiting for me to pick him up from a friend's."

"Yeah, yeah. Go be responsible and shit. I'll catch you later."

"Glad lunch went well."

"Thanks for asking. You texted *me*. That's almost as big a win as stopping a penalty shot with my jockstrap."

"Goodbye, Beck." He can probably hear me smiling.

"Goodbye, sexy."

The call ends and I sit for a minute, grinning like a dope and tapping my phone against my knee. My instincts are telling me to keep my distance, to protect the fragile peace I've created for myself and Charlie. But Beck keeps finding the gaps in my armor. He makes me ask dangerous questions, like—why *can't* I have this?

I pick up Charlie. And when he gets in the car, I ask him a casual question. "What would you think about checking out an Ice Cats game tomorrow night?"

Instead of answering right away, he gives me the side eye. "Wait, is this about that weird goalie who came over? The one who talked about penguins for like twenty minutes straight and then destroyed me in Reavers of the Void?"

He watches my face, and I can feel myself being read like a hockey stat sheet. Charlie's too perceptive for his own good.

"The one who kept looking at you like you were actual goals?" he continues. "That's why you suddenly want to go, isn't it?"

I try to keep my expression neutral. "He gave us good seats."

"Dad." He gives me that look—the one he inherited from his mother that makes me feel completely transparent. "I'm not ten anymore. You like this guy, don't you?"

I could lie, but what kind of example does that set? "Yeah. Kind of. But that doesn't mean anything's going to happen with him. I just... thought we could use a night out."

Charlie grins. "So we're going to watch your boyfriend play hockey?"

"He's not my boyfriend."

"But you want him to be," he says, not a question.

I hesitate, and then shake my head. "He and I are in different places in life. It's not a great fit."

"You're in different places," he repeats slowly. Like the words are so dumb he almost can't pronounce them. "Like, he's in a fun place, and you're in a place where you say no to everything and worry a lot."

I swallow a sigh. "Look—do you want to go see the Ice Cats play, or not?"

"Duh." He rolls his eyes. "Free hockey and watching you get all weird about your goalie? Count me in."

"He might not even play."

"Doesn't matter. I'm *so* there."

Unfortunately, Charlie's amusement hasn't worn away by the time we get to the arena. He snickers as we take our seats in row D, right behind the Ice Cats bench.

And because I'm not very smart, I offered the other two tickets to Scully and Divina, who tended bar at Sportsballs until she and her girlfriend opened up a brunch spot in LoDo.

I'd been positive that Scully would decline, on account of the bar. One of us is always there on a busy weekend night.

But no. "This will give the new guy a chance to prove himself," Scully had said. "Trix is shaping up to be a good manager, and I'll leave my phone on just in case."

So here's Scully, taking off his coat and eyeing the players on the ice with far too much interest.

"Which one is Forest's goalie?" Divina asks, cracking her gum.

"Neither of them," I say tightly, and Scully laughs.

"That one," he says, pointing at Beck, who's stretching on the ice. "Do we know yet who's in goal?"

"Nope. Maybe we can tell by who's getting the most attention during warmups," Charlie says, because he's watched approximately one million hockey games with his old man.

"Yeah, maybe," I say, keeping it casual. But I'm mentally crossing my fingers for Beck.

Charlie unwraps a chocolate bar from his Christmas stash. Or, more probably, from mine. "So where did you meet Beck, anyway? You never said."

Scully chuckles from beside me.

"Um, at the bar," I say.

"Makes sense. And you said—let's go on a date?"

"He's not a date," I correct automatically. "He was just a regular customer."

Charlie gives me a skeptical look. "A regular customer who gives you hockey tickets and comes over to play video games with me? Dad, I'm not stupid."

More laughter from Scully and Divina, and I sigh. "We met at the bar. He came in once a week for months before we actually talked much."

"Wait, so he was, like, stalking you?" Charlie's eyes widen with interest rather than concern.

"No, Charlie. He was just... shy, I guess." I watch as Beck drops into a butterfly stretch, then pops back up with that fluid grace that's so mesmerizing to watch.

"But then what? He finally asked you out?"

I rub my temples. "He offered to help out my hockey team one night when we needed a goalie. We became friends after that."

"Friends," Charlie repeats with air quotes. "Is that why you got all weird when he showed up at our house? Because you're 'friends'?"

My actual friends erupt with laughter.

"I got weird because I wasn't expecting company." I give him a pointed look. "And because I knew my son wouldn't act normal around guests."

"Bestie, I was the normal one. You were the one who kept finding excuses to go into the kitchen."

He's not wrong. I did keep finding reasons to escape that night, needing a moment to collect myself while Beck charmed my son with video game strategies and his theories on why goalies should be encouraged to take more shots on goal.

"And now you're literally checking out his butt," Charlie whispers, elbowing me in the ribs.

"Charlie." I keep my voice low but firm. "Enough."

"What? It's not like I'm judging your love life."

"This isn't my love life. It's hockey."

Scully finally takes mercy on me and changes the subject, asking Charlie about his own hockey team. While I watch the arena fill up around us, pregame music thumps through the speakers. Beck is in the net now, and his teammates are firing on him.

"Hey, Dad! That's a good sign, right?" Charlie says, pointing. "That he's going to play?"

"God, I hope so."

"Sir?"

When I look up, I find a guy in an Ice Cats jacket holding a tray out to me. "Are you Forest? This is for you and your guests."

I blink.

"That's us!" Charlie says, holding out his hands for the tray. The guy hands it over, and it contains two of those pretzels with the cheese, a basket of popcorn chicken, soda for Charlie and a few beers for the rest of us. "Whoa!"

"Um, are you sure this is for us?" I ask.

"Yup," he says. "Here's a jersey for your boy." He hands me the shopping bag that was looped over his wrist. "And here's the note. Have a good game."

"Omigod! A jersey?" Charlie hoots.

I fish it out of the bag. It's a men's small, and it says JAMES across the back.

"Cool! Hold the tray so I can put it on!"

I take the tray, and I also slide my finger into the envelope holding the note. The moment Charlie's head disappears inside the jersey, I flip it open and read.

Hey Forest—

You're always the one pouring me drinks, so here's one for you. Consider this a scientific experiment in fluid dynamics. Does beer taste better when you're not the one serving it? Let me know your findings.

I hope you don't mind that I got Charlie a jersey. They don't sell very many of mine so I'm basically funding my own fan club at this point. One member stronger! Woulda got you one, but that seemed a little presumptuous. Like "hey sexy, how about you wear nothing but this after the game while I demonstrate my superior puck-handling skills in your bedroom." Too much?

Thanks for coming. Now I have to get a shutout or I'll have to fake an injury and be carried off the ice to preserve my dignity. If I let in more than two goals, please pretend you don't know me. If I get a shutout, I expect you to tell *everyone within earshot that you're with the goalie. No pressure though.*

Later!
Beck

"Ooh, the note!" Charlie says. "Can I..."

"*No.*" I shove it in my pocket.

Charlie and Scully practically disintegrate with laughter. My son passes out food and dunks his pretzel in the cheese. "This is the best, Dad. I'm so glad we came. And look!" He points up at the Jumbotron.

STARTING LINEUP, it reads, followed by a bunch of jersey numbers.

Including number 6, Beck's jersey.

"It's on!" Charlie hoots.

"This *is* the best," Divina says, reaching around to poke me in the shoulder. "Thanks for inviting me."

"My pleasure."

"Puck drop!" Scully announces. "Now we get to watch Beck, and also watch Forest get all clenched up over this guy."

I shove a pretzel in my mouth, so I won't say anything I regret.

About five minutes later, I'm definitely clenched up. The game is off to a weird start. Beck makes an uncharacteristic fumble on the first shot—a lazy wrist shot from the point that somehow squeezes through his pads. The crowd groans, and I feel my stomach drop.

Even Charlie shoots me a look of concern.

"It's fine," I mutter, more to myself than my son. "Just nerves."

Beck slams his stick against the post in frustration, and I can practically feel his embarrassment. He glances toward our section briefly, then snaps his mask back down and settles into his stance.

But the next ten minutes are pure torture. Beck seems to be fighting the puck, making routine saves look difficult. The Ice Cats' defense is hanging him out to dry, allowing odd-man rushes that have me gripping my armrest with white knuckles.

"Dad, did we jinx him?" Charlie whispers as Beck gives up a second goal—this one a deflection he had no chance on, but still.

I shake my head, trying to appear more confident than I feel. "He'll settle in."

When Beck lets in a third goal—a shot that bounces off his glove and trickles over the line—I feel genuine concern. This isn't the same confident goalie who stonewalled the Plague. He looks rattled.

"Dad," Charlie says during intermission, "maybe you should text him or something?"

"What? No. That's not how this works."

"But he's totally bombing because you're here."

The thought had crossed my mind, but hearing Charlie say it makes my chest tighten. "That's ridiculous."

Charlie rolls his eyes. "You're so oblivious sometimes."

When the second period starts, Beck is still in goal. That has to mean something, right? His coach still believes in him.

But the same can't be said for Beck. He still looks shaky.

"We've got to do something," Scully announces.

"Like what? Drink another beer?" We've already crushed everything Beck sent us.

"That's not what he means," Charlie says. "We gotta turn this ship around, before they pull Beck."

"They can't pull Beck," I say automatically. That is the worse-case scenario. I'll feel guilty for no good reason, and I'll be reluctant to ever come to another game.

"Yeah, but I got a plan." Charlie tugs his jersey over his head. "We have to make a shirtless men section."

I play those words back again, and it still makes no sense. Except Charlie is shedding his sweatshirt, too. "Wait. No. That's a *football* thing, not a hockey thing."

"Omigod, Dad. The idea is the same."

"Your kid is a genius," Scully says, rising from his seat. He pulls off his sweatshirt, too.

"What are you *doing*?"

"Dad, let's goooo!" Charlie says, his pasty chest on display now. He raises his jersey over both our heads and swings it around.

"Charlie, jeez," I plead. "This isn't a shirtless men section! First of all, not everyone wants to be in a shirtless crowd. Women—"

"I'm into it," Divina says, popping up to unzip her coat. "IT'S RALLY TIME."

Oh my God. We're going to be arrested, aren't we?

What will my ex-wife say when she bails us out of jail?

FIFTEEN

Chanting Like Warriors

FOREST

DIVINA HAS IT COVERED, though. Literally. She strips down to a sports bra in a shade of blue that's not too far off the Ice Cats shade, and then twirls her sweatshirt overhead, joining Scully, who's now doing the same.

My face is on fire.

"*Dad*," Charlie hisses. "Come *on*. You're *embarrassing* us!"

"*I'm* the one—?"

"Do it for Beck," Scully says firmly (as well as half-nakedly). "He stuck his neck out for us. It's time to repay the favor."

My face is boiling, but I know the man has a point. And another thing? I *used* to be the guy at the party who had all the big ideas. The first one to pour the shots. The first one to turn up the music.

But now I'm *this* guy—the one who thinks of ten different reasons not to do something. The worrier who ruins everyone else's fun.

I've got my reasons. But Jesus. This is a real hockey emergency, and I've got to show some spirit. I drop my coat onto the seat and wrestle my sweater over my head.

"That's it, Dad!" Charlie hoots, jumping around. "Show some spirit. Now all we need is a chant."

"LET'S-GO-ICE-CATS!" Scully yells. Then he claps five times in a familiar rhythm.

"LET'S-GO-ICE-CATS!" the whole section yells after him.

With a sigh, I yank my T-shirt off, and the cold rink air slaps my chest. "LET'S-GO-ICE-CATS!" *Clap. Clap. Clap-clap-clap.*

Man, this better work, because I feel pretty ridiculous right now. A tiger doesn't change his stripes just because a goalie with dimples bought him a beer.

There are a lot of us, suddenly. Baring our chests and whirling our shirts. Chanting like warriors. "This is eighty percent stupid and twenty percent inspiring," I grumble.

"Like most things!" Scully says cheerily. "And look—your boy is about to notice us."

"It'd be kinda hard not to."

But Scully is right. There's a stop in play, and Beck rises to his full height. He pushes up the cage on his mask and swivels toward the sound of chanting.

I can tell precisely when he spots us. Charlie swings that jersey like he's trying to signal a plane down from the sky. Scully's yelling. Divina's got her sweatshirt overhead like a maniac cheerleader. And I'm standing here shirtless in a hockey arena, chanting like a frat boy with something to prove.

Beck's gaze finds mine, and he goes still in the net. Frozen. Just stunned.

And for a half second, I'm afraid we fucked up—that we might have yanked him even further out of the zone.

Then I watch a slow smile spread across his face. He shakes his head, lowers his mask's cage, and squares off his body toward the face-off circle.

He drops back into his stance, and in the next couple of minutes, something changes. Beck looks a little more solid somehow, and so do his teammates, the speed of their play ramping up a notch. The whole stadium is chanting now, as if this is the final three minutes of a Stanley Cup playoff game.

It seems to help, too. Their opponents lose a little of their confidence. They've still got the puck, but they look a little less dangerous.

The next shot comes—routine, low blocker—and Beck handles it like it's nothing. No scrambling, no second guessing. He steers the rebound right to his defenseman and slams his stick on the ice once, loud and sharp.

He's back.

No—he's better. He starts moving like he's skating on instinct again. Snapping up pucks, squaring up fast, tracking every shot like it personally offended him. He even chirps one of the forwards on the other team after a glove save, and I know he chirped him, because I can see the grin through his damn mask.

The Ice Cats score with only eight minutes into the period, and I feel like I'm watching a whole team light up from the inside. And maybe my judgment's been infected by the raucousness happening all around me, but I feel like we stoked that fire. Like maybe, just maybe, the half-naked fans in row D yelling our hearts out for a goalie who needed a lift, made an impact on this game.

Kinda funny that one of the reasons I came tonight was to prove I could be chill about this. That Beck was just a friend. But right now? Watching him move like he's got something to fight for? Yeah. I'm not chill at all.

The real test comes five minutes later, when the opposing team's star forward breaks in alone. Beck stays patient, doesn't bite on the fake, and somehow gets his pad on a shot that looked destined for the top corner.

"Holy shit!" Charlie exclaims.

"Language," I say automatically, but I'm thinking the same thing.

Beck builds from there, making one clean save after another. The Ice Cats seem energized by his performance, and they claw back with two more goals of their own.

Just one goal from victory heading into the third period, there's a rowdy tension in the arena. Charlie is practically vibrating with excitement beside me. Or maybe he's just shivering.

"He's locked in now," he says with the confidence of someone who's known Beck his whole life instead of for a few hours.

"Here, put your coat on, at least until the puck drops again," I insist. And I do the same.

I forget to take it off again, because the third period quickly becomes the Becker James Show. He stops a power-play shot with a lightning-quick save that has the crowd roaring. When a scrum breaks out in front of his net, he calmly stands his ground, somehow finding and dumping a puck that nobody else can see.

With five minutes left, Charlie grabs my arm. "Come on, Dad, you have to believe!"

And in that moment, I realize I do. I believe in Beck—not just as a goalie, but as the weird, wonderful guy who's been chipping away at my emotional fortress. The guy who sent me rambling texts from Canada and played video games with my son. The guy whose blue eyes light up when he sees me.

With two minutes left, the Ice Cats score to take the lead 4-3. The celebration is short-lived, though, because the other team pulls their goalie and mounts a furious attack.

For the final ninety seconds, I barely breathe. Beck makes three saves in rapid succession, each one more desperate than the last. A point shot with twenty seconds left hits him in the mask, knocking it sideways, but he somehow keeps the puck out of the net.

The final horn sounds, and the Ice Cats players mob Beck in his crease. He's just made 47 saves on 50 shots, stealing a win that seemed impossible after the first period.

"Your boyfriend's pretty good," Charlie says, nudging me.

I don't even bother correcting him this time. As Beck skates to center ice for his first star selection, he looks directly at our section and taps his chest twice before pointing right at us.

And damn it if my heart doesn't skip a beat.

SIXTEEN

You've Been Weirder

DURING THE POSTGAME RITUALS, I keep sneaking looks at my phone, in between celebrating, and showering, and my brief interview by a sports journalist who asks me about my game. "Looked like a shaky start, Mr. James. Any reason?"

"The start was rough," I agree. "But goalies are like thermostats, not light switches. We don't just turn on and off. Sometimes you need to adjust the settings until everything feels right. I got there eventually."

It's not like I'd admit that the presence of a hot, bearded bartender in row D had me feeling shaken. Hell, a hockey player *never* admits to nerves. No matter who causes them.

"That wasn't my worst quote, right?" I ask Rigsy as we head to the parking lot.

"Nah, man. You've been weirder."

"Thanks, I think."

He shrugs. "Can I ride with you to the bar? I want to drink. A lot."

"Sure. Whatever."

As Rigsy and I are tossing our stuff into the back of my Jeep, the phone finally lights up with Forest's name, and I stand there in the frigid parking lot to read it and reply.

FOREST

Wow, man. You were on fire tonight.

BECK:

Are you calling me hot? Who started the whole strip tease, anyway? That was a perk.

Would you believe me if I said it was me.

Nope.

You're right. It was Charlie and Scully.

Knew I liked those two.

Great to see you kicking ass, though. Charlie and I had a great time. Thanks for everything.

Now I'm grinning at my phone like a loser.

Feel free to thank me in person the next time you have a night alone.

Well…

I wait. Staring at the phone. *Please don't blow me off now. It's been such a great night.*

Full disclosure, here. I just dropped Charlie at his mother's house. Now I'm heading home.

Holy shit.

Are you inviting me over? You have to be clear. I'm bad at context cues.

…

...

...

Jesus Christ, is it that hard to make up your mind about whether you want to fuck me?

Of course I want to. Get over here before I change my mind.

Yessir! I'll chow down my ritual post-game fried chicken sandwich on the way. Want anything?

Just you.

Anticipation zings through me. I slam the back of the Jeep and tear around to the driver's side. I slide into my seat and find Rigsy in the passenger's seat, staring at me. "Dude. I could have walked there by now."

"You still can," I point out. "Look, I can drop you at the bar, but then I got somewhere else I need to go."

He blinks. Then he smiles. "Bruh! You're smashing twice in the same year?"

"Technically, it's a new year," I point out.

His grin widens. "Still. That's low-key wild. Drop me at the bar. I'll Uber home."

I start the engine and practically peel out of the parking lot.

Rigsy chuckles. "For real, I need to meet this person who's got you all twisted up."

"Not gonna happen," I murmur, gunning it through a yellow light. The bar is only another three blocks away.

"That's interesting. How come?"

I shake my head.

"Fuck's sake."

After turning into the bar's parking lot and pulling up by the door, I glance at Rigsy and say, "Sorry about the ride home."

He shakes his head. "Have a good night, Beck. With whoever."

"I will. Thanks." Not sure why he's acting weird. But whatever. I point the Jeep toward Erie before Forest can reconsider.

I get fried-chicken crumbs in my lap, and I probably break the speed limit on the way to Forest's house. When I finally pull into his driveway and kill the engine, I don't get out of the car right away. I need a minute to center myself.

It's great that Forest wants to see me again, but I'm still the same inexperienced weirdo I was the last time I was here. The more he sees of me, the harder it gets to disguise it.

And *this* time we might really have sex. Dirty, naked, penetrative sex. Even though I don't know what the hell I'm doing.

This is going to be such a disaster.

A knock on the window startles me, and I jump like a cat who just saw a cucumber. Forest is standing there, arms crossed, his beard doing that thing where it looks both soft and masculine at the same time. He raises an eyebrow at me through the glass.

I open the door sheepishly. "Hi."

"You coming inside?" he asks.

"I was hoping you'd be the one who does that."

He smirks. "Me too. But I'm too old to do you in your Jeep. So if you haven't changed your mind, you'd better come into the house before I'm eligible for an AARP membership."

I get out of the Jeep. "You can join AARP at any age. They don't check."

"Beck?"

"Yeah?"

He steps into my space. "Shut up."

"Oka—"

His mouth slams down onto mine.

Ooooooooh-kay.

Oh yeah. Yes*sir.*

I grab him by the sweater and pull him closer to me. His response is to nip my lower lip and then suck on it.

And, Jesus. My dick is open for business and suddenly trying to jab its way out of my suit pants. I jam my tongue into his mouth, and now we're just standing in the driveway going at it like horny goats on meth.

Until Forest pulls back to growl, "*Inside,*" and yanks me off the Jeep toward his door.

This time, we don't even stop in the kitchen. Forest tows me through to his bedroom and shucks my suit jacket off of me. Then he tugs at my shirt.

"Easy on those buttons," I babble. "I only have two good shirts, and I hate shopping."

Forest doesn't comment. He sucks on my neck instead. *Aw, yeah.* The feel of his beard against my skin is everything. Somehow, he's also simultaneously divesting me of my shirt, my belt, and then my trousers.

After those items hit the floor, he cups my ass in his hands and pulls me against his big body. "What do you want tonight? I could just devour you."

"If that's the same thing as fucking me, then sure. There are condoms in my jacket pocket."

He runs his thumb across my lips and laughs darkly. "Pretty confident, were you?"

"No, but I had to shoot my shot. So to speak. Even if that metaphor doesn't work so well for a goalie." I unbutton his shirt. "How did I convince you? Was it row D? The beer? The pretzel?"

He runs a hand down my bare chest, dipping to play with my

happy trail, and my skin tingles everywhere he touches. "It wasn't the fucking pretzels." He kisses me again.

I shiver as he slides his hand into my boxer briefs to palm my erection. "Fuck, I'm so keyed up. If you jerk me, I'm going to come like a T-shirt cannon."

His laugh is sudden and rich. "God, you're a good time." And he almost sounds like he means it.

After removing his hand from my shorts, he wrestles his own clothes off. Those glorious tattoo sleeves come into view, along with the mouth-watering dusting of hair across his strong pecs.

If I died right now, it would still have been a very full life.

"I want you on that bed," he says, pointing at it.

My pulse rate jumps another notch. "Yessir."

He gives me a hot look as he's unzipping himself. I can't follow his instructions, because I'm too busy watching as he strips off his jeans and his boxers in one go. Forest, naked, is a beautiful sight.

He peels the comforter off the carefully made bed, and even though I'm pretty busy admiring his ass, I pick up on one crucial detail. There are fold marks on the sheets.

"You changed your sheets tonight," I say.

His gaze flickers quickly from the mattress to me. "That illegal?"

"No." I shake my head, but I can't hold back a grin. "You *planned* this. You went to the game knowing you were going to invite me over later."

"It's laundry day." He skims his hand down my chest again.

My nipples harden, and my brain attempts to fuzz out. "That's...not a denial," I say as I step closer to his questing hand.

"Shut up, Beck," he says quietly. "You have your issues. I have mine. Let's not let 'em ruin the night."

"Okay," I whisper, reaching for his muscled arms. I love these arms. So strong and capable. I want to lick them.

He rubs his thumb over my lips again. "Fuck. Your mouth makes me crazy. I don't usually do this." He kisses me. Deeply.

"Do what?" I pant a minute later when we come up for air.

He looks me up and down. "Well, any of this."

And before I can ask him to explain, he pushes me down on the bed.

SEVENTEEN

Employee of the Month

FOREST

I NEED HIS MOUTH, but not for talking.

Back when I used to hook up, kissing was never part of it. That's just too intimate.

My body has forgotten this rule, though. I climb on top of Beck and kiss him like it's my job, and I'm running for employee of the month. I suck on his tongue until we're both panting like prizefighters.

"If you keep that up, I'm going to lose it," he says on a gasp.

"Don't," I say abruptly. I reach between our bodies and give the base of his dick a squeeze. "Not yet. I've got big plans for you."

He rests his head on my pillow and closes his eyes. "Hang on. I'll think about something boring. Like the certification requirements for goalie-mask impact testing. They use a specialized pneumatic cannon to fire pucks at three different velocities while measuring microscopic deformation patterns across seven distinct facial impact zones..."

I watch his handsome face and his squeezed-shut eyes, and something shifts inside my chest. Something dangerous. And I find myself kissing him softly on the jaw as he takes a deep breath.

The problem is that I *like* Becker James. It's not just that he was smoking hot on the ice tonight, and that naked, he's a work of art. All his nervous chatter ought to be annoying, but it isn't. It's real and it's raw. It's...*great*.

Fuck. A guy who's hot *and* earnest. That's my kryptonite. If I'm not careful, I'll get carried away and do something I'll regret later. Like invite him to stay over and then make him breakfast.

But nope. I can't lose focus. Tonight's tryst isn't meant to be cuddly. This is about sex and showing Beck a good time. I can do that. Starting now.

I open my bedside table and grab the lube and the condoms. "This still good idea?"

"A great idea. The *best* idea." He rubs his hand reverently down my biceps. "I just want you to *destroy* me."

That's a clear mandate. And, fuck, I admire this about Beck. Sure, he talks a lot, but it's a feature not a bug. He's honest as the day is long, and I need that in my life right now.

He watches as I open the lube and coat my fingers. "You ever play with yourself like this?" I ask as I dip my hand to his ass.

Lifting his hips for me, he nods. "Think about you when I'm doing it, too."

"*Fuck*." My dick throbs in response. "You're going to get it so good." I run a slicked finger over his hole, and he parts his legs, relaxing for me.

"Do it," he pants. And then he groans when I penetrate him.

"Breathe," I remind him as I slowly open him up.

"Yes...sir."

"You *trying* to kill me?" I rasp, thrusting my finger in deep. "Sure you haven't done this before?"

"Not unless toys count. If they do, I'm a total slut."

I re-lube my fingers and tease him some more. When I

nudge his spot, he moans my name. Yeah, even if I'm a little rusty, I'm good at this.

I lean down and taste the salty tip of his cock, and he bucks. "*Dude.*"

"I know," I say, backing off. "Waiting is hard."

"So hard," he agrees. "Hurry up. I can take more."

"But I'm having too much fun," I tease, lubing up again and giving him another finger.

He grits his teeth a moment and then relaxes again. "More."

"So impatient." We both are, though. So I stick to the plan and work him open until he's sweaty and begging, and my balls ache.

"God, look at you, hungry for it." I reach for the condoms. "I'm gonna give it to you now."

He lifts his hips, and when I line myself up against his hole, he bucks against me, so eager. "Yes, yes, yes," he chants. "Now, Forest."

I'd never want to hurt him, so I'd planned to go slow. But that's not okay with Beck. As soon as I breech him, he growls and bears down on my cock. And I'm the one who's left open-mouthed and struggling to adjust to the glove-like fit of our bodies, and the sudden, erotic embrace of him.

"Fuck," I gasp. "*Fuck.*"

"Yeah, we are," he agrees. "*Finally.* I've been thinking about this so much I could probably write a dissertation. 'An Analysis of Why Forest's Flannel Shirts Make Me Lose My Mind: A Study in Poor Life Choices.'"

I'm too turned on to process much of that. I've turned into a lower-order organism, the kind with only a couple of functions —breathing and thrusting. Although I try to take it slow, because I need this to last.

Beck grabs his knees, spreading them to give me space. He's so fucking flexible that I sink easily down onto his ripped body, moaning when he does an ab curl so he can lift his head to kiss me hotly.

It's almost like he's the one in the driver's seat now, and somehow, I don't mind that much. I thrust shallowly, so I can devour his mouth at the same time. His dick is trapped between us, hard and leaking onto my skin. And I never want it to end.

We kiss fast, and then slow. Like there might be a quiz later, and we need to review every detail. He makes desperate, horny sounds, and I swallow down every single one.

He manages to grunt, "So. Close," into my mouth, and when he says it, it's suddenly true for both of us.

I pull myself up and grab his legs, one in each arm. "Touch yourself," I pant. "Do it."

Beck, face red and lips swollen, wraps one big hand around his cock and stares up at me with heated eyes. He's so fucking beautiful. It's hard to believe that he's ever felt undesirable a minute in his life.

"You look at me like that, and you're gonna make me come," I growl.

His hand flies on his cock, and he tips his head back against the pillow, seeming to unspool in front of my eyes. "Fuck yes," he slurs. Then he bites his lip and shoots all over his own chest.

I follow him about a nanosecond later, because how could I not. All the tension leaves my body in several pulses of pure joy. And a few seconds later we're left staring at one another's sweating, wondrous faces.

Beck lets out a shuddering breath, and I feel like a god.

In the morning, I wake up slowly, consciousness filtering through layers of warmth and drowsiness. There's a weight against my side, the sound of breathing that isn't mine, and—

fuck—a hand threading gently through my hair. The touch is so pleasing that for a moment I forget where I am. Forget all the reasons this shouldn't be happening.

"Is it okay if I make some coffee?" Beck's voice is rough with sleep, barely above a whisper.

"Yeah," I manage, the word slurring past my lips. My head feels heavy, full of lazy, peaceful thoughts that I haven't allowed myself in months. Nobody ever touches me like this—gentle, reverent, like I'm something worth savoring.

I haven't done sleepovers since... My blurry mind takes a minute to consider it. Hell, since I was married. Ruby and I used to have lazy Saturday mornings in bed, back when we pretended we could still make it work.

Beck's hand abruptly disappears, and I hear his bare feet padding across my hardwood floors. Soon there's the distant sound of cabinet doors opening and closing, followed by soft whistling. I let myself drift again, floating in that space between sleep and waking where everything feels possible.

The whistling gets closer, and I force my eyes open. Beck appears in the doorway, fully dressed in yesterday's clothes, holding two mugs. His hair is sticking up on one side, and there's a crease on his cheek from my pillowcase. He looks rumpled and beautiful and completely at home in my space.

I struggle into a seated position against the headboard, and he hands me one of the mugs. It's the blue ceramic one with *World's Greatest Dad* printed on the side—a Father's Day gift from Charlie three years ago that I never use because it feels too presumptuous. Too hopeful.

The coffee smells good, but my heart starts pounding the moment the mug touches my hands. A bad memory hits me like a meteor—the last time someone made me a drink in my own kitchen, I woke up twelve hours later with my life in ruins.

The coffee turns to acid on my tongue. Suddenly, I'm

painfully awake, fully present, and confronted by the reality that this sleepover probably shouldn't have happened. Beck in my kitchen. Making coffee. Acting like he belongs here. Like this is normal. The panic running through my veins is *not* normal.

Why the hell didn't I send him home like I'd planned last night?

"Want to go out for breakfast?" Beck asks, settling cross-legged on the foot of my bed like he's done it a thousand times before. "Your fridge is kinda bare. I know this great diner about ten minutes away. They make these pancakes that are basically diabetes on a plate, but in the best possible way."

"I can't," I say, the words coming out sharper than I intended. I set the mug down on my nightstand without taking another sip.

His offer isn't outrageous, but that's part of the problem. I can't even afford to take myself out for brunch, let alone someone else. How pathetic is that? A thirty-four-year-old man who can't spare twenty bucks for eggs and coffee.

And riding hard on the heels of that thought is the larger problem of where this is headed. I don't want to lead him on.

"I've got errands." I swing my legs over the side of the bed and get up, reaching for yesterday's jeans. "It's my first day without Charlie in a week. Laundry, groceries, oil change. Boring adult shit."

Beck gives me a sideways glance, his coffee mug frozen halfway to his lips. "Okay, dude. It was just an idea. Don't get freaked out."

"I'm not freaked out," I lie, shoving my arms through the sleeves of a flannel shirt.

"No, I'll go," Beck says quietly, setting his mug down and standing up. There's something resigned in his voice that makes me hate myself. "There's only so much of the Beck Show that any one man can take."

The words hit me like a slap. "Hey, that's not it." The expression on his face—shuttered and trying so hard to be okay with rejection—makes my chest ache. I'm so bad at this stuff, but I try anyway. "If I didn't like you, you wouldn't have made it past the front door."

Beck rubs his forehead with the heel of his hand, not meeting my eyes. "Nah, I get it. I'm a lot."

Something clicks into place as I watch him retreat into himself. The way he assumes he's the problem. The way he's already apologizing for existing.

"You've got it all wrong," I insist, stepping closer. "You being you? That's actually *why* you're here."

He looks up, confusion clouding his blue eyes. "Because you have a thing for weirdos with no filter?"

"Nah, don't do that." The words come out harsher than I mean them to, but I need him to hear this. "There's plenty of people in the world ready to tear us all down. We don't have to help them."

His eyes go wide and vulnerable, like I've just told him something revolutionary instead of offering basic human decency.

"I wasn't kidding earlier. You don't have all the information about me. I don't do this anymore." I wave a hand between us. "Sleepovers, dating, any of it—because I got burned by someone who could charm the pants off a nun, and it fucked up my whole life."

I run a gentle hand through his hair. "The only reason you're here right now is because you're so *unlike* other guys. You're not slick. You don't put a lot of effort into being something you're not. I don't even think you're capable of it."

Beck's mouth opens slightly, like he wants to protest, but I keep going. "One hundred percent real is the only kind of guy who'd make it past hello with me right now, and I'm not even sorry about it. You're a rare breed, Beck, and I'm glad you came over last night."

"And yet you're so eager for me to leave?" The question cuts right to the heart of things.

I sit down heavily on the edge of the bed. "I'm not eager. Not really. But—and this isn't going to change anytime soon—I just don't have a lot to give." I look up at him, trying to make him understand. "But if I did? I'd give it to you."

The silence stretches between us, heavy with all the things neither of us knows how to say. Beck stands there in his wrinkled clothes, coffee-mussed and beautiful, and I want so badly to be the kind of man who could offer him breakfast and Sunday mornings.

But I'm not that man. Not yet. Maybe not ever.

He tilts that handsome face and considers me. "We're doing this again, though, right? The just-sex part. I know I want to. And I don't think you're sick of me."

"I'm not," I say immediately. "Not even close."

He smiles. And I feel like I finally did one thing right.

EIGHTEEN

Miss Your Stupid Beard

FEBRUARY

THREE GAMES IN A ROW. Three *starts* in a row. And not just starts—wins. My save percentage has climbed back above .920, which in goalie math translates to "Holy shit, I might actually have a career."

Coach Tanner pulls me aside after practice. "Keep this up, James, and we might have to have a conversation about what's next for your career."

It's wild. Meanwhile, Hennie, our usual number one, just grins and slaps my back as we head to the showers. "About time, rookie. Was getting tired of carrying this team on my back."

That's Hennie for you—zen master in goalie pads. The guy could probably stop pucks while meditating. When I was struggling earlier this season, he never once made me feel like shit about it. Just kept doing his thing, letting me figure out mine.

"You're not worried?" I ask, because I would be. Hell, *I'm* worried, and it's my hot streak.

"Worried about what?" He strips off his gear with the casual efficiency of someone who's been doing this for fifteen years.

"Good goalies make each other better. Besides, you think I want to play seventy-two games a year at my age? My knees are held together with duct tape and spite."

Right. This is why I like Hennie. Most goalies are territorial psychopaths who'd shank you for looking at their crease wrong. Hennie's just happy when the team wins, especially if he can drink a Corona afterward. The man loves his Mexican beer.

In other words, I should be floating on cloud nine. Three wins, Coach talking about starter minutes, and my confidence finally crawling out of whatever hole it's been hiding in for months.

Instead, I'm staring at my phone in the parking lot, reading the same three-word text for the hundredth time.

FOREST

Way to go.

That's it. That's his entire response to me telling him I had back-to-back shutouts and might actually have figured out how to stop a hockey puck again.

Way to go. Like I'm some kid who finally managed to tie his shoes.

I mean, what did I expect? A parade? Dirty texts about what he wants to do to celebrate?

Actually, yeah, that second one would've been nice. Because Forest has been spectacularly unavailable lately. And I'm starting to take it personally.

We've had more sex these past couple weeks. Once on the sofa. Once in his bed, and then in his shower.

But we aren't so great at planning it. One of us (okay, it's usually me) just texts "you free?" and if the answer is yes, we end up naked and sweaty and pretending it's no big deal.

It is, though—for me. For Forest... not so much. When we're together, he's all in. I'm treated to a few hours of his full-blast attention. Those brown eyes and that strong body and that rich laugh. It's intoxicating.

But in the morning, I always leave the second he starts looking antsy. I know I'm supposed to. But it always leaves me with an emotional hangover. Because, inevitably, Forest drops off the face of the earth for a while afterward.

Then the cycle starts again—me wondering if it's too soon to text him. Spending hours thinking about him and scouring the internet for exactly the right hockey meme to make him smile. I'll take photos on my road trips and then agonize over whether he wants to hear from me or not.

Sometimes he replies, and we'll have a half hour of chatter. I live for those times. The other day I'd mentioned that I didn't understand the phrase *under the weather*, because aren't we *all* just under the weather, except for a couple of astronauts up at the ISS?

And then he'd said he'd never understood why people say *the whole nine yards* "when everyone knows that in football, nine yards doesn't get you shit."

Another time I'd sent him a screen shot of a sporty edition of that "Connections" puzzle in *The New York Times*, and he called me to discuss. We sat up too late talking about everything and nothing, and I went to bed happier than ever.

But those moments are the exception, not the rule. Most of the time he doesn't return my messages for hours. And when he does, it's with a word or two, or a thumbs-up.

There's something uniquely soul crushing about a thumbs-up emoji. It should come with a warning label: *May cause existential crisis in people who overthink digital communication.* It's approval without engagement, acknowledgment without investment. It's the conversational equivalent of a polite golf clap—technically positive, but somehow more devastating than complete silence.

This week has been especially dire. Feeling reckless, I let my feelings fly.

> I stopped 37 pucks last night and only had one minor existential crisis between periods, which is personal growth.
>
> Also, you haven't said anything filthy to me in days and I'm starting to wilt like one of those plants that needs misting.
>
> Hope your night's good. Mine would be better if you were in it.
>
> PS: Miss your stupid beard.

He doesn't manage to reply for another couple of hours, after I've spent a lot of time doing laundry and driving to the grocery store and anxiously checking my phone for a response.

> FOREST
>
> You're right, okay? I'm sorry. Just really tied up.

I hope he doesn't mean literally. And now I feel stupid that I complained, and uncertain what I should say next. He's probably going to avoid me now. I can feel it through the phone, right here in the cereal aisle of King Soopers. Like a superpower I never wanted—the ability to detect emotional distance via text message.

Very useful for a guy who's already an expert at reading too much into everything.

My phone buzzes with a new message, and for a pathetic second my heart jumps. But it's just my roommate.

> RIGSY
>
> Dude where are you? Alien Genocide awaits.
> Martinez is coming over, too.

Right. Our Monday night gaming session. We're never on the

road on a Monday night, so this has become our sacred tradition. I add a case of beer to my shopping cart, check out, and then drive home.

Our little rental house looks exactly like every other rental house in Loveland—beige siding, dying lawn, and a front porch that's one strong wind away from collapsing. But it's cheap, and it's five minutes from the rink, and Rigsy doesn't leave dirty dishes in the sink for weeks at a time.

Well, not usually.

"Becks!" he calls when I walk in. "Perfect timing. I just hit level forty-seven and unlocked the plasma rifle. We're about to make some alien bastards very unhappy."

I drop my gear bag and put away my groceries. Then I grab a controller, settling onto our IKEA couch that's held together by prayers and hockey tape. The living room smells like the protein shakes Rigsy lives on and that vanilla candle his mom bought us for Christmas.

For twenty minutes, we blast our way through digital alien hordes, and I almost forget about three-word text messages and hot bartenders who apparently think I'm some kind of communicable disease.

Almost.

"Dude," Rigsy says during a loading screen, "you're not bringing your usual finesse to this alien genocide. What's up?"

I pause, controller in my lap. "It's just pixels on a screen. Don't you ever get frustrated by how meaningless it all is?"

He stares at me like I just suggested we take up competitive knitting. "Bro, it's a video game. Of course it's meaningless. That's the point."

"Right. But don't you get frustrated? Like, with real stuff?"

"Well, yeah. That's what sex is for." He grins and elbows me. "Speaking of which, I thought you had something good going on. Wasn't that why you were sneaking around like a teenager with a fake ID?"

My chest tightens. "I thought I did too."

"Ah." Rigsy's face goes serious, which is weird because I've never seen him be serious about anything except protein powder and his bench-press max. "Want to talk about it?"

"Not really."

"Cool. Want to blow up more aliens instead?"

"'Kay."

But my heart's not in it. When Martinez shows up, I hand off my controller with no remorse.

"Hey," Martinez says as I'm sneaking out of the room. "Some of the guys are hitting up Mulligan's tomorrow night. You should come."

I shake my head automatically. "I don't like that place."

"Then let's go to your bar instead. The one you disappear to every week. We can be flexible."

I freeze.

Martinez doesn't notice. "Not flexible like a goalie, I mean. Dude, that would be weird." He laughs at his own joke.

But I'm spiraling. "I, uh, go to that bar to get away from it all," I say, maybe a little too quickly.

Rigsy pulls his head out of the refrigerator. "Get this—Beck's hookup is a bartender. Explains why he goes to a bar without a wingman. He doesn't want us cutting in on his action."

"That's exactly right," I mumble.

Martinez's eyes light up with understanding. "Oh buddy, it all makes so much sense now. Bartenders are hot, am I right? Their titties bounce when they shake up the drinks." He mimes a shaker motion. "You don't want us cramping your style."

I nod and make some noncommittal noise, hating myself for the omission but not willing to fix it. Coming out to my teammates feels pointless when I don't even have a boyfriend.

"Respect, man," Martinez says, his voice following me down the corridor. "Keep your territory marked."

If only they knew my "territory" consisted of getting spectacular sex a few times and then being ghosted like I'm some kind of stage-five clinger.

My phone sits silent on the coffee table, mocking me with its lack of notifications.

Way to go, I think bitterly. Way to fucking go.

Maybe I am a stage five clinger, because I can't help but wonder what Forest is up to now.

But then I have an idea. So I pull out my phone and google "Stickhandlers Hockey Denver."

NINETEEN

Not Even a Thumbs Up

BECK

IT'S a frigid Thursday night when I walk into a public ice rink in nearby Fort Collins. The building smells like old Zamboni exhaust and teenage desperation, which seems about right for my current state of mind.

I shouldn't be here. I wasn't invited. But Forest hasn't answered my texts in two days, and when I saw the Stickhandlers' Instagram post about tonight's game—just a few miles from my house—my feet made the decision for me.

The first thing I notice is, of course, Forest. He's cycling through the offensive zone, his stick handling smooth and controlled as he draws two defenders toward him. Even on skates, he carries that quiet intensity that makes my stomach do stupid things. The way he bosses the puck around reminds me of the way he is in bed. Deliberate. Confident. Like he knows exactly what he's doing, even when I'm falling apart beneath his hands.

Not that I've done that lately. The truth is that Forest is keeping his distance in every practical way. Like tonight, for example. He's this close to my damn neighborhood, and he couldn't just reply to my texts?

But nope. Not even a goddamn thumbs-up.

So here I am, pacing the sidelines of this rink like a stalker. The scoreboard says HOME: 1 VISITORS: 3, so I hope the Stickhandlers are the visitors in this scenario. There are maybe two dozen other spectators, but if I had to guess, half are the partners of the players on the ice, and the other half are waiting for their own game after this one.

Lots of room in the bleachers, but I still don't take a seat. I stand near the plexi watching my favorite human outwit a big ox of a man who's trying to steal the puck.

Forest dekes the guy and flips the puck to Scully, who scores.

"YEAH!" I shout as the Stickhandlers celebrate.

And then it happens. Forest looks up at the sound of my voice. Our eyes meet through the glass, and I watch his expression shift. His eyebrows lift slightly, surprise flickering across his features before settling into something warmer. Something that looks almost like relief.

Then he smiles. Not his usual careful smirk or the polite bartender smile he gives customers. This is real—soft around the edges, reaching his eyes, transforming his whole face. It's the smile I only see in bed, when his guard is completely down.

He taps his stick once against the glass where I'm standing, before skating back to center ice for the face-off.

That simple gesture unties the knot in my chest. He's not mad that I'm here. He doesn't think I'm being clingy or weird. If anything, he looks... happy to see me.

The rest of the game flies by. Forest plays like he's got something to prove, making crisp passes and solid defensive plays. The Stickhandlers score again, then again. By the time the final buzzer sounds, they've won 6-1, and I'm hoarse from cheering.

The teams shake hands at center ice, and I watch Forest exchange the usual post-game pleasantries. But then, instead of heading straight to the bench with his teammates, he skates over to where I'm standing.

"Hey," he says through the glass, pulling off his helmet. His hair is sweaty and sticking up in all directions, and there's a flush of exertion across his cheekbones.

"Hey, yourself." I lean closer to the plexi. "Good game."

"You came." There's no irritation in his voice. If anything, he sounds almost shy.

"Saw it on social. I was bored. Plus, it's like down the road from my place."

"Ooh, Forest!" Scully's voice carries across the ice as he skates by. "Got yourself a fan!" He lets out a wolf whistle that makes my face burn and Forest roll his eyes.

Forest points toward the parking lot. "Give me twenty minutes to shower, and meet me outside?"

I try not to look as excited as I feel. "What if you came over? My dumbass roommate is out for the night." He and Martinez went to an overnight gaming tournament in Colorado Springs.

Forest looks intrigued. "Just down the road, you say?"

"I'll text you the address."

Then I make myself turn away from the plexi and head for the exit. He knows how I feel.

Either he shows or he doesn't.

TWENTY

Got Somewhere to Be

FOREST

THE LOCKER ROOM is loud with post-game energy, guys stripping off gear and talking smack about the goals they scored. I strip off my pads, but my mind keeps drifting to Beck's face through the glass. The way he lit up when I smiled at him. Like I'd given him something precious instead of just acknowledging he was there.

"Drinks at Murphy's?" Javier asks, toweling off his hair. "First round's on me since I got the hat trick."

"Can't," I say, shoving my skates into my bag. "Got somewhere to be."

Scully raises an eyebrow from across the bench. "Somewhere, huh? Wouldn't happen to involve a certain blond goalie who was eye-fucking you through the glass tonight?"

Heat crawls up my neck. "Shut up."

"Come on," Javier presses. "One beer. We crushed those guys."

I pull my compression shirt over my head and head for the showers. "Rain check."

The hot water feels good on my shoulders, washing away the sweat and adrenaline. But it doesn't wash away the memory of

Beck standing there, cheering for us. For me. I've been ignoring him, because there are too many other things in my life demanding attention. But he drove here anyway.

When I get back to my locker, most of the guys have cleared out. Scully's still getting dressed, taking his sweet time.

"So," he says casually. "This thing with Beck. Getting serious?"

"Fuck no." The words come out sharper than I intended. "It's just sex."

"Uh-huh." Scully pulls on his jeans. "Just sex. That's why you smiled like a toothpaste ad when you saw him?"

I yank on my flannel shirt. "We have an arrangement. No strings."

"And how's that working out for you?"

"Fine." I grab my gear bag. "It's where I'm at right now."

Scully shakes his head. "You're an idiot, you know that?"

"What's that supposed to mean?"

"That guy drove out on the coldest night of the year to watch you play beer league hockey. Is that part of 'just sex'?"

I shoulder my bag. "What Beck wants isn't something I can control."

"Jesus Christ, Forest." Scully stands up, giving me a look I've seen him give to drunk customers who are about to do something really stupid. "I never thought you were such a chickenshit."

"I'm not," I snap. "I'm protecting both of us."

"From what? Being happy?"

I don't have an answer for that, so I head for the door. "See you Friday."

Outside, I note that it really *is* cold as balls. We got a dusting of snow earlier in the day, before the temperature started dropping, and it makes that weird Styrofoam sound underfoot that you only hear when it's bitter.

My truck takes approximately seven years to heat up, so I wait, listening to the terrible grating sound the engine makes. "Come on, Bessie. Don't fail me now." I just need 'er to keep rolling for another two months or so.

Unfortunately, my finances are as precarious as ever. When I bought out one of the partners at Sportsballs, it gained me a significant share of a growing business. But it made me cash poor. *Very* cash poor.

I don't mind living thinly if it means I get to work with my friends while building my future. But then a certain incident last year cleaned out my savings, and I never really recovered. Every dime I have goes toward the business, or Charlie, or keeping this truck in motion, or keeping food on the table.

Scully, who really ought to mind his own beeswax, wasn't totally off base when he pointed out that Beck seems more devoted to our arrangement than me. But it isn't because I'm allergic to fun, and it isn't because I'm a stupid guy. I simply can't understand why he'd want a piece of this. He's a young guy going places, and I'm a single dad just trying to keep the wolves from my door.

And one of these days he'll meet someone else—someone younger and less of a disaster. And then his texts will just stop. I'm already bracing myself.

I put the truck into gear, wincing at the grinding noise, and drive two miles to the address that Beck sent me. I was expecting a shitty little condo development, but it's a little house on a snowy block. There's a warm glow coming from inside, and after I kill the engine, I sit still for a moment, thinking about how much I want to walk inside, but knowing I shouldn't.

The front door opens, though, and Beck gestures to me. His expression says, *this is the right house, idiot.* So I haul my carcass out, and it's not as easy as it should be. I didn't do any post-game stretching, and I'm paying for it now.

So sexy.

I trudge up the carefully shoveled walk and meet Beck in the front hall, where he takes my coat and hangs it on a peg.

Weirdly, he doesn't give me the happy puppy face I usually see when we're together. The glance he gives me is warier than that, even as he waves me toward the living room.

Hmm.

I step past him and immediately stop short. This isn't what I expected.

The living room is surprisingly grown-up—no pizza boxes or beer cans scattered around like I'd pictured. Instead, there's a decent couch in front of a solid wood coffee table, and the walls are painted a warm gray instead of rental white. But it's the details that catch me off guard.

There's a small shelf dedicated entirely to hockey-themed snow globes for various NHL teams. They're grouped by conference, of course. And the room is lit by string lights across the ceiling—in the shape of snowflakes.

Then there's the low, sexy lighting, and the heartbeat thump of a hidden speaker somewhere. The song is "Need You Tonight" by INXS.

"Nice place," I say, still taking it in.

"Thanks. Rigsy wanted to hang a neon beer sign, but I threatened to hide his protein powder." Beck kicks off his shoes by the door, where there's an actual shoe rack. "How about a drink? Fair warning—our fridge is like ninety percent energy drinks and Greek yogurt."

How about a drink? I wonder how old I'll have to be to hear that phrase and not suppress a shiver. "Just, uh, water would be great. Thank you for going to the trouble."

He gives me another stern look. "It's not trouble, Forest. Sit down. Let's talk."

Oh shit. Those words give everybody the shivers, right?

I take a seat on the sofa, and Beck disappears for a second, returning with two bottles of water. He sits down beside me and gives me a sideways glance. "Are you pissed I showed up at your game?"

"No," I say immediately. "That was fun."

He's quiet for a second, his long eyelashes dipping. "You didn't answer my texts, though. So that means I have to wonder whether showing up tonight makes me pathetic, or a stalker. Or, as you put it, *fun*."

"I'm sorry," I say immediately. "The week got away from me. The boiler at Sportsballs finally gave out, and I spent a lot of time trying to get it patched. And I'm trying to hire two new bartenders, so my text messages are like a portal to hell. Today I interviewed a guy who asked if we have WiFi for his laptop because he likes to work while he tends bar. *Work*. While bartending."

Beck blinks. "What kind of work?"

"His novel. He's writing a novel about vampires who play professional hockey."

There's a beat of silence, then Beck bursts out laughing. "Wait, that actually sounds kind of awesome. Like, do the vampires have an advantage because they sparkle and scare the other team? And is sunlight a problem during morning skate?"

"Don't encourage this," I growl, but I'm fighting a smile. "The woman I interviewed before him seemed promising until she asked if she could bring her emotional support pig to work." I pause. "A pig. Not a dog. Not even a cat. Anyway, I was going to call you, but I had Charlie's parent-teacher conferences at school, and..." I break off, rubbing my forehead. "I guess I could have just said that."

"You could have just said that," Beck repeats quietly.

"That was rude," I admit. "I'm sorry."

He puts his elbows on his knees and glances away from me.

"My mother brines her chicken for three hours. There's no cutting it short. If she gets a late start on dinner, we don't eat until nine."

I blink. "Your mother?" Is she *here*?

"Nah." He flips his blue eyes back to me. "But that's how you treat my texts—only responding after they're thoroughly seasoned."

Oh. I crack a smile, because I love the inside of Beck's brain. But he has a point. "I can do better. I don't mean to be such an ass."

"I *know* you don't." He swallows. "And I know the drill, man. I was listening when you explained your terms. But sometimes I get the distinct impression that you're *managing* me. Like you keep me at arm's length so that I won't forget my place."

My heart drops into my gut. "*Beck.*"

"Makes me feel like a loser and maybe I should just let go."

"You're *not* a loser," I say immediately. "Not one day in your life. You're right. I'm shitty at replying to messages. Always have been. But I'm also *not* a dude who has his life together. That's what you should take away from all this. And then you should fucking run."

He gives his head a shake. "Can't."

"Why not?"

"Because," he says. "Because of this." In one smooth motion he moves closer on the couch and grabs the flannel of my shirt. Then his mouth crashes against mine with zero warning, and my brain just... stops.

Holy shit.

The kiss is somehow desperate and slow at the same time, like he's trying to prove a point with his tongue. And fuck me, it's working. My hands find his face without permission, fingers threading into his hair as he licks into my mouth like he owns it.

Like he's trying to show me something I've been too stubborn to see.

When he finally pulls back, we're both breathing hard. His pupils are blown wide, and there's something fierce in his expression that I've never seen before.

"That's why," he says, voice rough. "Because every time we're in the same room, I forget how to think. Because you make me feel like I'm actually good for something besides stopping pucks. Because when you look at me like that—" He gestures vaguely at my face. "—I'd drive through a blizzard just to see it again."

I stare at him. My heart is hammering against my ribs, and there's heat pooling low in my gut that has nothing to do with the string lights casting everything in a warm glow.

Then I'm on him again, kissing him like I mean it. Which I do. Because it's like this every time. "Just sex" with Beck happens on a deeper level than I like to admit. Sure it's physical—hands sliding under his shirt. My tongue in his mouth. But as I flatten my palms against his chest, I can feel his heart hammering to the same rhythm as mine.

We're so in tune, and I don't even know what to do with that. Meanwhile, the music pulses through my bloodstream and straight to my cock. "Fuck," I breathe against his mouth. Because now I understand the problem. It's not just Beck who needs this —it's me.

That's why I don't answer his texts. Not because I'm managing him, but because I'm managing myself. Because every message from him makes my chest do this stupid fluttery thing that has nothing to do with my dick.

I told Scully it was just sex, as if Beck were just some hookup from my past. That's what I've been trying to tell myself, too.

Except it's not like that. Not at all. And I don't know what to do with this attachment we have for each other. I don't know how to process it. So I just haul him closer, my hands adventurous on his body. I tug his shirt off so I can see more. Touch more.

It's not just that he's gorgeous—though, Christ, he is. All lean muscle and sharp angles, with those blue eyes that see right through my bullshit. And the way he makes me laugh when I didn't even know I was capable of that anymore.

He makes me feel like I'm not just some washed-up bartender counting pennies. When I'm with Beck, I feel like the man I was before I learned to be scared.

"Forest," he whispers against my jaw, and I pull back just enough to look at him, at his flushed face and kiss-swollen lips. At the way he's looking at me like I'm everything he's ever wanted.

I'm so screwed. And I'm probably making a huge fucking mess of everything.

I just can't seem to stop.

TWENTY-ONE

Big Sexy Grizzly Bear

BECK

AS I UNBUTTON Forest's shirt with fumbling fingers, I'm trying to decode—for the millionth time—the intense expression in his dark-brown eyes. This man confuses the hell out of me.

He ignores my texts for days like he couldn't care less about me, but now, when we're together, he's kissing me like he's memorizing the taste of me, filing it away in some secret part of his brain labeled *Things Worth Keeping*.

What's a guy supposed to do with that?

Luckily, my brain shuts off again when he drops his mouth to my neck and starts sucking on it. It's a whole-body experience —like he's figured out the exact heat and pressure that makes my brain melt, weaponizing his mouth to prevent all coherent thought.

This must be how addiction feels—like there's only one important thing in your life and you know it's probably killing you, but it doesn't matter. You'll do anything for one more taste.

Can you blame me, though? Forest is slipping a hand into my sweatpants, with a hungry gleam in his eye. And now he's kissing me like we just invented it.

"Bedroom," I hiss between kisses. "Now." I yank us both into a standing position.

Forest's shirt hits the floor somewhere between the couch and the hallway, my sweatshirt following close behind. We're a disaster of hands and mouths, bumping into walls as we stumble toward my room like we're drunk on each other.

"Left," I gasp when Forest pins me against the wrong door-frame—that's Rigsy's room. Forest's laugh rumbles against my throat as he redirects us, his hands rough against my hips.

My socks get kicked off somewhere near the bathroom door. Forest's pants follow a few steps later, along with his socks, because apparently, we're both the kind of people who can't leave socks on during sex.

By the time we make it into my bedroom, we're down to boxers and desperation. Forest backs me toward the bed, and I catch a glimpse of us in my dresser mirror—hair messed up, lips swollen, chests flushed, looking like we just survived some kind of beautiful disaster.

I catch Forest looking back at me in the mirror, and his expression is feral. "Jesus, Beck," he breathes, and then shoves me down on the bed.

The roughness of it makes my heart leap. He leers down at me, grasping my hips in two hands and flipping me like a pancake. And I am not a small guy. "Hands and knees," he growls.

Fuck yes. I push up off the mattress, and he's on me like a bumper sticker. I feel his cock line up against my ass, while his muscular arms wrap around my body. The sense of being captured by him lights me up, as if a big, sexy grizzly bear has claimed me for his own.

I've always wanted to wrestle a bear, though, so I lock my muscles and push back against his bulk. His answering groan makes me leak against my briefs.

"Fuck," he whispers. He releases me, which ought to be a bummer, but he's yanking down my underwear, and I happily shift my knees to help. Forest is so impatient I hear the sound of fabric tearing as he scrapes the cotton from my body.

"Spread," he orders, knocking my knees farther apart with one of his.

Yowza. He roughly spreads my cheeks, exposing me. I let out another shaky breath as his thumbs slowly tease the sensitive skin of my crease. "Yes, go on," I babble. "There's lube in the bedside table."

But he doesn't reach for it. He palms my leaking cock, and then? He sinks to his knees. Oh wow. Is he...?

The next sensation is the pleasant scrape of his beard against my skin. Followed by the unhurried glide of his tongue at my rim.

"*Ohhh*," I gasp as he does it again. It's hot and dirty and perfect, and I forget to let out another breath, until my balls tighten and I exhale an unholy moan. That naughty tongue. It's exquisite. It's like he's found a nerve ending I didn't know existed, and now he's writing his name on it with his tongue.

I begin melting against the mattress, like an ice rink being hit by the summer sun. And then Forest gets even trickier, stroking my cock as he rims me. And I feel...

...

...

Never mind. It turns out there's a whole category of sensation that doesn't have words in English, probably because people's brains would spontaneously combust trying to describe it. All I can do is ride the wave of Forest's tongue, the blunt slide of his fingers, the scrape of his palm, and the brush of his beard against my back.

"Don't come," he says eventually, possibly after I've just threatened to do that very thing. "Condoms?"

"Um..." I honestly don't recall most of my vocabulary, and I sure as hell don't know where the condoms are. "Do we really need one?" I'm pretty sure Forest has been off the market a while, and I was never on it in the first place.

Apparently, Forest agrees, because there's a lubed-up cockhead pressing into me a beat later. I take a deep breath and push it out again, willing my body to take him. There's always a moment when it seems impossible, but then Forest presses a hand to the center of my back, fingers spread wide. The touch anchors me, and I steady myself in time for him to bottom out, soul deep.

I'm swimming in pleasure. Somebody makes a keening noise, and I think it might be me.

"Good boy," he says. "That's it."

The praise lights me up, and I flex back against his bulk, listening for his answering groan.

We find our rhythm immediately. I might be socially awkward, and Forest might be terrible at returning my texts, but our bodies communicate on a higher plane. It's so good that I have to squeeze my eyes shut. "I'm so close."

"Go on," he says. "I've got you."

Those are the sexiest words I'll ever hear.

I've got you.

If only.

I drop my head and roar with pleasure. I thought "seeing stars" was an exaggeration until I met Forest. His body does something to me that makes me question the fundamental laws of science, and I tilt forward onto the mattress.

Everything gets impossibly better when Forest's burly arm clamps around my body. He buries his face in the back of my neck and makes a noise of deep gratitude. I feel him shudder inside me, and every one of my muscles relaxes.

We end up in a sweaty heap on my bed. I'm still face down, my greedy heart thumping away against the mattress. I hold very still, hoping he won't get up and leave.

I know he has to. But just... not yet.

TWENTY-TWO

Think of Meatloaf

FOREST

I WAKE up but don't open my eyes yet. I'm pancaked against Beck. A month ago, I would have found that deeply confusing, but the lanky shape of him is familiar to me now, and I let myself drift.

When I eventually open my eyes, I'm a little surprised to find myself in his bedroom instead of my own. Which means it's happened again—I managed to take things further than ever with Beck.

Like sleeping over at his house.

And unprotected sex. Not that it's a danger. It's a precedent, though.

Don't panic, dummy. You'll figure it out. Beck is worth it.

I reluctantly extract myself from his warm body and sit up. It's Friday. I think. I have a million things to do, and a very full bladder, and I don't see my clothes anywhere.

While Beck sleeps on, I tiptoe naked to the door of his room and slip into the corridor. I avail myself of Beck's tidy bathroom and contemplate my day. More interviews. Ordering bar supplies, and bookkeeping. Shopping for trucks online.

First step—find all of my clothing. I vaguely remember

shedding some of it near the couch. I shuffle into the living room to find...

A man. On the couch. I freeze like Bambi in front of a semi.

Holy shit. What else can I fuck up for Beck? It isn't even eight a.m.

The guy—Beck's roommate I guess—looks up from the bowl of cereal he's eating. "Dude. Great ink. You get that done around here?"

"Uh..." I gulp. "Yup. Thanks?" Then, as if I could actually undo this disaster, I take a step backward, like that gif of Homer Simpson disappearing into the hedge. But there's no hedge, and I'm still naked.

"You know," the guy says, raising another spoonful of cereal. "I was wondering when Beck was gonna bring someone home. Dude's been moping around here for weeks." He shovels in the mouthful and chews. "You're the bartender, right? From that place he goes every week?" More chewing. "Cool. Just, uh, maybe grab some pants before you wander around? Not on my account, but my new girlfriend is coming by later to drop off groceries, and I'm in that stage when I'm tryna look classy."

"*You* have a *girlfriend*?" comes Beck's shocked voice from a distance behind me. I think he's still in his bedroom?

"Like, a living, breathing one?" Beck continues the conversation like he's standing right beside his roommate. "And why are you home already?"

"Dude, yes!" The guy stands up and actually brushes past my naked body to move into the corridor. He stops in the doorway of Beck's room. "We got knocked out of the tournament at three a.m. And also Lizzie wanted to see me today. Could you, like, avoid certain topics when she's here? Don't tell her I live on gas-station pizza and energy drinks. I want her to think I'm capable of adulting."

"Okay," Beck's voice says, but it's muffled.

"Now aren't you going to introduce me to your friend?" his roommate asks.

I use my moment alone to grab various articles of our clothing off the living room floor. I hold them in front of my package, like some kind of Garden of Eden farce, and then I head down the hall.

Through the open door, I can see Beck is still in bed, but now he's holding the pillow across his face, and this is why his speech is muffled. "His name is Forest. He's... We're..."

He yanks the pillow off his face and gestures wildly toward me, his face turning the color of a stop sign. "We have a lot of sex. Obviously. I mean, you probably figured that out because, uh, his dick is hanging out." He clears his throat. "I'm gay. Surprise? I should have mentioned that sooner, probably. But it never really came up in conversation, you know? Like, 'Hey Rigsy, pass the protein powder, also I'm attracted to men.'" He runs a hand through his hair, making it stick up even worse. "Are we... Is this weird now?"

Rigsy snorts. "Buddy, gotta fill you in on something—the weird don't start here, ya feel me? I don't give two fucks, though. When have I ever?"

Beck moves the pillow back onto his face, and says "Um..."

His roommate lets out a squawk. "No, really! Why dincha say something before now? I'm kind of offended. And I never call shit *gay*, and stuff. I know better."

"Almost never," Beck mumbles.

"No, *really*. Never!"

This conversation seems like it's going to last a while, and all I want is my underwear.

Beck sits up in bed suddenly. "Actually, not true. You and Booger and Martinez were talking on the bus on the way to a Bakersfield game and you literally said, *That's so gay*."

"No way!" Rigsy scoffs, leaning on the doorframe.

"Way. I heard you."

I sigh.

"Hang on." Rigsy scratches his ear. "Were we arguing about *Lovelorn*? That reality show?"

"Probably."

"Yeah, I was being *factual*. Brad and Isaac were vibing, and I totally called it. There was a make-out scene in the next episode, too. Total vindication."

Beck blinks. "Oh," he says softly. Then he lifts his pillow and covers his face again. "Thanks for explaining."

Rigsy finally leaves, and I close the bedroom door behind him. "Beck," I say quietly. "Can you breathe under there?"

"I guess." He doesn't move.

"I'm really sorry. I could've been more careful about getting dressed."

He gives a grunt of disagreement. "This isn't on you, and we both know it."

I locate my underwear hanging off a dresser drawer handle. I slip them on and sit down on the bed. I put my hand in the center of Beck's warm chest, spreading my fingers across his smooth skin. "Are you ever coming out of there?"

"I don't see why I should."

"Your save percentage will suffer."

He yanks the pillow away and gives me a grumpy look. "I didn't think Rigsy would be home before practice. Sorry you flashed him."

"'S'okay. For what it's worth, he didn't really blink."

"I noticed that." He rubs his forehead. "I should've talked to him a long time ago. He's not a bad guy. Just had no idea that *Come Out to the Whole Team* was on my bingo card for today." He reaches for his phone and starts tapping out a text.

"Wait. What are you doing?"

"Ripping the Band-Aid off."

Panic grips me. "What does that mean?"

His thumbs move furiously. "I'd already decided that when I finally came out to my team, I would do it on the group text. Just seems efficient."

Oh God. "Are you sure?"

"Yup." He gives me a calm glance. "This will only take a second."

Jesus. I already knew Beck was fearless, but now he's gaining hero status.

"There," he says. "It's done. See?"

He hands me the phone, and I take it with a sweaty hand.

BECK

Let's play Two Truths and a Lie. I'll start:

1. I'm super gay

2. I've never even tasted ketchup

3. I once got a penalty for arguing with the Zamboni driver

I laugh immediately. "Oh my God. That's the most Beck thing I've ever read."

He sighs, then puts his phone face down on the bedside table. "I hate talking about myself. Distract me with your hot body."

I put my hand on his thigh and give it a squeeze. "Not with your roommate on the other side of that door."

He smirks. "Ah, well. Then tell me a story. Who did you have to come out to first?"

"Oh. Hell. You sure you want to hear this? It didn't go all that well."

Beck grabs my hand with his. "Yeah, I want to hear it. You don't talk about yourself very much."

He isn't wrong. "Well, the first person I came out to was my wife. Charlie was about five years old at that point, and she freaked out."

"Wait, what?" He sits up straighter. "She didn't know you're bi?"

I shake my head, because he doesn't get it. "Beck, *I* didn't know it myself. Or I guess it's more accurate to say that I hadn't acknowledged it. She and I started dating when I was only eighteen. We got pregnant when she was twenty, and I was twenty-one. Then we got married."

"Oh," he says heavily. "Wow."

I shrug, because this is all water under the bridge. "Took me a while to figure myself out. I'd always suppressed my attraction to men. And after I got married, entertaining those thoughts felt dishonest.

"But then I met a guy at work who's a bisexual married to a woman. He and I became friends. And one time when we were stuck at an airport for hours, he told me the story of his own realization, and it hit me like a slap. I spent the next few months processing it. Then I told my wife, because I didn't want any secrets in my marriage."

Beck reaches up to absently stroke my beard. It feels ridiculously good. "Is that why you got divorced?"

I lean into his touch without even meaning to. "Eh, yes, but also, no. Things got rough between us. She asked a lot of pointed questions about whether I felt like our marriage was a trap. I didn't—not in the way that she meant. She kept asking me if I was tempted to cheat."

Beck groans. "That's not fair."

"No, it wasn't. But she wouldn't let it go, and she ended up asking for a divorce. But wait for the punchline—a few years later, she went into therapy and ended up apologizing to me. Turns out *she* was the one who felt like getting married so young was a trap, and I just sort of opened the door on all her issues."

He strokes my beard again. "And what about your parents?"

"Well, it's complicated." I let out a sigh. "They're not homophobes, but they hate that my marriage blew up. They think it's probably my fault somehow, and they think buying a queer bar is some kind of extended midlife crisis. They don't say any of that out loud, but I hear it anyway."

"Aw, Forest. How come you never told me any of that?"

I laugh. "Beck, believe it or not, I'm more like Rigsy than you know—still trying to make you think I'm cool."

He smiles, and then I find myself getting hugged by six-footthree inches of hockey goalie. It's awesome, honestly. My arms wrap around him without my permission, and we just hold on. I take a deep, slow breath, memorizing the scent of his skin.

"Beck," I whisper. "Were you out to anyone before today?"

"Oh, sure," he says. "My mom and her new family. Also my high school coach. Just not anyone in Colorado."

"Your mom has a new family?"

"Yup. She was single when she got pregnant with me on a one-night stand in the Netherlands."

I pull back an inch and eye him. "Your father was Dutch?"

"Probably." He gives me a sneaky smile. "There's some Dutch guy out there with a weird sense of humor and good hand-eye coordination. She never even knew his last name. But that's the wildest thing my mother ever did. She's been making up for it ever since with an aggressively normal life. Which doesn't overlap with mine very much."

"Oh," I say as my heart sags. I've always sensed a deep-seated loneliness in Beck, and I hate knowing that it was true.

"She's not cold, exactly. Just tuned into a different channel. Like she's living in a different sitcom where I'm the quirky neighbor who pops in every few episodes."

I don't know what to say to that, so I just kiss his neck. His phone buzzes with a text. And then another one. And another.

"Do you want to look?" I ask as the phone keeps up the buzzing.

"In a minute," he says, scraping his stubble against mine. "How bad could it be, really? I'm already the team weirdo."

"You're a goalie," I remind him. "It's your job to be weird. Your obsession with new wave music from the Eighties is totally on brand."

He snorts, and then he lets me go. He picks up the phone, which is still intermittently buzzing like a frantic mosquito. He unlocks it, and we both lean in to see the screen.

DIETZ

No way on the Zamboni thing. That's not even possible. Zamboni driver isn't an official

RIGSY

Bro. Beck would 100% argue with the Zamboni driver. I've seen him yell at a vending machine.

MARTINEZ

Wait hold up. He's NEVER had ketchup?? How is that even physically possible

HENNIE

@Martinez the Zamboni thing is definitely the lie. You can't get a penalty from arguing with ice crew

RIGSY

But seriously Beck what do you eat fries with??? Mayo like some kind of psychopath?

KOWALSKI

My cousin got a bench minor for chirping the timekeeper once so maybe Zamboni guy could take it up the chain of command?

MARTINEZ

No but think about it - ketchup is in
EVERYTHING. Thousand island dressing.
Cocktail sauce. BBQ sauce has ketchup

RIGSY

Those don't count as ketchup Martinez

HENNIE

They totally count. If he's never had ketchup
he's never had Big Mac sauce

MARTINEZ

EXACTLY. Beck you telling me you've never had
a Big Mac???

We both look up at the same time, and there's a question in his blue eyes. "Not a single one of them questions the gay thing."

"Uh, nope. Not yet."

The phone buzzes in his hand, three more times.

"Why do you think that is?" he asks. "Do I really want to know?"

I laugh. And then we return to the screen again.

KOWALSKI:

Still think the penalty thing is possible. Ice crew
has more power than people think

HENNIE

I'm googling Zamboni driver penalty rules brb

MARTINEZ

Beck answer the Big Mac question this is
important

MARTINEZ

OH SHIT what about when your mom made meatloaf? Ketchup glaze Beck. KETCHUP GLAZE.

COACH

This is the dumbest conversation you've ever had. And ketchup is life.

HENNIE

Coach HAS ENTERED THE CHAT

GORD

Guys, hold up. Not one of you thinks the gay thing was the lie?

COACH

Nobody thinks that, Gord. That's the motherfucking point.

GORD

Ohhhhhh. Got it.

COACH

Get off your phones and get to practice! We're doing 3-on-2 drills today.

RIGSY

Beck? You going to put us out of our misery, here? Or do I have to come in there? Assuming your bedroom door is closed for a reason.

RIGSY

Also, the coffee is ready.

Beck picks up his phone and I watch over his shoulder as he types a response.

BECK

> Ketchup is disgusting, which I know because
> I've tasted it. Unwillingly. It's a bullshit
> condiment.

MARTINEZ

I KNEW IT. But you like mustard? That's weird.

BECK

Mustard is elite. It knows what it is.

DIETZ

SO THE ZAMBONI THING IS REAL

Beck, looking slightly shellshocked, puts down his phone. "That could have gone worse."

"Yeah, it could." I put a hand on his warm stomach. "We should get up. But... the Zamboni thing?"

"It happened in high school. I wouldn't shut up about the shitty ice in my crease. Guy was so sick of listening to me bitch that he got the ref to penalize me."

"Asshole."

He grins. "Totally. I'll put your coffee in a to-go cup. Milk, no sugar?"

"Thanks."

He grabs a pair of briefs from a drawer and steps into them while I admire his ass. Then he strides out of his room in search of coffee, and I watch him go.

Beck is goddamn fearless. I'm proud to know him. I might even be falling for him.

I just don't know what to do about it.

TWENTY-THREE

Ringing Any Bells?

FOREST

SURPRISING NOBODY, Beck and I have trouble seeing each other for a while after our eventful night together.

It's not all my fault. The Ice Cats take a couple of road trips. I receive chipper texts from Grand Rapids and then from San Jose.

BECK

Did you know Eggo waffles were invented in San Jose? And Chuck E Cheese. Also, the band Smashmouth is from here.

Holy shit! They have a life-size monopoly board!

Then, a couple hours later, I get a photo of Beck and Rigsy standing on Park Place beside a pair of giant dice in the sunshine.

Beck looks so fucking happy. Even though he deserves a reply, I have nothing fun to add to the conversation. I'm busy plowing the bar's parking lot with a truck that makes a horrible grinding sound. We just got a foot of snow, and it's heavy, wet stuff. The lights on my truck dashboard flicker every time I engage the plow.

Even worse—the weather is so bad that receipts in the bar are down. People don't want to slog through the cold and the snow after work, I guess.

Also, Charlie flunked a math test. He needs tutoring, so now Ruby and I are bickering about whose fault it is and what we're going to do about it.

"He *failed*, Seth," Ruby'd hollered on the phone. "He got a forty-seven percent! We don't fail subjects in this family."

"It's middle school," I'd sputtered at her. "And it's one test, not a subject."

She hadn't been soothed by this clarification. Now she's on the warpath, and we're both unsure how to find a tutor.

The subtext, unless I'm projecting, is that math-flunking genes are from my side of Charlie's genetics, and I should really be more concerned.

When Beck returns from his trips, my schedule doesn't magically clear. The bartender that I eventually hire lasts three shifts before moving to L.A. with his new boyfriend.

So now I'm interviewing bartenders again, and covering shifts that I thought would be someone else's problem. And then everything gets suddenly worse one cloudy afternoon as I'm cruising toward the grocery store. I press the gas pedal and get nothing but a horrible metal-on-metal shriek while the RPMs spin uselessly.

I manage to coast into a Walmart parking lot before the thing seizes up completely, steam rising from under the hood like a funeral pyre. I sit there for a long moment, hands still gripping the steering wheel, watching other people go about their normal lives while mine officially falls apart.

Two hours later, I'm waiting in the mechanic's shop, hoping for a miracle.

"Have a cup of coffee," Craig says when he catches me staring into the garage again. "Give us a minute to take a look."

I'm too keyed up for coffee, so I take a seat in one of the unoccupied chairs and unlock my phone. I find texts from three people. One is my ex. One is Scully. And the other one is Beck.

I'd like to open them in reverse order, but duty calls.

> **RUBY**
>
> Hey Forest, I'm sorry but I might need a favor. Another doctor is down with the flu so I can't get away. You need to pick up Charlie after hockey, and I'll get to your place when I can.

That's how she does these things—it's an order, not a request.

I check the time. Practice ends in less than an hour. *Shit*.

Moving on to Scully's text, he asks if I can fill in tonight. The easy answer is no. I've worked so many nights lately that I am practically making drinks in my sleep. But I could really use the money.

Except... If I have to pick up Charlie, then I won't be able to open the bar. And if my truck is toast, I don't know how I'll pick him up at all.

I stand up and do a lap around the waiting room, peering into the bay again as if somehow it would move things along faster.

Then I read Beck's message, because I could really use a smile right now.

> **BECK**
>
> Hi, remember me? I pop up in your texts once a day or so. And sometimes I suck your dick? Ringing any bells?

Uh-oh. I *have* been awfully uncommunicative this week.

> Just wanted you to know I'm back in town. And
> free to see you. In case you missed it when I
> said that last night. And a couple hours ago.
>
> Even a thumbs up would be an improvement at
> this point.
>
> Actually it probably wouldn't. I hate that fucker.

I let out a quiet groan. There's no part of me that wouldn't like a night with Beck and his adventurous hands. And, if I'm honest, I want the following morning, too. Coffee in bed. His wacky sense of humor. A few hours with him feels like taking a two week vacation from my life.

But my current reality is this expensive repair shop and maybe an extra shift at work.

FOREST

> So sorry. Tonight isn't going to work out. Wish
> that weren't the case.

He starts typing a response immediately, like maybe he's been waiting for my text. So I feel even worse.

BECK

> OK. I get it. But Wednesday is your inviolable
> monthly poker night. And Thursday I'm already
> gone on my road trip. So I guess I'll see you
> next week.
>
> I mean, I hope I will.

Oof. I sink down on a chair. Then I google *inviolable*. It means *never to be broken, infringed, or dishonored.*

Yeah, I guess he would see it that way. He doesn't realize that this poker game is my last link to my former life—the one where

I worked a corporate job and was married to a woman. The poker guys are my Dad Friends—the club of divorced dads who all have kids in the youth hockey program.

The thing is? I need those guys for this whole it-takes-a-village thing. In fact, I might be calling one of them in the next few minutes to beg him to pick up Charlie from practice.

I start composing another text. ***I'm sorry. I had some hiccups this week but hopefully I'll be more fun by the time you get back from your next road trip.***

But then my thumb hovers over the Send button. I can't bring myself to hit it. I reread the text and realize I'm still keeping Beck on ice, still keeping my distance despite the fact I know it hurts him.

He deserves better.

I pull up his number in my call log.

"Hey, Forest?"

My chin jerks up to find Craig standing in front of me. "Yeah?"

"I've got some bad news and some just irritating news."

Fuck. "Hit me with it."

"Your transmission is toast. And fixing it is going to cost more than you should pay. Also, your axel is cracked. It's time, man. We gotta take 'er out back and shoot 'er."

My stomach drops again. "I see. That better be the bad news. What's the irritating part?"

"I won't have a rental vehicle available for..." He looks at his watch. "Another hour and a half. But then I can put you in a Honda CRV, at least for a few days. Give you time to buy a truck or negotiate a lease."

My bank account lets out a painful whimper. "Right. I see."

He gives my shoulder a quick squeeze. "Save me a seat at the bar for Friday night's game, and I'll give you a house discount on the rental."

I force a smile, because Craig is the best. It's not his fault my life is a dumpster fire. "Sure thing, boss."

He leaves me alone again with my troubled thoughts. I've got more issues to deal with, including Beck. No time like the present. I tap his number.

He answers after just one ring. "Hey. An actual phone call? Damn."

The sound of his voice makes me close my eyes. I can picture him with his lanky legs crossed on the coffee table, thinking deep thoughts. "Hi. How are you?"

"Kinda bored," he says. "I'm not allowed to practice this week. Muscle strain."

"Oh shit," I breathe. "Where?"

He chuckles. "My groin, if you must know. It's not serious. The trainers are just resting me. Honestly, I'm taking all their caution as a win. They want me to start against Texas on Friday."

"Ah."

"What, no groin jokes? I expected more from you."

He's teasing, but I find it sobering. *Just do it, Forrester.* He deserves better.

I inhale.

TWENTY-FOUR

This Isn't a Booty Call

BECK

"LISTEN, BECK," Forest says, and my mind wheels. It's unusual to get a three o'clock call from Forest. This isn't a booty-call time. This is either a something-is-wrong time or a butt-dial time, and Forest doesn't seem like a butt-dial kind of guy.

"I'm having a difficult time. My truck just fucking died. For good." His voice is gruff, frustrated.

"Oh *shit*." He doesn't ever complain to me, but it's obvious that money is tight. "Look—I know you're allergic to asking for favors. But are you stranded? I'll come pick you up." There's almost nothing I wouldn't do for this man. Even if he asked me to root for the Ducks against an Original Six team. It would hurt me, but I'd do it.

The line gets very quiet for a second. "It's both. I'm stranded. And also allergic to asking for favors."

"If I offered you a ride, are we talking hives? Or anaphylactic shock? Where are you, by the way?"

Another pause. "I'm waiting for a rental car, but it's gonna be a while, and, well..." He sighs. "It's Charlie who needs a pickup from hockey practice."

My heart does this weird skip. Forest asking for help is like spotting a unicorn. If unicorns were grumpy and had commitment issues. "I'll go get him." I say quickly. "It's no bother."

Another long pause, and I wonder if he's about to change his mind. "I'll text you the address. They just walk outside after it's over at four. He's supposed to be at his mom's tonight, but she's stuck at the hospital..."

I'm already pocketing my keys. "No problem. I got this. I'll just bring him to your place?"

"That makes the most sense," he agrees. "Are you sure I'm not tearing you away from something?"

"Well yeah—video games and masturbation. But not at the same time."

A snort of laughter. "You kill me."

I guess I'll take that as a win, too.

He sighs. "Thank you. I'll be stuck here for another hour at least. Charlie has a key. As long as he's safely inside, you don't need to stay."

"Don't worry about a thing."

Twenty-five minutes later, I'm pulling up to a hockey rink where a few kids lurk near the drive circle. I roll down the passenger window and wave at Charlie.

He lights up when he spots me, like I just announced that school's been canceled for the rest of the year. "Beck!" He picks up a backpack and hockey bag that's almost as big as he is and bounces toward the Jeep. "What are you doing here? Where's Dad?" He drops his gear and yanks the door open.

"His truck died, so he asked me to pick you up. Did you get the text?"

Charlie shrugs. "Nah, no text."

I get out to stash his gear in the back of the Jeep. "So you're going to jump into a strange car just because I said your dad sent me?"

Charlie laughs, but I pull out my phone and text Forest.

BECK

Got Charlie. Did you text him to tell him I'm coming? He seems fine with it but maybe it's better to close the loop.

FOREST

Fuck me. I forget to text everyone. Even my own kid. **Headdesk** I'll do it now.

Huh. Forest seems a little stressed out.

Once the gear is squared away, and I've checked to make sure Charlie is buckled, I pull away from the curb.

A moment later I hear Charlie's phone ping. He reads the text and then groans.

"Problem?"

"Did you *make* him text me? Because it says—*Beck is picking you up today. Say thank you and NO VIDEO GAMES UNTIL MATH IS DONE.*"

"Oh man, I'm sorry."

Charlie sighs. "Beck, you don't give serial killer vibes. We could have done without the text."

I snort. "That's the nicest thing anyone said to me today. Maybe I'll put it on my Grindr profile. *No serial killer vibes.*"

Oh shit. I shouldn't mention Grindr to a child.

"You should delete that app," Charlie says sagely. "And just date my dad."

"It was a poor joke," I admit. "I deleted that app a long time ago, mostly because it's full of—" I just barely stop myself from saying *assholes*, which would be an unfortunate double entendre. "Jerks."

"My dad needs a boyfriend," Charlie presses. "I mean, my

mom has one. His name is Mick, and all he talks about is pickleball."

"Hmm," I say, wondering how to get off this topic. "So what's the deal with your math homework?"

Another teenage groan. "Math is a BFD all of a sudden. Ever since I failed that test. I'm supposed to redo the whole test as homework, and my parents are *all* freaked out. Especially my mom." His voice goes all high and he says, "*In this family we don't fail tests, Charlie.*"

"Ouch, buddy. What was on this test anyway?"

"Variables."

"What kind of variables?"

"X. Y. What difference does it make? I do fine in math. It's just this one chapter that's killing me. Math is supposed to be about numbers, and now there's this letter right in the middle of everything. And I'm supposed to know what that means? I'll just do better on the next unit. It'll be fine. There can't be a lot of letters in math."

Oh, little man. I turn at the next light. It's only another five minutes to Forest's house, so I have to think fast. "So... want some help knocking out that test? I remember variables." *From every single math class since eighth grade.*

"Really? You'd help me?" He sits up straighter. "If I got it done tonight, everyone will finally shut up about it."

"Sure," I say, wondering just how uncomfortable Forest will be if he finds me hanging out with his kid. "Let's knock it out. No problem. Maybe we can get it done before your dad comes home."

Okay. Well. This is going to take a little longer than I thought.

"The answer is four," Charlie says. "Why can't I just write down *four* and be done with it?"

The first math problem is: X + 3 = 7. Four is, of course, the answer. But until Charlie learns to manipulate expressions, he's going to keep on failing. "They need you to show your work."

"Why?" he complains. "This is stupid." He has the panicked look on his face of someone who's deeply in the weeds and doesn't want to admit it.

We've all been there. And maybe I'm an asshole for imagining I could solve this problem so easily. "Let's look at the next one. 2X + 5 = 11."

Charlie's face turns red. He looks away from the page. "This is stupid," he repeats in a small voice. "I'll never get it."

"That's not true, pal," I say, feeling a little sweaty, myself. "This whole thing is just like a hockey team."

He gives me a dark look. "Not hardly. If this were hockey, I'd know what to do."

"But you will," I insist. "Just follow my lead here for a second. You need the same number of players on every team, right?"

"Well, yeah, unless there's a penalty."

"Right. But there aren't any penalties in math. And the equals sign? It's like the center line, okay? You need the same number of players on each side. Look at this problem again." I tap the page at 2X + 5 = 11. "Whatever happens to one team also has to happen to the other one. So, what if I took these five players away from the left side?"

Charlie frowns down at the test. "You better take five away from the right side."

"*Yes.*" I cross out the "5" and then write "-5" on the other side. "Now how many players remain for righty?"

"Six," he says easily, and we're left with 2X = 6.

I write that down. "Now here's the thing—I want you to think of

X as a player with a blank jersey on. He's, like, wearing a disguise, and we have to move the other players around until we can figure out who he is. That's all a variable is—a guy in a blank jersey."

Charlie chews his lip. "So who is he?"

"Let's try the same trick one more time. If we divide 2X by two…"

"Then you have to do it again over here." He points at the other side of the equation.

I push the test in his direction. "You do it."

Charlie divides each side by two.

"Great!" I say, relieved. "So now who is X?"

"Uh, three?"

"YES!" I shout. "Go on. Do another one. How about this one down here?"

"That one looks hard. Is Y the same as X?"

"Yup, just another imposter. Treat him the same. You got this."

And he does. It's all going great until the door suddenly opens.

TWENTY-FIVE

Uh, Hi.

FOREST

I DRIVE HOME in the worst mood. The rental car I'm driving is already eating into my inadequate savings, and I'm about to confront a hungry kid about math homework. Also, I'm giving myself whiplash about whether asking Beck for a favor was a great idea or an asshole move.

When I pull into my driveway, Beck's Jeep is there. I trudge inside, expecting to find a video game session in progress. But when I'm kicking off my wet boots in the garage, I overhear a conversation I don't understand.

"Yes! Move that five over the center line. Now divide by... yes! You're doing great, Coach. Okay—now what's his jersey number supposed to be?"

"Seven," Charlie says with a snort. "This isn't really all that hard."

I yank open the door, and I find Charlie and Beck sitting at the kitchen table. "Uh, hey," Beck says. He looks oddly guilty.

"Dad, guess what? I'm almost done."

"Almost done with...?" I can't even guess. He can't mean that damn test—the bane of our existence.

"The math!" Charlie says. "*Duh*. It's not that bad. Beck showed me how to do it the hockey way."

"The...*what*?" I'm struggling to catch up.

Beck gives me an embarrassed smile. "I just, uh, knew Charlie could do it. With a little change of the coaching strategy."

"Number nine is done!" Charlie announces. He waves the paper in my face as I approach. "Dad, can you order Mexican? I only have four problems to go."

"Well..." Unfortunately, our takeout food habit will have to end if I'm buying a new truck tomorrow.

"Pleeeeeeease? We should treat Beck."

"No, it's fine," Beck says. "Totally unnecessary."

I glance at Charlie. "We can't have takeout anyway, bud, because your mom is on her way, and I probably have to go to work. But if your mom is late, I'll make some pasta."

The enthusiasm drains from Charlie's face like air from a punctured tire. "Seriously? Beck just saved my life, and we can't even order burritos to say thank you?"

"Charlie." I try to keep my voice level, but there's an edge creeping in. "I said I already had a plan for dinner."

"Pasta again?" His voice cracks with disappointment. "Dad, this is like... a big deal. I actually get it now. And Beck drove all the way over here to help me, and you won't even—"

"*I said no.*" The words come out sharper than I intended, and Charlie's expression crumbles.

Beck pushes back in his chair. "Hey, I have to head out anyway—"

"God!" Charlie snaps. "This is so stupid. Mom would totally let us order food. Mick probably would have gotten us dessert too."

The comparison hits like a slap. Of course Mick can afford dessert. Mick gets paid high six figures as an anesthesiologist.

"Well, I'm not Mick," I say, my voice flat. "And this is my house."

Charlie stares at me for a long moment, something hurt and confused flickering across his face. Then he grabs his pencil and paper and stomps into the living room to finish the work there. At least I hope that's his plan.

I sit down in his chair and put my head in my hands. "Thank you," I tell Beck. "Seriously. I didn't know how I was going to find and pay for a fucking tutor."

"Hey," he says, his voice soft and low. He puts a hand on my thigh and squeezes. "It was nothing. I was listening to him grumble about the math in the car, and I thought maybe I could help."

"Seems like you helped a lot. But..." I bow my head, wishing I could throw the celebratory dinner that Charlie wants. And wishing I could just let this happen. Meals together. Math homework and video games and easy fun together. If I squint, I can *almost* see it. I sigh. "I'm sorry."

"For what?"

Rising from the table, I say, "Let me walk you to your car."

His face falls. "Okay, sure." He puts his coat on and follows me out to the driveway.

"That a loaner?" he asks, glancing at the Honda.

"Yup. I have to buy something tomorrow, whether I'm ready or not."

He winces. "Sorry."

"That makes two of us. I was a few months from having the down payment I need." We stop at Beck's Jeep, and I park my hip against it. "It pisses me off that I can't even buy you dinner to thank you for what you did for me today."

He throws his arms out to the sides. "When did I ever give you the impression that I give a crap about who picks up the dinner check?"

"You haven't," I admit. "But *I* fucking care." He solved two problems for me in one afternoon, but I can't even express my gratitude. "Look, I really do have to work tonight," I tell him. "And you're right that I have poker tomorrow. I can't blow it off this week, because—" *Oh jeez.* "Because it's my birthday, and they're getting me a cake."

He stares. "Your *birthday*? You weren't going to mention it?"

"Fuck no. My birthday isn't something I care about." It's not a lie. "When you're my age..."

He laughs. "Your age, huh. So tomorrow you turn... fifty-seven?"

"Thirty-five, you ass."

He smiles, then he takes a step closer. And fuck me, my pulse kicks into a higher gear like it always does around this guy. He knows it, too. He puts a warm hand on my neck and gives me a firm squeeze. "I'm glad *someone* is going to wish you a happy birthday, you old grump. Wish it could be me."

There's a wall made of stubbornness inside my chest, and I can almost hear a few of the bricks crumbling when I ask, "Do you happen to play poker?"

"Do I play poker?" Beck scoffs. "I've memorized the statistical probability tables for Texas Hold 'em. Did you know that pocket aces only win about eighty-five percent of the time in heads-up play because variance is a cruel mistress?"

Figures. I smile in spite of myself. "So. You busy tomorrow? Want to come with me to my Wednesday-night game?"

"You know I do." He leans in and brushes his lips against my cheekbone.

And because I'm not a lucky man, my ex pulls up to the house.

TWENTY-SIX

Who's Your Friend?

BECK

I FEEL FOREST STIFFEN, and I quickly step back. "What now?"

Then I spot the BMW at the foot of the driveway. A pretty woman with shiny brown hair hops out. She's wearing a chic coat and the kind of stiletto leather boots that say *I have somewhere important to be, and you're not invited.*

The ex-wife, I presume. She does not look happy to see me. This is the first time I've ever been glad that Forest is too classy to shove his tongue in my mouth in the driveway. Because it's clear that she feels she's caught us in some illicit tryst.

"Hello," she says crisply. "What's going on? Where's your truck, Forest?"

"May she rest in peace."

"Ah." She winces. "Sorry. And who's your friend? Am I interrupting a... date?" She pronounces the word like it's dirty.

And, to be fair, my "dates" with Forest usually are.

Forest sighs. "Ruby, this is Becker. He's just on his way out, after spending his afternoon helping us out."

She looks alarmed. "By...?"

"Well, first he picked up Charlie from hockey."

"He picked Charlie up?" she repeats. "In..." She glances at

the two unfamiliar vehicles in the driveway, and, demonstrating classic mom instincts, her gaze falls onto my heap. "That?"

"The seatbelts function fine, ma'am," I say, starting to get offended. "Just got my license last week, so I'm being extra careful."

Her lips turn white.

"*Beck.*" Forest closes his eyes. "He's *kidding*, Ruby. You should also know that Beck just tutored Charlie all the way through the math test redo."

She blinks. "Seriously? The whole test?"

Her expression is so dubious, I actually laugh. "It's not multi-variable calculus. Charlie isn't bad at math, either. He caught on quick enough." I leave the word *bitch* off the end of the sentence, but it's implied.

"Well, that's a relief," she says coolly. "Where is he?"

Like it's not obvious?

"Beck," Forest says with forced patience, "would you mind letting Charlie know his mother has arrived?"

"Sure." I head back to the house, not missing the way Forest steps closer to his ex, dropping his voice so he can quietly give her a piece of his mind.

I open the house's door from the garage and step inside. "Charlie? Your mom is here. She's looking for you."

"Already?"

"Sad, but true."

He emerges a minute later, shoving stuff into a messy back-pack. "Uh, thanks for your help with everything. You made vari-able stuff easy."

"So did you, dude. You got this."

He gives me a faint smile.

When we emerge, Forest's ex-wife is standing stiffly in the driveway, arms crossed. "Hi, Charlie. I hear congratulations are in order."

"You heard right! Can we get Mexican?"

"Sure, honey," she says.

I feel Forest's flinch like a stab.

"Becker," she says as her son throws his gear into the back of her car, "Thank you for your help today. Charlie really needed the support."

"It was fun," I say lightly.

She opens the driver's door. "Charlie, thank your dad's friend for helping you."

"He did about sixty seconds ago," I say. "Without any prompting from Forest, too."

Oops. That last bit just slipped out, and I probably deserve the dark look I'm getting now.

Worth it, though, especially because Forest is trying not to smile.

Forest says goodbye to Charlie, and then the ex drives away. Finally.

Forest turns to me. "I'm sorry. She's actually not a horrible person. I'm about to get a whole bunch of questions about you, though."

"What does she want? Psychiatric workup? DNA sample on file? Criminal history?"

He flinches. "Something like that. I had a rough patch last year and now she has trust issues."

Hmm. That's not the first time he's referenced some trouble, but whenever I ask, he clams up. "Don't worry about it. I get it. Exes are hard." Not that I have any.

And at this pace, I never will. Forest had made it clear that he's not boyfriend material. Which is not something I want to think about right now. Or ever.

"So, what's the buy-in for poker night?" I ask.

"Twenty bucks," he says. "That is what divorced dads can afford."

"Cool. Sounds fun. You'll tell me when and where?"

"Seven o'clock. I'll send you the address."

I start to walk to my Jeep but then turn back. "Wait. I forgot something."

"What? Mphff..." he says when I kiss him, right here in his driveway.

"Hang in there, tough guy. See you tomorrow."

I drive home wondering what I can get Forest for his birthday that doesn't look like I'm trying too hard.

TWENTY-SEVEN

Got a Confession to Make

FOREST

DENNY and I are putting chips and pretzels into bowls in his kitchen in preparation for poker night. He's our ringleader, and he has the nicest house and a custom poker table, so we usually meet up here.

"Happy birthday, man!" he says. "Has it been a good one?"

"Sort of? Bought a truck today."

"What did you buy?"

"A Nissan Frontier. Picking it up tomorrow after rust-proofing."

"Sweet ride!"

"Sort of. It's five years old, and it's got forty thousand miles on it already." It was a lucky find, though. It's better for my budget than a new truck, and it already had a plow hookup, too, which will save me several hundred more dollars.

No stereo system at all, though, which is a bummer. There's just an empty hole in the dash where it should be.

"I thought you were getting a new truck?"

"Yeah, so did I."

"Oh."

"It's fine," I say quickly. "Now I don't have to think about it anymore."

I hear a car outside, and my gaze flicks nervously toward the kitchen door, wondering if it's Beck. But Kenji steps through the door instead, shaking snow off his boots. "Hey guys!" Of all the divorced dads, he seems the happiest. He's big into snowboarding and is often jetting off somewhere to bag another sick peak and then posting on Instagram. He's always wearing a big grin, with his long black hair spilling out of his helmet.

And behind him is CJ, who wears a lot of plaid and has an unfortunate mustache. "What's news?" CJ asks.

Denny points at me with a pretzel. "Forest bought himself a truck for his birthday."

"Score!" Kenji says. "Happy birthday, man." He slaps me on the shoulder. "Who's coming tonight?"

"Everybody," Denny says. Our full roster is just five guys. "Big Bob got the night off, after all."

"Cool."

I take a breath, because I haven't mentioned Beck yet, and I know I'm just making it weird now. The truth is I feel awkward mixing these parts of my life. My Dad Friends are all straight. They know I'm queer, and that I run a queer bar. They aren't the least bit bothered by my sexuality.

It's just that I never talk about dates or hookups with this crowd, and I sure as hell haven't mentioned Beck.

"Um, guys?" I let out an awkward laugh. "Got a confession to make. I kind of invited someone tonight. Just this once. It's someone I'm dating."

Instant silence as they all gawk at me.

"Really?" Kenji says eventually. "Okay."

"I know we don't really do that," I stammer. "But I had to mention my birthday..."

They're still staring. "This person," Denny says slowly. "Is it a…"

"A guy," I say firmly.

That's when the tension breaks.

"*Oh!*" CJ hoots. "Why dincha just say so?"

"I mean…" Denny says with a shake of his head. "If you invited a chick to poker night, that would just be weird. Wait—is that terrible? Am I being an asshole?"

"No, no," Kenji says, looking relieved. "I had the same thought. So maybe I'm an asshole, too. But poker night has a *vibe*, you know? I mean—I *love* women."

"So do I," Denny insists. "Almost anywhere, anytime."

"But not poker night," CJ agrees. "Phew."

And now I have emotional whiplash.

"So who is this guy?" Denny demands. "Where'd you meet him?"

"At my bar, of course. He was a regular."

Kenji grins. "And then one night you took him home after work?"

"Aww, our little Forest is thawing out," coos Denny.

"Well no," I admit. "He asked me out, and I said no."

"Of course you did," CJ scoffs. "Who's surprised?"

Nobody raises a hand.

"But then we were short a goalie for one of our games," I add. "And guess who's a goalie?"

They all crack up. "No way," Kenji says. "He seduced you with his moves in the crease?"

"Something like that."

They roar as Denny shoes us into the great room, where the poker table lives.

"Tell us more," Kenji demands. "Can't wait to see what kind of guy is Forest's type."

"He's..." How do I even describe Beck? "Well, he's younger than I am." That'll be the first thing anyone will notice. "And more fun. But we both have crazy schedules, so we don't get to see much of each other. And this week he bailed me out twice. Picked up Charlie from hockey and then tutored him for an hour. And then Ruby gave him a hard time."

There's a collective groan—the same one we make whenever someone mentions their ex.

"He play poker?" Denny asks. "That's all that really matters here."

"Of course," I say.

The doorbell rings, and everyone turns toward the front of the house with matching curious grins. They're practically salivating. Kenji even rubs his hands together.

How do I get into these situations?

I move toward the door, but Kenji leaps forward, winning the race. He swings open the door with a flourish. "Hey, man! You must be Forest's date. We could not be more curious."

"Thanks, I think."

I find myself smiling. Typical Beck.

He looks good, unzipping his parka to reveal a blue button-down shirt with little white flowers all over it. It's dapper in a way that catches me off-guard. And dark jeans that fit like they were tailored just for his strong body.

"I'm Kenji, and you are...?"

"*Becker James*?" yells Denny with obvious disbelief. He actually shoves me out of the way for a better view. "The Ice Cats' goalie?"

"Yup," says Beck, shifting a box under one arm so he can shake hands all around. "Some of the time, anyway."

"Holy shit, Forest!" Denny yelps. "You bagged yourself a younger man, and he happens to be a professional athlete?"

I sigh. "Could you not sound quite so surprised?"

Another roar of laughter.

Beck sidesteps my friends and ends up in front of me. I'm trying to decide on how to greet him in this situation. I feel like we're onstage. But Beck solves this problem by pulling me into a one-armed man hug for a half second. "Happy birthday, old man. Wasn't sure what to bring a bartender on his birthday, so I went with some cocktail fixings." He hands me the box. "Cheers."

"Oh, cool," I say, looking down into the open box. It's full of mixers from an artisanal cocktail place in Boulder, plus a couple of small bottles of liquor. "I love this stuff."

"Fancy," Kenji agrees. "We can start with a blood-orange margarita or a mojito."

"Mojitos!" yells Big Bob from the front hall where he's removing his coat. "I'll mix! Let's get our poker on."

"In a second," Denny says. "What are your intentions with our friend Forest?"

"Oh God, Denny," I moan, wanting to die.

Beck gives me a fond glance. "I intend to destroy him in poker. Birthday be damned."

I grin.

What follows are some of the most entertaining poker games of my life.

In the first place, Kenji uses Beck's gourmet ingredients to make us all a blood-orange margarita that's so good I almost cry.

Then there's the game itself. Beck is a proficient poker player with a few professional-level skills. He doesn't showboat. He doesn't take chances. And—I really should have seen this coming—*nobody* can tell when he's bluffing.

"You sneaky fucker," Big Bob complains for the third time as

Beck wins another big pot with nothing but a pair of fours. "I'll get you next time."

Beck hums like he's considering this. "Statistically, you won't. But I support your optimism," he says, while I try not to notice the way his shirt is unbuttoned at the top, showing off just a V of skin that I can't stop staring at.

I mean, it *is* my birthday. I don't think it's unreasonable to assume I'll be unbuttoning that shirt later and peeling it off his body.

Big Bob wins some chips off Beck, finally, and crows about it.

Beck tips his head. "Nice. I love watching underdog documentaries in real time."

Kenji snorts into his cocktail glass, and then somebody breaks out the cigars. And also a chocolate cake.

"Don't sing to me," I mutter. "I'm not seven. Just deal me a decent hand, Kenji."

"Sure thing, bud."

But I just don't have the cards tonight—which, let's be honest, is just how my life has been working out lately. Even on my birthday. I run out of chips eventually, and so does Denny. The game comes down to a final standoff between Big Bob and Beck.

I can tell from Big Bob's face that he thinks he's got a winning hand. "I'll raise you fifty," he says, pushing his chips toward Beck.

The look Beck gives him says: *you sure about that?* "I'll call," Beck says with enough composure that Big Bob is probably shitting himself already.

And, yeah, it's all over a minute later. Beck wins with a pair of tens.

Big Bob flips over ace-high. "Christ!" he hollers. "How did you know I was bluffing? I thought you'd fold, for sure."

"Reading guys who are trying to take advantage of me is my day job."

"You must be a fantastic goalie," he mutters. "We got time for one more cocktail?"

"Sure," Kenji says. "I'll whip something new up. Hold, please." He gets out of his chair and heads for the kitchen.

TWENTY-EIGHT

It Was a Whiskey Sour

BECK

AFTER I STACK MY WINNINGS, I gather up the cards and let my hands do what they do best. The cards flow between my fingers in perfect arcs, making that soft whisking sound as they cascade together. I do a bridge shuffle, letting the cards waterfall in a controlled stream, then split the deck and weave them back together with a rhythmic *flick-flick-flick*.

"Show off," Forest mutters, but he's giving me a sly, sexy smile.

I don't need to look down as the cards dance between my hands—riffle, bridge, cut, repeat. The sound is soothing, like rain on a roof. I glance at Forest and find that he's still watching me with warm eyes. Sometimes I catch that look from Forest and I just *know* we could be more. I'm not supposed to have those thoughts, though. It's against the rules.

Then again, he invited me tonight. It has to mean something, doesn't it?

Denny puts on a hockey game on the giant screen above his fireplace, and Kenji comes back with a new set of cocktails.

"I shouldn't really drink this," Forest says. "I've had plenty."

"You go ahead," I offer. "It's your birthday. I'll be the sober driver."

"Aw, Forest. I like this one." Denny asks. "Can we keep him?"

If only, buddy.

Forest just smiles blandly.

"To Forest!" Kenji says, raising his cocktail in the air. "And many more trips around the sun."

"Hear hear!" CJ says.

I dutifully raise the glass that Kenji has set down beside me. It's rude not to take a sip after *cheers*. And it's a tasty concoction. Kenji has used the sour mix from my kit to make some kind of elevated whiskey sour, I think.

But when I look over at Forest, he seems to have a different opinion. I watch his glass stop right under his nose. Something flickers across his face. Then he finally takes a sip, and the look on his face is pure revulsion.

Odd.

"What do you think?" Kenji asks.

Forest takes a shallow breath. "I need some air," he says, pushing back from the table.

"What?" Big Bob looks up from his phone. "Dude, it's like twenty degrees out there."

"Just... need a minute." Forest is already standing, one hand gripping the back of his chair. "I'll be right back." Forest gestures vaguely toward the sliding door that leads to Denny's back deck. "Hot in here."

It's not hot in here. If anything, Denny keeps his place on the cool side.

Forest is already moving toward the door, leaving his jacket behind. Through the glass, I watch him step out onto the snow-covered deck in just his flannel shirt, his breath immediately visible in the frigid air.

The table goes quiet for a moment, everyone exchanging looks.

"That was weird," Kenji mutters.

Yes, it was. My heart thumps with a warning that something is very wrong. So I head to the mudroom off the kitchen, grab both our jackets, and follow Forest outside.

I find him leaning up against the back of the house his arms crossed against the cold, breathing purposefully, as if trying to stay calm.

He glances up when I come out the door and I offer his jacket wordlessly. "Thanks." He gives me a wary look. "Is there any world in which you turn around now and go back into the house?"

"Nope."

"I didn't think so." He heaves a sigh. "It was a whiskey sour."

"The drink? I figured." *But what am I missing?*

"It was a whiskey sour that fucked up my whole life," he says heavily.

Oh wow.

"Right after my last birthday, actually. There was this guy..." He looks away, and his body language is... broken. I've never seen him look defeated before. "We both swiped right on an app. I invited him over to my place for sex. He pretended to be really interested in all of my bartending supplies. What he was really interested in doing was drugging my drink."

"*Holy shit.* Forest."

He gives me an angry glance, the kind that says: *don't you dare feel sorry for me.* "I woke up the next morning, no memory of any of it. Except—before you ask—I was still wearing all my clothes."

I sag with relief.

"Yeah, in this case, it wasn't that kind of violence. Instead, he emptied my bank account. I lost more than thirty grand.

Money I'd been saving for a down payment on a new truck, plus what I was supposed to be living on for the next few months."

Jesus. "Can't they… Did you call the police?"

He gives me a look like it's a stupid question. "Of course I did. Two cops showed up, and I spent the most embarrassing couple hours of my life explaining how I let a stranger into my house to poison me. Like the biggest dumbass that ever lived." His voice is pure bitterness. "And even after all that, it didn't help. I can't recover *anything*. It turns out if you authorize a wire transfer with your fingerprint—even if you're minimally conscious—the bank isn't always liable."

"Oh my fucking God. And they couldn't find the guy?"

He shakes his head slowly. "He was slick. His account on the dating app wasn't connected to anything traceable. They couldn't find his license plate on any neighborhood cameras. And he'd wired my savings into a foreign bank account before I woke up, so it's gone forever. I even paid some forensic accountants money that I don't have to dig a little deeper. But it didn't matter. The bank isn't liable for the transaction."

I lean back against the wall and look up into the starry sky. I'm not very good at saying exactly the right thing. Everybody knows that. But I give it a shot anyway. "I'm so sorry. That's so… violating."

He hangs his head. "Yeah, it fucked me up. It's not really even about the money. It's knowing I let him do that to me. I had to explain to Charlie that his gaming console was stolen, as well as his Bluetooth speaker. Then I had to explain to his mother why I couldn't take him at the usual time, because I had to be drug-tested at the ER. She was actually really helpful, but now, of course, she is afraid for me all the time."

"Fuck. I mean—you only did what millions of guys do every day."

"Yeah, I'm just lucky like that." He gives a bitter laugh, and it ends up as a sigh.

The night is quiet around us, except for Denny's laugh from inside the house.

"Look, can I drive you home?" I ask. "I'll make some excuse inside."

I expect him to protest. "Thank you," he says softly instead. "Let's go."

TWENTY-NINE

It Explains a Lot

FOREST

IT'S A QUIET RIDE HOME. I can't believe I ruined my birthday. I'd been having *fun*, damn it. I don't regret talking it through with Beck, though. I trust him.

We're nearing my street when he breaks our silence. "Thank you for telling me, Forest. I'm sure you didn't want to."

Ain't that the truth. "This is in the vault, okay? Even Scully doesn't know the whole story. Nobody does, except for Ruby."

He gives me a sideways glance. "I guess I understand now. Why she's wary of me."

"Yeah. Honestly, it explains a whole lot, right? Like when I had such a shitty reaction to you hitting on me."

He reaches over and places a hand briefly on my knee. "Glad to know I'm not just ugly."

I snort. "You are the opposite of ugly. Which is probably why you're the only guy I've been with in almost a year."

He squeezes my leg before returning his hand to the wheel. "I thought it was my sexy conversation style."

"Now you're just fishing for compliments. You know I like the whole package. I wasn't lying when I said I wasn't in a good place to date anyone. This past year was all rage and financial instability."

"Yeah, I get that now. But..." He frowns.

"But?"

"A year is a long time to be so hard on yourself," he says quietly.

"Not really." I snort. "It'll take me longer than that to rebuild. And even when I make back all that money, I'll still be pissed off at myself."

"You could be," Beck says, turning onto my street. "Or you could apply goalie rules."

"I...what?"

He rolls slowly up to my house and pulls into the driveway. Then he kills the engine and turns to study me. "Goalie rules," Beck says, unbuckling his seatbelt. "Like, the worst game of my life was in college. Against Michigan. I let in seven goals. *Seven*. On twenty-three shots. That's a save percentage that most twelve-year-olds can beat."

He runs a hand through his hair, and I can see the memory still stings.

"The fourth goal went right through my five-hole—a weak shot from the point that I should have stopped with my eyes closed. The fifth one bounced off my glove and trickled over the line. The sixth was a rebound I kicked right to their center. By the seventh, the crowd was booing every time I touched the puck."

"Jesus, Beck."

"Coach pulled me halfway through the second period. I'd never been pulled that early in my life. When I got to the bench, my teammates wouldn't even look at me. I sat there watching our backup try to salvage what was left of the game, and I just... I wanted to disappear. Like, actually cease to exist."

He stares out the windshield at my front door, lost in the memory.

"That night I called my high school coach, whining like a ten-year-old. Told him I was thinking about quitting. That maybe I just wasn't good enough. He cut me off after a few minutes of bitching and said the thing I needed to hear."

"Which was?"

He turns to me with those clear eyes, and they are deep pools of empathy. "He said, James, the only save that matters is the next one. That's goalie rules—you can't carry the last goal with you into the next play. You forgive yourself, reset, and focus forward.' I started the next game three days later. Thirty-seven saves, shutout victory. But none of that would have happened if I was still beating myself up about Michigan."

I knew Beck was a stud, but he's making a logical error, here. "My life isn't a game. I don't get eighty chances in a season to get it right. And that asshole still has tens of thousands of my dollars."

"No, I disagree." He reaches over and touches my hand. "Every day is a fresh start, no matter what your bank balance says. The point of goalie rules isn't that you have to forget the shitty things that happened. The point is that if you don't *forgive* yourself, the asshole who violated you keeps winning. You gave him enough of your happiness already, don't you think?"

"Shit." I lift a shaking hand to cover my eyes, which are suddenly hot.

"Hey, hey," he says, leaning across the console and pulling me into his arms. "It's okay, man. That's what I'm trying to tell you. Just let that shit out. Let it go."

I make a noise that sounds suspiciously like a sob. And I cling to Beck like I'm drowning in the ocean, and he's a life preserver.

Beck just holds me. I can feel his steady heartbeat against my chest.

Getting a grip, I try to even out my breathing, but he doesn't release me. We just stay here a while as I take gulps of the night air and let the warmth of him seep into my cold heart.

Just when it might get embarrassing, he tips his head a fraction and kisses my neck. Then he does it again.

It feels so good that I have to squeeze my eyes shut against another flood of emotion. I coast a hand between the unzipped halves of his jacket and curve my hand around his waist. The crisp cotton of his shirt is smooth against my palm. His hot mouth on my neck is a balm to my soul, and I let out a groan that makes sure he knows it. Then all I have to do is turn my head a few degrees to find his mouth with my own.

Before long we're steaming up his Jeep. I thought I'd killed the mood for sure, but apparently not. His kiss is deep and his hands are magic.

I want to stay here forever. It seems like goalie rules apply to sex, too, because whenever we're alone together I seem to lose track of my past failings and focus on only heat and urgency. And then Beck's whispered plea. "Why don't we head inside."

THIRTY

Like Seeing the Face of God

FOREST

I WAKE up to the smell of coffee and the sensation of the bed dipping under someone's weight.

"Coffee?" Beck says. His knuckles take a leisurely trip through my beard.

I blink against the morning light, taking in his handsome face with the pillow crease still pressed into his left cheek. His hair is sticking up at odd angles, and somehow that makes him even more beautiful.

"You were out of bread, so I ran out to pick up some breakfast."

"Out...of the house?"

"Yeah, we're both surprised." He grins. "It's wet and gross out there. Quick, warm me up."

He sheds a pair of sweatpants that I recognize as my own, and I get a glimpse of those long legs before he climbs back under the covers, immediately wrapping himself around me in a full-body embrace. His skin is cool from the morning air, and I automatically pull him closer.

"That's more like it," he says, planting his cold feet against my warmer ones.

I'm getting way too used to this. To *him*. To the way he makes everything feel lighter. "What did you get us?" I ask, hoping it wasn't expensive.

"My treat," he says, reading my mind like he always does. "It's just egg sandwiches from this deli I like."

"Thank you," I say.

"I know you hate it when I pay for things, but I have to eat before practice or I'll die."

"When do you have to leave?"

"An hour? Today's a late one. Coach must have had a meeting." He nuzzles against my shoulder. "So, honestly, it's a huge conundrum."

"What is?"

"Eat the eggs while they're hot, or…" He starts kissing my neck, his lips warm against my skin. "More sex."

Ohhhh. I close my eyes as he nibbles at the sensitive skin beneath my jaw and I only feel contentment as Beck's warm body presses against mine and his messy blond hair tickles my shoulder.

But then the kisses stop abruptly. He pulls back slightly, those blue eyes bright with mischief. "On second thought, egg sandwiches aren't as good when they're cold."

"Seriously? You tease."

"Always leave 'em wanting more. Hey—grab my arm? I think I can just reach the bag without getting out of bed. We'll eat here where it's warm."

Gamely, I hold onto him while he stretches down to snag our breakfast off the floor, enjoying the view as his muscles ripple under his golden skin.

A minute later we're both sitting up against my headboard, unwrapping warm egg sandwiches, mostly naked beneath the covers. "This is a level of debauchery that I could never get away with when I was married," I confess.

"In a good way?"

"Yeah, buddy, in a good way." I run a toe down his muscular calf.

Beck smiles, and my heart cracks open a little further. That smile is more dangerous than crumbs in the bed.

Beside me, he lets out a happy sigh. "When I taste bacon, it's like seeing the face of God."

"Truth. And it's even better when you don't have to clean the frying pan after."

"Facts."

We're almost done eating when I hear Beck's phone ping from the nightstand. He grabs it and squints at the screen. Then I see his blue eyes widen. "Oh shit!"

"Problem?"

"I have to go." He leaps out of bed, and I can't help but admire his form as he hops around my room, looking for various pieces of his clothing.

"Did you get the time wrong?"

"No. Better. Look." He tosses the phone onto the bed, eyes bright with excitement.

I pick it up and read the text message on the screen.

COACH POWERS

We're keeping Volkov out of practice today to rest a muscle strain. Can you scrimmage with us at the Boulder facility? Scrimmage starts at 11 but come in when you can to warm up.

"Whoa!" I say. "You're practicing with the Cougars? How often does this happen?"

"Never. That's how often. I have a two-way contract, but I've never been recalled." He's trying to cram a sock on one foot from a standing position, looking a little like a flustered flamingo. "I have to get my gear from home."

"I know, Beck. But take a breath. You have plenty of time to get there. Finish your sandwich."

He grabs the remainder and shoves it into his mouth in one enormous bite, and I laugh.

"Now drink your coffee. And we need to get you some water, too."

"Okay. Yeah. Good point," he chatters. "Thanks."

"Hey." I step into his space and force him to look at me. "What kind of energy do you want to bring to this practice. The frantic kind?"

His clear eyes lock onto mine, and he shakes his head.

"Then do me a favor." I place a hand on his sternum, where his heart is beating wildly. "Take a slow breath. Fill your lungs from bottom—" I press the heel of my hand into his chest. "—to top. Come on, now. Just take a moment for yourself."

Watching me, he takes a slow breath and sighs it out.

"Again."

He closes his eyes and breathes deeply.

"There you go. That's it. Now remember that feeling." I pick up his to-go cup off the nightstand. "Let me get you a bottle of water to drink. Stay hydrated, okay?"

He gives me a nervous smile, and a few minutes later, I'm alone in my kitchen, listening to the sound of his Jeep pulling out of my driveway. Then silence. I listen to the heat cycle on, and picture him heading speedily toward home to grab his gear.

And I'm almost as excited as he is.

THIRTY-ONE

It's Only a Scrimmage

BECK

I DRIVE TOWARD THE HIGHWAY, trying to remember the sensation of Forest's hand on my chest. *Breathe.* When I have myself under control, I dictate a reply to Coach Powers's message.

BECK

I'll be there. Flying towards Boulder like a greyhound who heard the treat bag rattle.

COACH:

Awesome. We'll be skating drills when you get here. Just head into the dressing room and Banks will sort you out with a practice jersey. Warm up and stretch all you need.

And drive safe, okay? We'll wait.

I take another deep breath and try to visualize the next couple of hours, but it only makes me more nervous. So I ask my phone to text Forest with a couple of thoughts.

BECK

Question for you. Would it be bad karma to
steal the Cougars jersey after this practice?

Related: is it bad luck if I throw up beforehand?

FOREST

You're not going to throw up. And don't steal
the jersey, because only a guy who doesn't
think he's ever going to be invited back would
need to take it.

That's not you, Beck. This is just Thursday for a
professional athlete who's on his way to the top.

That seems like a generous interpretation. Still, it calms me down.

It's only a scrimmage, I remind myself. Besides—the Boulder rink has good juju. It's where I skated with Forest for the first time when I practiced with the Stickhandlers.

By the time I pull into the lot—parking in the farthest row so my hunk of metal doesn't stand out beside all their luxury cars —I'm calm enough. Sort of.

The lobby is empty when I walk in, except for a young woman in a sharp suit who's perched on a bench, typing furiously on her laptop. She looks up at me with a serious frown. "Becker James?"

"Yes ma'am."

"I'm Liana, Coach's assistant. Thank you for coming in on short notice."

"Happy to help," I say, as more nerves swirl through my bloodstream.

She rises from her seat, closes the laptop, and grabs a file folder out of her briefcase. My name is on the label. "Has any of your personal contact information changed since development camp this past summer?"

"Nope." I shake my head. "Same address. Haven't even repainted the mailbox. It's still puke green."

She gives me a strange look, but let's face it—we're both lucky I didn't say something even weirder. "Okay, then you'll receive a check in the mail for today. Now, off you go."

She leads me to a door that says *PLAYERS ONLY* and pushes it open. "Banks?" she calls. "He's here."

The young equipment manager appears a moment later. "Oh hey, Mr. James. I put you over here." He waves me toward a stall near the door. There's a grey practice jersey hanging there with the Cougars logo right on the chest.

Luckily, practice jerseys don't have names on them, because if I saw JAMES on that thing, I'd probably stroke out.

I drop my bag and start pulling out my base layers.

"Just let me know if you need anything at all," Banks says. "And go see the trainer when you're ready."

"Thanks." I hang up my jacket and start the long process of gearing up. This part is the same no matter who you're playing for, and the familiar procedure calms me down.

Thirty minutes later, I've warmed up my body on an exercise bike, I've stretched, and I've had my ankles taped up by a nice trainer named Kevin. He didn't even blink when I started babbling about the luckiest colors of tape.

At long last, an assistant coach sticks his head into the room. "Scrimmage in ten."

Gulp. Then I'm strapping on pads and tying my laces and internally saying a prayer that contains only four words: *don't fuck this up.*

The equipment guy hands me my stick and a water bottle, and I trundle out the door and down the black rubber path toward the ice. Coach Powers waves me toward the bench. "Hey, Beck! Thanks for your hustle. You're doing us a favor. We just needed to rest one guy for the weekend. That's in the vault, of course."

"Of course," I agree. They don't want me yapping that something is wrong with Volkov.

"Thanks, man. Strap in. Take the far end, okay?" He waves me toward one of the nets.

"Yessir." I step onto the ice, feeling like the new kid at school. The team is on a water break. Guys stand in twos and threes talking about whatever. This is just an ordinary Thursday for them, while my heart is doing laps around my ribcage.

I skate toward my net and drop my water bottle onto it. Then I drop to the ice for a couple more stretches, while surreptitiously glancing around at the players.

All the big names are here. I spot the team captain talking to defenseman Tommaso DiCosta. And there's Hudson Newgate chatting with Dougherty.

I've shared ice with a few of these guys before. In fact, now the backup goalie—Zack Walcott—is skating toward me, which is kind of surprising. I'm not a fan of this dude. He's always been way too smug.

So I'm not prepared for him to greet me with a friendly smile and say, "Beck! Great to see you. Gonna stop some pucks for us today?"

"That's the idea." I pick myself up off the ice so we're eye to eye.

"Cool, cool," he says, sounding ten degrees warmer than I ever thought him capable of. "Gotta guess that your first time getting called up can't possibly go as bad as mine. So you might as well relax."

"Wait, really?"

"Really." He thumps my shoulder pad. "I'll tell you sometime. Good story."

We're interrupted by David Stoneman, one of the alternate

captains and a fan favorite. He arrives with a spray of ice and a smile. "Hey, dude. I'm Stoney. You like burgers?"

Just be cool, Beck. "Doesn't everyone?"

"Well, no. Vegetarians exist. Not usually in this building, but still. And—this is even harder for me to process—not everybody drinks beer, either. Hale doesn't."

He points, and I spot Jethro Hale—my idol, and Coach Powers's boyfriend—taking a seat in the bleachers. He's not dressed to work out. He's holding a clipboard and a pen.

"Hale's first night with the team, I invited him to get drunk. But he doesn't drink any alcohol, so I've learned to ask."

"Uh, smart." Where is this conversation going, by the way? I've never met someone with a conversation style that's half as odd as my own.

Also...why is Hale here? It can't be to watch *me.*

Can it?

"So you and beer are friends?" Stoney asks, oblivious to my rioting nerves.

"We're more like drinking buddies who only see each other on weekends," I chatter. "But burgers and I are *tight.*"

He grins. "Cool! We'll get one after this, then."

I sneak another glance at Hale and see an older man sitting down beside him. "So, um, does Hale come to every practice?"

Stoney glances at the retired goalie again and frowns, like he's never thought about it before. "Nah, he's a scout. We rarely see him. The goalie coach is here, too. Huh. Maybe that's because of you? But hey, no pressure. See you after!"

He skates off, and I take a deep breath.

Our Father who art in hockey heaven, if you could get me through this without embarrassing myself, I'll let my subscription to Dude-Porn lapse, and I'll donate the money to a soup kitchen. Or an animal shelter. Or a soup kitchen for dogs. Is that a thing?

Coach blows his whistle. Every nerve ending fires inside me as I skate into the crease.

This is it. Time to prove I belong here, even if my stomach feels like it's hosting its own scrimmage.

Coach divides the team into squads, while I do a couple more last-minute stretches. The forwards line up for a simple drill—shots from the slot. Nothing fancy. I bounce on my toes, trying to shake out the jitters.

First shot comes from Hudson Newgate. Clean wrist shot, low blocker side. I catch it square in the chest, absorbing the rubber with a satisfying thump. The rebound bounces harmlessly to the corner.

"Nice!" someone calls out. Maybe Stoney.

The second shot comes from a guy I don't recognize—probably a fourth-liner. He winds up like he's trying to put the puck through the back wall but telegraphs it so obviously that I'm already there before he releases. Simple glove save.

"Easy there, cannon," I say, tossing the puck back to center. "Save some ice for the rest of us."

A few guys chuckle, and I feel myself relaxing by degrees. This is just hockey. I know how to do this.

They start cycling through more complex drills. Two-on-ones, breakaways, screens in front. My glove starts to sing. My positioning feels crisp, and I stop more shots than I let in.

The last shooter is Kapski, and when he comes in alone and tries to go five-hole, I snap my pads together like a bear trap.

I get a weighty nod from Coach. Then he claps his hands. "Nice warmup! Let's scrimmage!"

My heart hammers as they set up for a face-off, like I've watched them do on TV.

Don't fuck this up, don't fuck this up, don't fuck this up.

The puck drops and chaos erupts. Bodies crash into the corners. Sticks clash. I follow it all like my life depends on it.

The goalie's job isn't just saving pucks. I've got a view they don't have, and I'm supposed to share the wisdom.

"Heads up, Stoney!" I call as an opposing forward sneaks behind him. "Ghost on your six!"

Stoney spins and picks up the man just in time, breaking up the play.

"Back door!" I bark when I spot Wheeler drifting toward the weak side.

The defenseman adjusts, closing off the passing lane.

Then suddenly there's a loose puck sliding toward the slot where Dougherty is lurking like a vulture.

Time slows. He winds up for a one-timer. I slide across my crease, reading his eyes, his shoulders, the angle of his blade. When he releases, I'm already there. The puck smacks into my blocker and wings safely into the corner.

"Fucker," Dougherty says, shaking his head.

"That's *Mister* Fucker to you," I mutter, and he snorts as he skates off.

I'm in it now. I've got this. I face shot after shot, each save building my confidence. A sprawling pad save on Wheeler. A glove robbery on some defenseman's point shot. When Newgate tries to stuff a rebound past me, I slide post-to-post and swallow it up.

My inner voice finally shuts up. This is what I was born to do.

With five minutes left, they get a two-on-one. I stay patient, forcing the pass, and when it comes, I throw myself across to stop it. The sound of the puck hitting my pad echoes through the rink like a gunshot.

"Holy shit!" someone yells from the bench.

My thoughts exactly.

When Coach Powers blows his whistle, ending the scrimmage, I can't believe it—nothing went in.

I have an honest-to-God shutout.

Holy shit.

As I skate to the bench, guys are tapping their sticks on the ice—the hockey equivalent of applause.

Stoney skates over and bumps my mask with his glove. "Dude, nice showing."

"Thanks," I say quietly. But inside, I'm dancing.

And my next thought is, *I can't wait to tell Forest about this.*

Two hours later I'm climbing back into my Jeep after lunch with Stoney and a couple of his teammates, and I'm still feeling high on life.

I grab my phone out of the cupholder and look to see who's messaged me. I'm hoping to see Forest's name, but instead, I see my roommate's.

RIGSY

Dude. I got a keg! Be home by seven.

I read it twice, but I don't remember making any plans with him.

BECK

What? Did you meant to text me?

RIGSY

OF COURSE I DID YOU DUMBASS. We're
going to celebrate your rise to power!

Rigsy isn't the smartest tool in the shed. Maybe he thinks I got called up for real.

BECK

Um it was one practice? I'm still your
roommate. Don't rent out my room.

RIGSY

Duuuuuude. And I thought I was the dense one.
One practice in the big league is still one more
than the rest of us got. You're living my dream
right now. So we're doing this. Be home at
seven for beer and gaming. Invite Forest over.
He'll want to celebrate too.

Will he, though?

I hold my phone against my chest and try to take all this in.
Rigsy wants to celebrate with me? And he thinks Forest should
join us.

Honestly, I can't picture it.

But I text him anyways. Because hope is a megabitch.

THIRTY-TWO

Maybe Don't Be That Guy

FOREST

MY PHONE LIGHTS UP while I'm sitting outside Charlie's school, waiting for him to come out so I can take him to the dentist. I grab it and read:

BECK

Hey. You won't believe this, but I got a shutout at the scrimmage.

I take a deep breath and read it again. It still says what I thought it said, and suddenly my eyes feel weird and prickly.

Holy shit. A fucking shutout. This is going to change everything.

For once in my sorry life, I'm able to text him back immediately.

FOREST

THAT IS GODDAMN LEGENDARY! You absolute beast. A shutout?

BECK

Straight-up facts.

Holy… I mean, I'm not *that* surprised. I knew
you had the goods. Just as hot in the net as you
are in my bed. JFC, Beck.

Thanks. I'll be more excited once the shock
wears off. David Stoneman just bought me
lunch, can you believe that? And I wasn't even
weird.

Actually I was, but Stoney is also weird. I think
we canceled each other out, or something.

I'm grinning like a madman in the front seat of my car. I
barely register that Charlie is climbing in, because Beck texts me
one more time.

BECK

Hey, Rigsy is forcing me to celebrate tonight.
Beers at seven o'clock. He made a point to say
you should join us.

Beers? I have a much more wicked idea for how to celebrate,
and I'm just about to say so, when Charlie says, "Dad? Hi?"

My chin snaps up. "Hey, buddy."

"Who you texting?"

He slams the door of my new-to-me truck a little harder than
he should, and I hold back a sigh as I put down my phone and
put the truck in gear.

"Who was it?" Charlie demands. "Was it Beck? You had that
weird look on your face."

"What weird look?"

"The face you make when you're talking about him. Like this."

I risk a glance at the passenger seat to see Charlie make a
completely stupid face. "Buddy, please. I was just talking to Beck
because he had a big day, and we're friends."

"Friends." I can hear the smirk in his voice. I don't even have to look. "Is that what we're calling it?"

"*Yes*," I growl. "Because that's the right word." I mentally add *with benefits*. But it's still true.

And yes—I can admit that I care about Beck and that I was wrong to ever think he was too young to understand my life, or to matter to me.

His life and mine will diverge, though, sooner rather than later. Today's performance insures that.

"Why haven't we been to another Ice Cats game?" Charlie demands. "If he's your *friend*, we should watch him play."

"Only half his games are in Colorado," I point out. "The other times I've been at work, or at one of *your* games."

Charlie makes a disgruntled face. "But do you still see him?"

"Sometimes," I admit. But I won't be tonight.

As soon as I reach my driveway, I reply to Beck's invitation.

> Sorry I can't celebrate with you guys. I'm
> picking up a shift at work tonight.

Work and more work. That's the reality of the situation.

The next morning, though, when I pluck my phone off the bedside table, I find several texts from a strange number.

RIGSY

> Hey man, this is Beck's roommate. Remember
> me? You probably do, because you flashed me
> your package in my living room.

> Did you not get the invite last night? Because it
> was kind of a big deal. I mean—I'm trying to
> give you the benefit of the doubt. Maybe you
> don't follow hockey.

> But he talks about you sometimes, especially
> after a couple brews. What a good guy you are.
> How much he likes your bar. And you.

He would kill me for this. But you seem kinda like a girlfriend I had once—great girl but she just wasn't that into me. She let me dangle on the line instead of just throwing me back in the river. Low-key cruel.

Maybe don't be that guy, okay?

Thanks for coming to my Ted Talk.

I read all of this as shame pools in my gut. I don't want to be "low-key cruel" to Beck. I've been honest this whole time. Beck knows I'm not just keeping my options open so I can date other guys. He knows I care about him.

Doesn't he?

FOREST

I respect what you're doing here. Although you don't have all the information. And I will think about what you said.

I'll probably think of nothing else.

THIRTY-THREE

Best Seat in the House

FOREST

THE DREGS of winter bring a snowstorm, and I plow the parking lot of the bar with the help of my new truck. Then we're treated to a preview of spring with a thaw that turns the snowbanks into ugly piles of sludge.

The Stickhandlers make it to the beer league playoffs, where we lose in the first round. But so does the Plague, so I'm mostly okay with it.

Charlie's hockey season also ends, which means he has more free time for video games and sass. Not necessarily in that order.

I, on the other hand, have no free time at all. Another bartender quits, so I'm stuck on a work treadmill that just won't quit. Either I'm picking up extra shifts or interviewing prospective hires.

Beck and I manage a couple of sleepovers. Once at his place, where I avoid looking Rigsy in the eye on my way out. And once at my place, where I make Beck a fantastic brunch the next morning on his day off.

He seems happy—as sunny as ever when we're together—but Rigsy's message still stings a little.

Then, in the middle of another busy week, I'm training a new server one Thursday at the bar, when my phone starts dancing a jig in my pocket.

BECK

Hola

This text was scheduled to pop up on your phone just after the puck drops on the Cougars.

I need you to watch the bench.

Where I have the best seat in the house tonight.

Also, would it jinx me if you took a pic of the screen?

I've forgotten how to breathe, and when I remember again, all I can say is "Holy. Shit."

Ignoring the customer who just sat down with an expectant look on his face, I grab the TV remote. Aiming it at a nearby screen, I switch the channel away from the basketball game in a big fat hurry.

"I was *watching* that!" yelps Fregular, but I couldn't care less.

The Cougars are only three minutes into their game, but I'm glued to the action, waiting for the camera to pan the bench.

"Buddy?" Scully says, putting a hand on my shoulder. "Something wrong? Or are you just in the mood to ignore all our customers?"

"Watch the bench," I bark. "I think Beck is the backup tonight."

"No shit?" Scully says, his eyes zipping up to the screen.

"Can I get a Sierra Nevada?" someone says.

"In a minute," Scully thunders. "Pay attention! We got a friend having his first call up to Denver tonight."

The whole bar turns toward the hockey game. "Who is it?" Fregular demands. "Wait—that sexy Ice Cats goalie with the cute smile? I'd like to see him use his stick."

I growl, but Scully says, "Yup, that's our guy! Stay sharp, everyone. We need the camera to..."

A view of the bench pops onto the screen—a line of Cougars with their coach standing attentively behind them. And there he is. I let out a shout when I spot Beck, geared up and ready, watching the game from the bench.

The bar lets out a roar of applause and luckily Scully is filming it all on his phone, because I'm too overwhelmed to react.

Beck is up there on that screen, like I always knew he'd be. My throat is suddenly very tight, and when Scully claps me on the back, I struggle to make all the right noises.

He *did it*. Never mind that it's only an emergency call-up to sit on the bench. It's another stepping stone to greatness. He's on his way, and now everybody knows it.

Scully's phone looms into my face, and I lift a hand to push it out of my way. "What are you doing?"

"Had to preserve this for posterity. Forest gets all emotional over the goalie."

"I didn't get all emotional," I grunt, turning back to the bar to serve some drinks. I probably do a shitty job, because it's hard to be a good bartender when you're keeping an eye on the game.

And does it make me an asshole to hope that Walcott gets a bad cramp and comes off the ice?

At intermission I take my phone out and reply to Beck's text.

FOREST

Words cannot express how happy I am for you. Come over later, if you want to. Maybe you have other plans. But I'll leave the front door unlocked just in case.

I get back to my job, because one of us isn't going anywhere. Spoiler: it's me.

THIRTY-FOUR

Like a Sleeping Bear

BECK

IT'S the dead of night when I slip through Forest's unlocked door, kicking off my shoes to move as quietly as I can manage after a few beers with the team. He's left the kitchen lights on the lowest dimmer setting for me, and I flip them off as I pad toward his bedroom.

The door's open, and there he is—sprawled across the bed like a sleeping bear, his bare body covered by the blankets to his waist.

I don't get that many opportunities to observe him like this. Hell, I don't get that many opportunities to be in the same post code as Forest. But my heart just doesn't care. He's the most beautiful man I've ever seen, and the yearning I feel for him doesn't ever take a day off.

I strip down to my boxer briefs and slide under the covers as carefully as possible. The mattress dips slightly, and I hold my breath, but Forest doesn't stir. He's really out—mouth slightly open, one arm flung over his head. It's the most relaxed I've ever seen him.

Settling against the pillow, I give myself one more long look. His beard looks soft, and I have to resist the urge to run my hand across it. There's a small scar on his shoulder that I want to ask about someday.

The urge to touch him is overwhelming, but I don't want to wake him. He needs his sleep. So I close my eyes and let the warmth of his body next to mine sink in.

I'm almost asleep when Forest shifts beside me, rolling over until we're face to face. His eyes flutter open, unfocused and sleepy.

"Hi," I whisper.

"Hi," he whispers back. "You should have woken me up."

"Didn't want to disturb you," I say, already feeling my eyes closing again. "You were sacked out."

"Sorry."

I smile without opening my eyes. "I didn't mind. It's late. They took me out for a beer. Not at my favorite bar, but a guy can't have everything."

He chuckles softly and slings an arm over me, and fuck, that feels good. Like I belong here.

"You have fun tonight?" he asks.

"You know it."

"Any nerves?"

I shake my head against the pillow. "I knew Walcott wouldn't blow his chance to keep me on the bench. He's healthy, and he's having a great season."

"Dare I ask what's wrong with Volkov?"

"His back flares up sometimes. Don't tell a soul, okay? The team will never call me again."

"I'm a rock." He kisses my jaw, and my whole body comes alive. "Especially when you're around."

That gets my attention. I press up on an elbow and look down at him, trying to read his expression in the dim light. "Is that so? Show me."

He flips the covers back to reveal his naked body and his growing semi, and I hiss through my teeth.

Then, because I'm not a fool, I kick off my boxers and straddle him.

"Fuck," he says, running a hand up my chest. "You're a sight for sore eyes."

"Miss me when I'm gone?" I place my hands on his big shoulders and rock my hips.

"You know I do," he grunts.

I don't, in fact, know that for sure. I mean—I know Forest enjoys my company. I know he enjoys my body, which is why he's rock hard already and pulling me down for a kiss.

In fact, I suspect he likes me a lot. Which is why Scully texted me a pic of Forest staring at the TV screen tonight when he was supposed to be mixing drinks.

But Forest won't admit how he feels. Not in words. I get a soft, hungry sigh as our mouths come together. And I get his greedy hands all over my body as we kiss. Those big, blunt fingers exploring my ass. His soft beard against my face.

The thump of his heart against mine.

But this is all I'm going to get. No *I love yous*. No *let's meet each other's families*.

Regardless, when he takes control, rolling on top of me, I spread myself for him anyway. I do it willingly. I accept the terms of our arrangement with each brush of my cock against his.

I do it because I know that getting two thirds of Forest is better than getting a hundred percent of anyone else.

Do I wish things were different? Yes. But it doesn't make me a fool. It makes me a realist. Because there's nothing more real than the heated look on his face as he yanks the bedside table open and reaches for the lube. Or the perfect, rumbly groans he makes as he pounds into me.

It helps that I know we're both getting more than we

bargained for. I would have done anything for a single night with him. But I've gotten so much more than that.

And so has Forest. Again—not a fool. He gives himself to me in spite of his better judgment. Till the day I die, I'll carry the memory of the look on his face when I kissed him that first time. The shock. The excitement. The pure hunger.

Staring up at his sweaty face. I see my own awe reflected back at me. He's trying to resist. He's trying to hold on. "Fuck, Becker," he pants. "You're making me—"

"Come," I gasp. "Do it."

He bites his kiss-bruised lip, and his face fills with peace. The groan sounds like a prayer.

And that's it for me, too. Forest just does it for me, every time. Even as he reaches for my cock, I erupt all over us both.

Afterward, we're nothing but two wet noodles in a heap in the center of his bed. Breath sawing in and out. Sweat cooling.

This is almost my favorite part. Forest goes so still beside me. He's stroking my hand absently. His hip touches mine.

"You undo me," he whispers, and my heart skips a beat. It's so close to perfect.

I don't say it back, because I have to be careful. Always. I just squeeze his hand instead.

"Gotta deal with this condom," he says sleepily.

My sex-addled brain says, "Why'd you bother, anyway?" He's gone without before. Well, once. But we don't need condoms to be safe.

I can tell I've fucked up when his forehead creases. "It's respectful."

"You know I'm not sleeping around." In for a penny, etcetera.

"But you could be," he says quietly. "I got no right to assume otherwise."

For once, I'm glad he gets up and goes into the bathroom, because I don't know if I can control my expression.

I'm the idiot who brought it up, after all. I have no right to feel hurt by this. Not tonight of all nights.

Be cool, James. Everything is fine. Everything is *great.*

Five minutes later he brings me a warm, damp cloth to clean up, and we arrange ourselves in his bed to sleep.

"Beck," he whispers softly, a hand on my hip. "Congrats on your big night."

"Thanks," I say, moving my feet to tangle with his.

For some stupid reason, my eyes are stinging.

THIRTY-FIVE

A Cry for Help

FOREST

MARCH

"I GOT THIS," Davie, my newest employee, says. "Seriously. I know how to make a French 75."

"Okay, cool. Sorry." I back away, and he reaches for the gin while simultaneously shimmying his hips to the music.

It's a damp Wednesday in early March, and there's an engagement party in full swing at the game-room end of the bar. Two of our regulars decided to get hitched, and they're celebrating here. The cocktail orders are rolling in.

Luckily, we're fully staffed for the first time in forever. I should be ecstatic, but after months of unlucky breaks, I'm conditioned to believe the next crisis will pop up any minute.

"Maybe go home?" Scully says, nodding toward the hockey game on the screen above the bar. "You've worked more shifts than the Cougars' captain during the run-up to the playoffs."

"Home?" I echo. That's a dramatic idea. Especially when there's a box of tax documents in our office that's yelling my name.

"Yeah, remember that place? Where your bed is?" He winks. "Maybe call your guy and see if he's free."

I pat my pocket absently, where my phone lives. Come to think of it, I haven't heard from Beck in a couple of days. Have I? My heart does a weird little flop, and I duck under the bar and wander toward the office, where I pull out my phone.

I find my text thread with Beck and plop down in the shoddy office chair that's held together with duct tape. The last message is from three whole days ago.

What is happening?

FOREST

Hey man. You okay? It's been a minute since we talked.

I hit Send, and then immediately feel three or four different kinds of uneasy. I get unhelpful flashbacks to our past conversations when I've told Beck I'm not long-term relationship material. Hell, I once told him he ought to meet someone closer to his age—someone with more time and less baggage.

My gut gives a twist that I don't want to analyze.

Glancing at the computer on the desk in front of me, I shake the mouse to wake it up. When the screen lights up, I google the Ice Cats game schedule. Their next away game is Saturday night. Which means Beck has been home all week.

And not texting me.

I stare at our text thread again. There's nothing much to go on, here. No smoking gun. Our last exchange involved Beck sending me a picture of a massive cheeseburger and asking if I thought it looked "elite or just desperate."

I hadn't replied. And that was it. Nothing since. No dumb jokes. No unsolicited opinions about sandwich structure or condiments or cat cafés.

Which means either his phone's at the bottom of a lake, or I said something that scared him off and didn't notice doing it.

Or he met someone.

He'd tell me, though.

Wouldn't he?

For reasons I don't wish to examine, I send him one more text.

> Hey, I might clock out early tonight. You around?

I set the phone down on the desk and open the box of receipts. Rifling through it, I attempt to impose some order on them, while keeping one eye on the phone.

It lights up five minutes later.

> BECK
>
> Hey
>
> Busy

I blink. The chilly response is so unlike Beck.

My first thought is to worry. Maybe he's been kidnapped, and the one-word responses are a cry for help.

But that's dumb. There's another explanation that's far more likely.

Maybe he's finally giving me a taste of what it's like to communicate with *me*.

THIRTY-SIX

That Wiggling Thing

BECK

"ARE YOU EVEN *LISTENING?*" Rigsy asks. He's using his authoritative voice—the one he usually saves for intimidating our opponents.

"I'm listening," I lie. But my ears hurt, along with everything else in my body. I just need Rigsy to leave me alone so I can go back to wallowing in peace.

Until two days ago, I was having the best month of my life—playing great hockey, getting call-ups from the Cougars. That all came to a screeching halt when I started to feel sick. Then I had a positive Covid test. Now the team is leaving on a road trip without me.

"Okay, here's the setup." Rigsy sounds like he's so far away. "The pain relievers are on the kitchen counter. There are Popsicles in the freezer. There are four cans of soup in the cupboard and a lot of drinks in the fridge. You know the drill. You've had Covid before, right?"

I shake my head, and it's a huge mistake. Pain wings across my temples.

"Wait, really? You've *never* had Covid? What planet are you from?"

"This one," I mumble, even though everything feels alien right now. My head is hot, my throat is on fire and even my sheets feel scratchy. "Just go to California, already. Unless you can stop the walls from doing that...wiggling thing. Then do that first."

"Uh, wiggling thing?" He glances around the room, looking uneasy. "Beck, who you gonna call if you feel worse? Or if you need help?"

"I won't need help." I close my eyes to end the conversation. "I just need sleep."

"Your mom is all the way in Maine. But you could call Forest, right?"

"Sure." As if I'd ever do that. The last thing he needs is to get sick, and he sure doesn't need one more person to take care of. "You'll miss the bus."

"Okay, okay. I'm going. Call me tonight, though. I need proof of life."

Just make it stop. "Why are you giving mother hen vibes, dude?"

"Because you seem so..." He bites his lip.

"Sick?" I cough, and my ribs hurt from the violence of it.

"Yeah, man." He runs a hand through his hair. "Hang in there. Keep that fever down. Drink your ice water. And your next dose of Advil is in one hour."

"Will do." My eyes drift closed.

He finally leaves, and I lie very still, conserving my strength. I can't afford to be sick. The Ice Cats will lose games, and the Cougars will forget my phone number.

I'm not taking that medicine, either. Fever is a natural process. I'm just gonna let the sickness burn right out of me.

Besides, it's not all bad. I can hear colors now. Red and orange are nice. And the gray of my comforter makes kind of a hum. Blue is too fucking loud, though. "Keep that shit down," I yell at my bathrobe, where it hangs on the back of my closet door.

It yells louder, and the walls do that shaky thing again. But whatever.

I'd drink the ice water, except it hurts to swallow.

Fuck it. Fuck the whole world.

It's very dark in my room when I feel a presence. My eyes snap open. "Who's there?" I croak, but my throat hurts so bad I hardly make a noise. I free my hands from the covers, just in case I need to fight off the bathrobe. After all that yelling, it might be coming for me.

God, it's heavy, too, because I feel the mattress dip. I make two fists and punch in that direction.

"Whoa, buddy," says a deep voice. A wonderful voice, actually. My favorite voice.

"Stop it," I snarl. "You're not Forest."

There's a low chuckle, and two strong hands catch mine. "It's dark in here, I'll give you that. It's me, though. Promise."

I take a deep breath, and his woodsy scent is right here. But it could still be a trick. "But I didn't text you." I think that over. "Did I?"

"No." Kind fingers push the hair off my forehead, and then he sucks in a breath. "Jesus, you're hot."

"I know. That's why Forest fucks me. I'd be history, otherwise."

He makes a noise of dismay. "Beck, hon. I mean your temperature. It's through the roof."

"Oh. That's just a fever."

"*Just* a fever." He sighs. "You feel like a Texas sidewalk in July. When's the last time you had Advil?"

"Whenever Rigsy made me. What are you even doing here?" I ask the stranger who's imitating Forest. It's totally not cool that this guy is in my room. Except his hands in my hair feel really nice.

"Got a text from Rigsy," the guy says. "Told me you were sick, and he left the key under the mat."

"Oh." That's plausible. Or else my delusions are super detailed. Could really go either way.

"Where's the medicine, Beck?" He uses his dad voice.

"Don't need it." I close my eyes as those gentle fingers push the sweaty hair off my forehead. "Fever is a natural process."

"Okay. Sure. But either you take the stuff, or you come to the ER with me just for a check-in on this *natural process*. Your call."

Ugh. No. "Nice of you to stop by, but it's all good. Now that it's dark out, I can't hear the bathrobe yelling at me anymore. I can sleep it off."

There's a silence, which hopefully means this guy has decided to see things my way. But then he speaks again, in another voice. It's quiet, but it's somehow even scarier than the dad voice, if I'm honest. "Beck, I'm going to find the Advil, and you're going to take it. Or we go to the urgent care immediately."

He gets up and disappears on quiet feet. I drift a little, my brain taking me on a strange tour of my junior high school. I whirl down the corridor toward the nurse's office.

Becker James, you have a fever, the nurse says.

I turn and run from her, heading for the gymnasium, which is set up for bowling, instead of one of the cool activities like kickball or rock climbing.

"Bowling," I mutter. "Almost as stupid as square dancing."

"What's wrong with bowling?" asks Forest's voice. "I'm going to need you to sit up and explain."

God it's so obvious, so I do sit up to explain. "Gutter balls.

Rental shoes. So much bacteria. But mostly there's no goalie. What the fuck? The pins are just sitting there asking for it."

Low laughter. And then somehow there are pills in my palm, and my hand is guided toward my mouth. I taste their sweet coatings a second later, and the only obvious solution is to swallow them.

A cold glass of water finds its way into my hand after that, and I take a sip to wash away the nasty taste of the pills. "Ugh. You happy?"

"I will be, once your temperature goes down. You own a thermometer?"

"No? Is that a thing people have?"

He sighs. "I'd feel better if a doctor saw you."

"*You'd* feel better, but I wouldn't." I flop back onto my sweat-dampened pillow. "And who's the priority here?"

My visitor lets out another sigh, and his hand finds its way onto my damp forehead again. "Okay. We'll give it a couple hours."

"Before what?"

"Before I panic," he says tightly.

"Nah." I yawn. "You won't panic. You're a stranger. Why would you care?"

The fingers go still on my head. "Beck, I'm not a stranger. Hey. You're scaring me."

"Well, you're certainly not Forest. He wouldn't be here. He doesn't love me."

Stunned silence.

"I mean..." I sigh. "It's not his job to love me. It's nobody's job. I know this. The problem is that I love *him*, and that's not allowed. I mean—if Forest was super sick, I'd lose my mind. Like, I can't even think about it. Not sure what I'd do. Not supposed to care like that. It's against the rules. I cheat all the time, though. It's not like you can tell. Hockey rules? Break 'em and the ref is on your ass. But sex rules are easier. I can love Forest without anyone calling the penalty. I mean—even when it hurts. It hurts a lot lately."

Only silence from fake-Forest. It must not really be him, then. Phew. Because I'm probably not supposed to talk like that. I yawn.

"We'll sleep now," comes a whisper. "More drugs in four hours."

"You can't sleep in this bed with me," I argue. "If you were really Forest, you'll get sick. If you're not, then that's just creepy."

A sigh, and one more brush of those tender fingers. "I'll be on the couch. Yell if you need me."

I'd say something back, but I'm back in the middle school gymnasium again, looking for a bowling ball.

My fever finally breaks the next morning, and I wake up suddenly, blinking at my walls, wondering what time it is. I'm damp from sweat and woozy. But my brain works again.

It's something.

I push myself up to a seated position and take inventory. The house is deeply quiet. Rigsy isn't back from his road trip yet.

I swing my legs over the edge of the bed. Everything hurts— my spine, my ribs, my fragile pride. The air in my room smells stale, like sickness and regret. But also...cedar?

My head snaps up.

I drag myself to the bathroom, because I feel disgusting. But halfway down the hall I stop short.

There's a soda can on the kitchen counter. Not a brand that I buy. This one is Spindrift, and the flavor is Nojito.

Forest's favorite.

My soul detaches from my body. He was *here*?

I stumble backward like I've been punched, and then wander into the living room. That's where I notice a folded dish towel on the couch. Neatly laid across one of the cushions. As if someone used it as a pillow.

Oh God. He slept here.

Forest.

The couch. The can. The cedar smell in my room.

The memory pokes me in the brain.

"I said I love him," I whisper, mortified. "Out loud. With my actual mouth." While sweating like a baked ham and hallucinating about gym class.

I cover my face with both hands. The horror is immediate and all-consuming. How much of my broken heart did I fling at him like a feverish raccoon?

Hurrying back to my room, I grab my phone off the bedside table, where someone has plugged it in for me.

Feeling like I've been steamrolled, I open my favorite chatbot and dictate a question. "Help! How can I undo a fever-induced confession of love?"

It thinks for a second. Then:

Based on extensive linguistic analysis, you have several options:

*1. Blame it on a dream. Tell him you thought *he* said it first and you were sleep-repeating. Dreams are weird. People forgive dreams.*

2. Make it a metaphor. Say you were talking about how much you love his neutral zone play. Romantic miscommunication, classic hockey blunder.

3. Distract with something weirder. Divert attention by revealing your belief in Bigfoot. Or that you eat kiwi fruit like a baked potato. Ideally both.

4. Fake your own death. Bold, but effective. Change your name and your entire personality.

5. Relocate to a distant place, such as Tahiti. Out of sight, out of mind. Also, piña coladas.

"NOT HELPFUL!" I yell before tossing the phone down on the bed. My heart is racing with embarrassment. Unless... Maybe it wasn't as bad as I thought. Maybe I mumbled it, and Forest couldn't even understand me.

I pick up the phone again.

BECK

Hey. I hope you're not going to get sick. You should have stayed away.

For once, Forest immediately starts typing his reply.

FOREST

Hey! Look who's up! I'm glad you're feeling more lucid. Will you take your temperature? I left a thermometer on your bathroom sink. And some orange juice in your fridge.

I take a deep, shaky breath. He must have spent some serious hours at my house. And I repay him with emotional vomit?

He must have *hated* that.

BECK

Thank you. But I have to ask. Did I say anything weird last night?

FOREST

Isn't that a loaded question? Weird is a strong word. I heard a lot about your views on bowling.

I groan in the silence of my bedroom. Then I bite the bullet and call him. "Hey," I say when he answers. "I don't mean normal weird. I mean..." I take a breath. "Sometimes I get emotional and, uh, clingy when I'm sick. You shouldn't take it seriously."

There's a deep silence on his end of the call, and then I hear a sigh. "Beck," he says. My heart drops a mile. He's using his dad voice again, and I brace myself. "It's all valid…"

Oh *God.*

"But I'm just not in a place…"

"*Stop,*" I break in, exasperated. "Just… Don't, okay? I get it. Promise. So long as I don't have another fever above 103, we can go back to the way things were, right? With me being the guy who loves bad jokes and your beard, and you pretending not to notice when I'm needy."

"*Beck,*" he says, his voice strained. "That genie won't go back into the bottle."

Distress shoots through me. "So? What are you saying? Are you trying to tell me we're done?"

There's hesitation on the other end of the line.

And, fuck, that pause tells me everything I need to know. "Fine," I say tightly. "I get it. So I guess this is it. Thank you for not letting me, like, die alone in my own sweat. But I'll let you get back to your life now."

Then I actually end the call before I start begging, and I set my phone down with a shaking hand.

Except. Except. I stare at it for a few long minutes, willing it to ring again, with Forest saying, *No, Beck, we're not done. That's not what I want at all.* And then, *I need you.* And maybe even, *I love you.*

But it doesn't happen. The phone remains silent. And the truth starts to sink in: I gave him an out, and that gutless fucker took it.

I'm crushed. Really crushed. But I guess it's better to know where I stand than to keep waiting for a sign that will never come.

You're the Problem

FOREST

I DON'T CALL Beck back.

I could. My thumb hovers over his name.

Instead, I shut off my phone and toss it onto the coffee table like it's radioactive. Then I sit very still on my couch and stare at nothing for a long time.

I never lied to him. I told him very clearly that I don't have a lot to give. We could have sex, but nothing more.

But then I broke my own rules, didn't I? The sleepovers. The kissing. Dropping by when he's sick to make sure he'll be okay.

And he *is* okay. That's what matters. He's upright. Lucid. Breathing. Fever's down.

Everything is fine, right? Except I don't feel fine.

But... What was I supposed to say? Like, seriously, when he told me he loved me last night. In the dark, with sweat on his neck and pain in his voice and my name in his mouth like it meant something?

He was a mess, I remind myself. Sick and emotional and not thinking clearly. It was just fever talk. He even said so.

We can go back to the way things were, he'd said. But I know that's a lie, and I like him too much to keep things where they need to be. I'm still me—still in debt, still unavailable most days and nights. Still treading water while he slices through his season like a champion.

It's wrong of me to maintain this on-off, will-I-or-won't-I cycle again. It's hurting us both. I'll do the standup thing and let him go. Like a good guy.

Because I am a good guy.

Mostly.

I try to be, anyway.

Fuck.

I spend the next few days drowning myself in my work. I update every single spreadsheet. I go over the bar's first-quarter financial results. I make the payment on my new truck.

The loss of Beck in my life aches, and I glance at the lock screen of my phone a thousand times to see if he's texted me. But of course he hasn't.

When his team goes on another road trip, Beck is healthy enough to start one of the games. The Ice Cats win, of course. They're going to make a deep bid in the Calder Cup this year. I can just tell.

I roll through another weekend of late nights behind the bar, and Scully takes a couple of well-deserved days off.

See? This is just how my life works. No time for a boyfriend. The boiler at Sportsballs breaks *again,* and I get tied up dealing with the emergency plumber even on my day off. Then Ruby flies off for a medical conference, which puts Charlie at my place for the rest of the week.

It's good having him, and I make three healthy dinners in a row and bake chocolate-chip banana bread, which makes the whole house smell delicious. And I make sure he does his homework.

"You're, like, super dad this week," Charlie says on Thursday night.

"Glad you think so." I'm tidying up the living room, keeping busy while Charlie plays a video game. My house is clean. My kid is well fed. Everything is great, right? This is what I was meant to do.

I glance at the TV and, in the corner of the screen where the player's icons are displayed, I see an unfamiliar avatar. It's a blue cat and my gaze freezes on the name beneath it, like my brain has been programmed to seek it out. *Beckstopper*.

"Charlie, are you playing a game with Beck?"

"Yeah," he says.

"Do you do that a lot?"

Charlie shakes his head. "I texted him and asked if he wanted to come over..."

My heart does a weird little flip, even though it shouldn't.

"He said he couldn't. He was super nice, though. He said he'd play with me online for an hour instead." Charlie gives me a sideways glance. "It's weird he couldn't come over, right? He doesn't even have a game tonight."

"His team is all young hockey players, Charlie. They probably party together several nights a week."

My son's expression is dubious. "If he has time to play online, he has time to come over here."

Shit. "Where did you even get his number?"

He shrugs. "Off your phone. Duh."

Jesus. My text thread with Beck has been mostly PG, I think. Mostly. But there have been some exchanges between us that I wouldn't want Charlie to see.

I don't growl at him for invading my privacy, though, because this is on me. I broke my own rules. I introduced him to Beck, and now it's awkward. Beck is probably pissed off at me and feels obligated to navigate Charlie's questions.

Heart thumping, all I can do is walk out of the room. I end up in my super-clean bedroom, sitting on the edge of the bed, taking a slow breath. Then I pull out my phone and find my last text exchange with Beck. It's totally fine—just me inquiring about his health the morning after he was sick.

Now I send him one more message.

> Hey. Thanks for playing with Charlie. I know I put you in that position. He looks up to you, and we both appreciate your generosity toward him.

Ugh. Sounds like a press release.

I put the phone face down and bury my head in my hands. I miss Beck. In this house. In this room. He's fun. He's sexy. He's decent to the core.

And he hasn't been texting me. He doesn't beg, which somehow makes me feel even shittier. I drew a line, and he sees it clearly. He even respects it.

Any second now, he'll finally meet some guy with cash in his pocket and fewer obligations and more free time.

So why do I feel so awful right now? There's a heavy spot in the center of my chest—like I've made a huge mistake.

I'm just sitting here drowning in my own misery when my phone vibrates with a notification. And before I can stop myself, I've picked it up to look.

There's no new text. There's just... Beck has given my text a thumb's up.

The most polite middle finger in the whole damn world.

Early on the following Tuesday evening, I'm starting my shift at the bar when I look up and find Kenji and Denny seated in front of me. It's so surprising that I actually jump a little. "Where'd you two come from?"

"We've been here for, like, five minutes," Kenji says with a wide smile. "We're going to a Cougars game, and we thought we'd stop in to see your bar first."

"Wow, okay." For a millisecond I'm sad they didn't ask me to go to the game, too. But just as quickly I realize I would have had to say no, and that they already know this. "Cool, cool. How about a drink? You want—?"

"I got it already." Scully plunks two beers down on the bar. "You've been obliviously restocking the beer fridge for, like, an eon."

"Sorry," I mutter. "I'm just a little distracted."

Denny snorts. "That's like saying Travis Kelce likes the spotlight a *little*. You misplayed half your hands at poker last week."

"You're shitting me," Scully says, propping an elbow on the bar. "Forest is trash at poker? I woulda thought he was a shark."

"He's usually great," Kenji says. "But last week he couldn't seem to pay attention. We were all kind of worried about you after."

Oh hell. "I'm fine. Seriously." And it would be great if we could change the subject now.

Scully has a familiar nosy look on his face. "He's been kind of a wreck here, too," he says. "I think it's because of…"

"Beck," all three of my friends say at once. Then they laugh.

"Guys, come *on*. My private life isn't open for discussion."

"It is when you folded top pair to a check-raise from Big Bob," Kenji says. "Which, come on. His bluff face looks like he's trying to take a shit."

Scully whistles. "Oof. That's not distracted. That's lovesick."

"I'm not *lovesick*," I whine. "I was tired. And maybe a little drunk."

"And *that* was weird," Denny says. "Mr. Responsible drank all my gin and had to Uber home."

"Is that why you came in tonight?" I grouse. "Because I owe you some Plymouth?"

"I think it's probably because you're being fucking stupid," my so-called friend says.

"*Scully*. Tell me how you really feel."

"You let that perfectly great guy go, didn't you? Because of some misplaced instinct to hurt him before he hurts you."

"Ohh," Kenji says heavily. "Is that what's happening here?"

"No," I say loudly at the same time that Scully says, "Exactly."

Denny sips his beer. "I dunno, Forest. Never met any of your other guys, but he seemed like a keeper. And he's super into you. Nice kid. Going places, too."

"Exactly," I say heavily. "That's pretty much the problem."

"You'd rather have a freeloading deadbeat?" Kenji asks. "Those exist. We could find you one."

Scully, mixing a drink that I'm supposed to be mixing, snickers. "We'll put up a flyer. 'Wanted: emotionally unavailable man with no ambition and a mediocre dick. Must be okay with resentment and half-assed hand jobs.'"

That earns a laugh, even from me. I scrub a hand over my beard, suddenly exhausted.

"I don't know what I'm doing," I mutter. "He's so damn young. And bright. And good. And I'm..." I gesture vaguely toward myself. "A broken-down bartender with trust issues."

Kenji shrugs. "You're also a great dad. Solid friend. Ridiculously hot. And according to Denny, you make a decent omelet."

"Better than decent," Denny confirms.

"You make him laugh," Scully says, quieter now. "I saw it. You made him feel seen."

"That's a pretty low bar," I point out. "He won't have much trouble finding someone else to clear it."

"Dammit, Forest." Denny thumps his fist into his forehead. "I'd better stock up on more gin. This problem isn't going to solve itself anytime soon, is it?"

"No," I say, because at least he understands now.

"He means *you*," Scully says, hip-checking me. "You're the problem that needs solving."

"Nothing new there."

THIRTY-EIGHT

Knew This Would Happen

BECK

APRIL

"JAMES!" Martinez calls out to me as I walk into the gym. "You're up today on the music rotation."

"Noooooo," yells another hockey player from the squat rack. "God, I can't take that techno crap today. I got *goals* to achieve, here."

"Simmer down," I grumble. "I'll take it easy on you."

Usually, taking my turn in the music rotation brings me great joy. Forcing my playlists on the masses is something I look forward to.

Today, though, I'm too depressed to explain the Cure or Depeche Mode to the undereducated, so I put on my Madonna playlist instead. It's still 80s music, but more accessible than my usual picks. Then I stomp over to the leg press.

Nobody complains about the music, though. I spot at least two guys shaking their asses to "True Blue."

And I feel nothing. Even though I'm starting in goal tomorrow again. Even though my team is on a winning streak, and springtime has finally arrived in Colorado.

None of that matters. The sky remains gray, at least in my mind. Because Forest is still an idiot, and because I ruined everything by telling him how I really feel.

If I could go back in time and take it all back, I would. Just for a couple more nights of his company.

I load the plates onto the machine like I'm mad at gravity itself, then slump into the seat with a grunt. Webster walks by, towel around his neck, and gives me a once-over.

"Damn, you look like someone ate your last Pop-Tart."

"Worse," I mutter. "Someone emotionally withdrew after mutual orgasms and excellent cuddling."

Webster flinches. "That answer was... surprisingly specific."

"It's fine. I'm processing. With Madonna. And quadriceps."

He snorts. "You're a weird little man."

"Incorrect," I grunt, pushing the plates with more enthusiasm than necessary. "I'm a tall goalie with feelings and elite musical taste."

"You gonna cry-lift through the whole workout?"

"Only if 'Oh Father' comes on. That song wrecks me."

Webster laughs as he wanders off. I keep pressing. Each rep feels like I'm trying to push Forest out of my system. So far, it's not working.

The session is almost over when Coach Tanner stomps into the room with a snarl on his face. "Where's James? I gotta problem with him."

Oh great. Another satisfied customer. "Over here, Coach. What did I do now?"

Coach stops in front of the Bluetooth speaker and snaps it off. The gym goes silent, so I guess the whole crew is about to witness my latest humiliation.

"Get up, James. Get out of here. You're wanted in Denver tonight."

"Holy *shit*," Rigsy whispers.

But I'm still trying to process. "Wanted…by the cops?"

Coach tips his head back and howls with laughter. "You were always such a smartass. Gonna have to tell those jokes in the Cougars' locker room tonight, though. You're in the net against Calgary."

It's like the air pressure changes suddenly. There's a swoopy sound in my ears.

"I shouldn't even be surprised," Coach says, oblivious to my shock. "Late season game, so Powers wants to rest both his goalies for the playoffs. Get on outta here, James. They want you for a pregame meeting with the goalie coach at the Four Seasons by the arena, okay? Then you'll get some downtime in a hotel room before you head into the arena. Make us proud. Don't fuck this up."

My teammates launch into furious applause and cheering. "Get 'em, Beck! Woot! Make the magic happen!"

Still reeling, I rise from the leg press. I suddenly have a million things to do. I make my way to the door, interrupted by back slaps and awkward high-fives from the other Ice Cats.

My mind spins. I've got to sharpen my skates.

I've got to find my luckiest water bottle.

I've got to make sure I know where to park at the arena in Denver.

I've got to call my mom, because that's an automatic. But I've *really* got to tell Forest. He'll—

Oh.

"Beck?" Rigsy has followed me into the dressing room. "Something the matter?"

I take a breath. "No. Of course not." This is supposed to be the biggest moment of my life. No—it *is* the biggest moment.

Rigsy grins. "I'm gonna find some tickets on StubHub. So is Martinez."

"Really?" I give him a nervous smile. "But no pressure."

"Duuuude." He leans in and slaps me on the arm. "I'd be there no matter what. This is *big*."

I take a calming breath. "Yeah, it is."

Rigsy folds his arms and leans against the door frame. "You call your mom?"

"I'll call her from the car." *She might care.* I grab my hockey bag and unzip it.

"Cool. Are you gonna tell *him*? Forest, I mean?"

I take another deep breath. "Not sure. I mean—it's tempting. He'd lose his mind." I *know* Forest would be thrilled about this. He'd be excited for me, and he'd mean it.

Rigsy looks troubled. "He should lose his mind, right? He should be, like, drop-everything-and-run-for-the arena happy. Because if a guy is really on your team, then he shows up for all the important stuff, yeah?"

"Yeah," I echo, looking away.

"Tough call," Rigsy says quietly. "Either way, I'll see you tonight, okay? I'll be screaming from the cheap seats." He gives me a mock salute and then disappears back into the weight room.

I toss some gear into my hockey bag. I need to get out of here and head for that meeting in Denver. But I sink down onto a bench instead and pick up my phone, Forest's smile swimming in my mind. If I call him right now with this news, he'll say something like, *Way to go! Knew this would happen someday.*

He wants me to succeed. He cares about me even if he won't really admit it. I know this. He knows this.

And yet he won't acknowledge it. Not in the way that I need. Yes, *need*.

I finger the edges of my phone and stare at Forest's avatar, my thumb hovering.

How did Rigsy put it? *If a guy is really on your team, then he should show up for the important stuff.*

I kept telling myself Forest would meet me in the middle, while he kept telling me in plain English that he couldn't change his stripes.

I take another deep breath. "Okay, Forest," I say to the empty room. "I'm listening. Finally." I drop the phone into my bag.

THIRTY-NINE

It Was a Sex Injury

FOREST

THE BAR IS PACKED tonight with Cougars fans, half of them in jerseys, all of them drinking. It's going to be a good night for drink sales. It will also be a long one, because Scully has a sprained wrist with a splint on it, and he's pouring drinks at half speed.

When I asked what happened, he told me it was a sex injury. Then he winked, which made him look like there was something in his eye.

I'm not sure if he was joking, but I was too busy making drinks to ask for details.

"Izzy!" I holler to our cocktail server. "Can you spare a few minutes to clean some glassware?"

"Sure, pal." She cracks her gum and ducks under the bar. "I can't deliver the drinks, anyway, if you guys don't start mixin' 'em faster."

"Sorry," Scully mutters. "It's a shame we don't have an injured reserve list, like in hockey."

"What would that even look like?" I ask, slamming a shaker down.

"Are you kidding? I'd be day-to-day with 'shaker wrist.' Izzy's got 'chronic tray shoulder.' You've definitely got 'bourbon elbow.'"

Izzy pops up from under the bar. "Don't forget Todd's 'garnish thumb.' He almost sliced it off last week cutting lime wedges."

I grimace, thinking of how much our workers comp insurance would go up if that really happened.

"Can I get a refill?" someone at the bar asks. "Puck drops in one minute."

"Sure." The Cougars are playing Calgary tonight, and everyone's got playoff fever. I grab the guy a clean glass and fill it with beer.

Fregular leans halfway across the bar, waving his arms like he's coaching from the rail. "If Powers starts Vitek with DiCosta on D again, I swear to God I'm walking out."

"You say that every week," I mutter, shaking up a martini like it owes me money.

"They have no chemistry!" he yells. "Vitek couldn't clear the puck out of a cardboard box."

Onscreen, the arena lights flash and the Cougars' announcer starts bellowing into the mic:

"*Starting on defense, number 51, Jiri Vitek!*"

Fregular throws his hands in the air. "You see?! That's it. I'm done. I'm done!"

"Uh-huh." I pour the martini into a chilled glass, toss in an olive, and pick up the glass to deliver it.

"Last but not least, starting in goal tonight," the announcer continues, "in his NHL debut—number 90, Becker James!"

I drop the martini. It just slides right out of my hand and onto the floor, treating the whole bar to the sound of breaking glass.

But nobody looks in my direction. They're all watching the screen.

"What the fuck," Fregular breathes.

"I've seen that guy in *here*," someone else says in a shocked voice.

Nobody is more shocked than I am. I'm staring up at the screen, and there's Beck, in a literal spotlight on center ice, lined up with the other starters for the Cougars.

Then the arena's house lights come back on, and Beck skates toward the goal. I'd know that lanky stride anywhere. He's got a weird, little hunch when he's nervous. Like the weight of the world just dropped onto his shoulders.

And I didn't know he'd be there tonight.

I *didn't know*.

"Holy shit," Scully says beside me. He's staring up at the screen. "Did he tell you?"

"No."

"He didn't call?" He sounds like he doesn't believe me.

"No," I say again, quieter this time.

On the screen, Beck drops into the crease, taps each post with his stick, and pulls down his mask. Ready to play.

His first big league game, and I'm not there. I'm behind the bar, with gin on my shoes.

"I...I have to go," I say suddenly.

"Yes you do," Scully agrees, voice sharp with urgency. "Izzy! Check StubHub. What's the cheapest seat in the building?"

She already has her phone out. "We don't want the cheapest. We want the best. Here's one in row fourteen for three hundred."

"Oof," I say, because I can't not say it.

Izzy shrugs. "You can Venmo me later." I watch her hit the Purchase button. "It's a good seat. You'll be able to see if he blinks behind the mask."

"Guys, I know I shouldn't leave you like this." My heart is hammering. "I've got a bar full of people. Scully's wrist is in a brace. This is—"

"I'll tend bar," Izzy interrupts. She's already moving behind it, tying on her apron with zero hesitation. "I know the register. I know enough."

"And I'll carry drinks," Fregular adds, puffing up his chest. "How hard can it be? I got good hands!"

"You've literally never won a game of pool," I point out.

Izzy's already pouring someone a pint of beer. "We'll be fine. And if we're not, we'll lie about it later."

I look at Scully, my last chance at reason.

He doesn't even flinch. Just smiles. "You going to worry about the bar, or are you going to go support your guy?"

Ouch. "I think I already fucked this up. It'll be an hour before I can even get there. Maybe he doesn't even *want* me there."

Everyone in earshot groans.

Scully grabs my shoulder with his good hand. "This is your *moment*, Forest. Are you going to stand behind the bar and let it pass? Or are you going to go show him you actually care?"

I don't move.

He leans in, quiet now. "It's now or never, man. Why is this so hard for you? I know you care about him just as much as you care about this bar. Maybe even more."

My eyes travel to the screen, where Beck is already settling into the crease in front of ten thousand spectators. "I do care. I always have. But he's so..." My voice is gravel. "He's a fucking shooting star. And I'm trivia night and drink specials."

"Stop it, dumbass," Scully says. "He's a grown man. He knows his favorite flavor, and you're it. So get the fuck out of here. You're ruining a very romantic moment for me."

Then he gives me a shove.

And I do it. I go.

FORTY

Feels Like My Fault

BECK

THE TUNNEL SMELLS like rubber and nerves. My nerves, specifically.

I'm carrying my helmet in one hand and a towel in the other, trying not to look like I'm spiraling. Even though I am. A little.

The first period went okay. One goal. Just one. It was a weird bounce off a deflection—guy fired it from the point, it tipped off our D-man's skate, and fluttered in like a sad little pigeon.

Not a highlight-reel goal, and not exactly my fault it went in.

Doesn't matter. It feels like my fault, because that's how this works.

Clay Powers pulls me aside just before we go back out. He's calm, which helps. He's always calm. He's got that thing head coaches have—like he could guide a sinking ship to shore just by narrowing his eyes.

"Talk more," he says, looking me right in the face. "That's the only note I've got for you right now."

I blink. "Okay?"

"You're seeing everything out there," he says. "Your reads are sharp. Positioning's great. But these guys don't know you yet. They need to hear you. Doesn't matter if you're the new guy. Call out screens, call out rebounds, call out the back door. Doesn't have to be poetry." He claps a hand on my shoulder. "You know what to do, and you're doing it. So now let them *hear* you doing it."

"Okay," I say. "Yeah."

He nods. "We'll figure out how to score this period. You just keep doing what you're doing, and we'll get you the W." He turns toward the bench.

The W.

I let that roll around in my chest for a second like it might crack open something warm inside me.

Because this is it. My shot. My fucking NHL debut.

And it's only one goal. One weird, dumb, unfortunate goal that doesn't get to define me. I take a breath, jam my helmet back on, and step out onto the ice.

Stoney skates up to me. "I haven't forgotten."

"Um, what?"

He skates a circle around me. "I told you after your first start that we'd celebrate at your favorite bar. So which one is it?"

I got bigger things to worry about right now, so I blurt the name automatically. "It's Sportsballs. North Denver."

"Cool," he says. "Love that place. Let's gooooooo!" He skates away.

Heart pounding, I go to the crease like I've been doing since I was seven. I tap the posts and rough up the resurfaced ice under my feet.

It's just hockey. Same shit, different building. I hum "True Faith" by New Order, and I watch the face-off. Then I do my best to turn up the volume.

"SCREEN RIGHT!" I yell, loud enough to rattle my own mask. "I got eyes on it."

"No lane, no lane, don't let him shoot that!"

"Cover..." I don't know that player's name. "No shot for Ugly Mustache!"

"Newgate! Take his stick, not his body!"

"Stoney, shoot the puck!"

It's a little like casting a spell. The more I holler, the less I think, and the better we play. The guys start yelling back. They trust me. They listen.

"DON'T BLOCK ME, VITEK, YOU'RE SHAPED LIKE A FRIDGE!"

"STONEY, I SWEAR TO GOD, SHOOT THE PUCK."

He does, and we tie it up halfway through the second on a gritty rebound goal, and it feels like the world exhales.

The second intermission is a sweaty blur, but Powers seems happy with me, and less happy with his forwards. "Shoot, you fuckers. Calgary skates like their butts are made of lead, and we're still tied?"

Third period he gets his wish. Kapski lights the lantern with a snap from the left circle—clean, gorgeous, highlight-reel shit. The bench goes electric.

Be careful what you wish for, though. A few minutes later, Calgary pulls their goalie and throws everything they've got at me. But that's how this game works, and I'm ready.

One at a time, I shut them down.

Pads, blocker, glove, stick. Rinse and repeat. I play on pure reflex. Pure fire.

When the buzzer goes, I'm actually surprised. The crowd roars like it's playoff hockey instead of late-season grit. I drop to my knees in the crease for a second, chest heaving.

I did it. I fucking did it. My mom is probably watching, so I get to my feet to look around for a TV camera, but I'm suddenly mobbed by a pack of Cougars.

"Great game, rookie!" says the captain.

"Good hustle!" growls DiCosta, one of their best D-men.

"Yaaaaas, kids!" Stoney yells as we skate toward the hand-shake line. "I'm buying a round at Sportsballs! Hey, Calgary! You're invited, too—if you've never been to a gay sports bar, you haven't lived. I'm *super* popular there." He says this all with a big smile.

This team is *#goals*. I'd better be invited back someday, and I think I just improved my chances of that.

"I'm good for a beer, if Stoney's buying," Kapski says. He thwacks me on the back. "Right after your press interviews, rookie. I see 'em hovering in the tunnel already."

Oh God. Interviews? I have the brain power of a sea sponge right now. And that might be an insult to sea sponges.

This could get very awkward, very fast.

Kapski takes the first interviews in the tunnel, and I manage to slide past the cameras and microphones and make it to the showers.

The Cougars have a *sweet* locker room, by the way, with a sound system playing tunes even in the shower and premium men's products in the stall. I don't know what tonka bean is, but I smell like it now.

I dry off with a big, fluffy towel and make my way back to my stall where I start to get dressed. My adrenaline is crashing, and I need my post-game chicken sandwich really badly.

A quick glance at my phone shows me twelve excited texts from my Ice Cats teammates and a *Good job honey* from my mother.

Not one from Forest though. Not a single one.

I turn my phone face down, so I don't have to think about it, and I pull on my shirt.

The PR guy hustles over. I know who he is even before he introduces himself, because his suit is perfectly pressed and his teeth are extra shiny. He confirms his identity by informing me that the press conference starts in seven minutes. "And you're the guest of honor," he says.

"Press conference," I say dully. "With, like, chairs and a lectern?"

His expression wonders which planet I've dropped in from. "That's the general setup, yes. Don't sweat it, though. They just want to hear you say how excited you were to get the call-up, and how good it feels to help the Cougars win a game. Someone will probably ask if you feel ready to support the team into the playoffs, and you'll say yes."

"See, you make it sound so easy. But as soon as someone shoves a microphone in my face, I lose feeling in my face. That's when the word vomit starts."

His smile dulls a fraction. "But not *actual* vomit, right?"

"If I weren't so hungry right now, we couldn't rule that out."

He gives me a weird look and then stands there *watching* me tie my tie, as if he isn't sure I can do it myself.

As soon as I'm presentable, he has me follow him into a windowless room where the postgame pressers happen. Honestly, I feel a little cheated, because this place looks more glamorous on television. I sit down in my metal folding chair, feeling like a prisoner in front of the firing squad. A number of journalists and photographers crowd in, and then Coach Powers and Kapski take the seats on either side of me.

Coach Powers opens with a short, no-nonsense intro. "We're proud of the team tonight. Everyone battled. Becker James gave us a hell of a performance in his NHL debut—big stops, calm presence, and a well-earned win. We'll open it up to questions now."

The first question comes fast. "Beck, what was going through your head when you stepped onto NHL ice for the first time tonight?"

I open my mouth. Close it again.

The real answer is something like: *Don't fall. Don't forget how to play hockey. Why does my helmet feel like it's on sideways?*

But none of that will sound good in print. "Um…" I swallow hard. "I was hoping the regulars at my favorite bar were watching."

Polite laughter follows, so I guess that wasn't too terrible.

The next question comes immediately from a guy with a notebook instead of a handheld recorder and a voice like he's been doing this since before I was born. "Beck, there's been some chatter on the AHL circuit about your uneven performance this season. But you were a rock tonight. Did you have something to prove?"

And my brain just… blanks.

My mouth opens again, but this time nothing comes out. I glance at Coach Powers, but he stays politely still, letting me handle it. Kapski doesn't move either. They're letting me stand on my own two feet here.

Oh God. Seconds tick by. The silence throbs.

That's when I spot a guy easing into the door at the back of the room. He's standing against the wall, and he's wearing a flannel shirt.

Forest.

He's *here* in this room.

It's not even a low-blood-sugar hallucination. That calm, brown gaze is one hundred percent real when it lands on me, and he puts a hand to his chest and takes a slow breath in. *Relax, Beck.*

He lifts his hand. Not like a wave. More like a lifeline. He's holding a paper bag with the beginnings of a grease stain on the side—the kind that might hold a postgame chicken sandwich.

The message is clear. *Survive this interview, and you can have the sandwich.*

Something settles in my chest. I clear my throat and turn back to the reporter. "Yeah. I did have something to prove tonight. But not to anyone in this room. To myself, I guess."

"And how'd you accomplish that?" the reporter asks. "How did you turn your season around?"

"Well actually..." I let out an awkward laugh, thinking about the game that turned my season around—the beer league game against the Plague. "I remembered why I used to play hockey— for fun, as a team. And I surrounded myself with good people." I give Forest a pointed glance. "Nobody does well in this sport in a vacuum. Coach Powers helped me figure that out, and I've been super grateful."

Lord, that better be the last question, because I'm holding it together like a champ, here, and I'm too emotional to take any more deep questions.

Luckily, the next one is for Kapski, and I survive the next seven minutes on adrenaline, plus a few more hockey platitudes.

Then it's finally over. The reporters get up and start to file out. Coach Powers shakes my hand and tells me he'll see me at Sportsballs.

"Oh, you're coming?" I babble.

He looks at his watch. "I've got time for a couple beers. Wouldn't miss it. Kinda wonder who's behind the bar, though, because doesn't that guy own the place?"

I swivel my head, and here comes Forest, threading his way through the bodies in the room, a determined look in his eye.

I can't look anywhere else. I'm locked onto him like a laser beam. Then he's right in front of me, gripping the shoulder of my suit jacket. The pressure of his hand, combined with the intensity in his brown eyes, is like medicine.

"Look, I'm still angry at you," I say. Although, right this second, it's hard to remember why. "I didn't even tell you about tonight because..."

"I *know* why you didn't tell me," he says. "I get it. And I'm sorry."

We're sort of gaping at each other, and then Coach Powers clears his throat. I realize with horror that the head coach of the most important hockey franchise on the continent has just been third-wheeled by our staredown.

"See you at the bar, Beck," he says.

I swallow hard. "Thanks, Coach."

He chuckles and passes me with a thump on the back. "Good game, by the way. We'll be seeing more of that here, I hope."

Even those career-boosting words aren't enough to make me look away from Forest, who suddenly pulls me into a hug. "God, I've missed you," he says, and his voice is rough.

"You... have?" My own voice catches a little.

"So much," he whispers, pulling me in. "It's bad. My friends even tried to stage an intervention."

"I didn't think you...you..." I have trouble swallowing again.

"Cared? Aw, Beck. I always did. I still do. And it messed me up."

"But you..." A little flare of latent anger curls inside my chest, even as I revel in the grip of his hug. "Why'd you do me dirty like that? It's... It's insulting."

"Yeah." He sighs and pulls back. "That was just me being an idiot. I was fucking scared to put myself on the line again."

"James!" yells a voice from the corridor. "Where are you, buddy? Time to get drunk with Uncle Stoney!"

"Shit," I whisper.

"Go," Forest says. He puts the paper bag in my hand and then turns me toward the door. "Eat this chicken sandwich. Go on. We'll talk later. Ride with Stoneman to the bar, okay? I'll make sure you get home safe."

After one more soul-breaking glance at Forest, I turn and go.

FORTY-ONE

Having a Huge Night

FOREST

SPORTSBALLS ENDS up having a huge night. As soon as the first couple of Cougars walked into the bar, Scully put the news on blast. Which meant that a hoard of regulars turned up to rub elbows with greatness and ask for autographs.

By the time I get there, Scully and Izzy are deep in the weeds.

"Forest!" Izzy yells. "Happy to see you! How was the game?"

"Legendary." I tie on an apron. "I'll never forget it."

She gives me a warm smile and hurries to wash some of the dirty glasses piling up in the sink.

Hudson Newgate—jersey number 68, hot as blazes, and the first out bisexual player for the Cougars—approaches the bar. "Hey, man. What do you have for light beer these days?"

"Lagunitas Daytime—carb count is three grams. Devil's Backbone Bright Tangerine Ale is our new one, with just two grams of carbs. It's fruitier than a regular beer. Then again, fruity is a theme around here." I wink.

Newgate laughs. "Fine—you sold me. One of those, please."

He pulls out his phone to pay, and I push it away. "Cougars

drink free tonight. How's your kid? She have a good hockey season?"

"She did!" He grins. "High scorer for her team. I tried to talk her into playing D, but she wants the glory."

"Kids, amirite?"

He takes his drink and I get back to work, making drink after drink, before *finally* catching a glimpse of Beck near the door. He's a sight for sore eyes, too. Smiling. Dimple on display. His roommate stands proudly beside him. It's almost certainly Rigsy's first trip to a queer bar, but he looks like he's having a blast.

I send Izzy over there with a whole bucket full of Beck's favorite beer and over the next several minutes, watch it rapidly disappear. Beck is surrounded—literally—by famous hockey players and people who love him.

I fight a familiar reflex of disbelief. He's got life by the balls, and yet he chooses to love *me*?

"He's in his glory," Scully says, following my gaze. "And somehow, you're the one he's going home with tonight."

"Yeah, there's no accounting for taste."

He gives me a stern look. "Stop that."

"I'm *joking*."

"You're not, though," he says. "That's the problem. Last year, some guy stole your joy. You downplay it, but he got away with more than your wallet, Seth."

I gulp. "That's not something I talk about."

"You don't have to." He grips me by the arm. "Your friends can see it anyway. That guy stole your will to live. If I ever find him, I'm gonna end him. Or at least knee him in the nuts. If you could just learn to accept help, consider starting there."

"Scully. We have a bar full of thirsty customers. Maybe we could have this conversation later?"

"Nah, man." Without releasing my arm, he shakes his head

slowly. "Did we learn nothing tonight? No more putting the important stuff off. That era is *over*. Tell me you understand."

Instinctively, I glance toward Beck, who's deep in conversation with Volkov, the Cougars' veteran goalie. They might be talking about glove-hand positioning. Or, knowing Beck, they might be ranking gas-station breakfast burritos by their effect on lateral movement.

I care about him *so much*.

Scully chuckles knowingly and goes to serve a customer, leaving me to watch Beck with soft eyes.

"Hey, barkeep."

I snap to attention, finding David Stoneman in front of me. "Yessir. What can I get you?"

"How about a round of shots?" He puts his credit card on the counter.

"Cool," I say, reaching for some shot glasses. "But your money's no good here. How many, and what kind?"

"How many glasses you got? What does our new rookie go for? Whiskey? Tequila?"

"Actually, the weirder the better." I grab a bottle of pickle-flavored vodka. "It's a local thing. Kinda briny. Very polarizing."

Stoney hoots. "Let's gooooo! If I get 'im drunk, I'll make sure he gets home safe."

"Actually, that's my job tonight."

He shrugs. "Awesome. Then I can get drunk too."

And then he does, right along with most of the bar.

The exceptions are Coach Powers, who always keeps up appearances, and his boyfriend, Jethro Hale, who doesn't drink. They're sitting at the bar in front of me watching a tied West Coast game that's headed for a shootout.

"You want me to turn it up?" I offer. It's so loud in here tonight.

"No need," Hale says. "The sloppy positioning is loud enough without the announcer's voice."

Powers gives him a fond glance, and I grab Hale's glass and refill it with soda water. "Thanks for your hospitality tonight," Coach says.

"Trust me, you guys are worth every penny." I put a fresh lemon wedge in his boyfriend's drink. "Every time you all come in here, I get a bump in traffic. It matters to this cash-strapped small business that you show us some love."

Powers gives me a thoughtful nod. "We always have a good time here. Are you still planning a new screening room in back?" He tips his head in the direction of my latent dreams. "It'd be easier to throw more business your way if you did."

"I consider it every day," I promise him. "But I don't like the sky-high interest rate the bank is offering me, and I don't have the cash just now."

Hale looks away from the screen and frowns at me. "How much money would you even need? Maybe let some of us invest? Can't be much more than a half million."

"A half..." I sputter. "It's so much less than that. For two-fifty I could build something great and fix the leaky roof all in one go."

Hale shrugs. "Two-fifty, split a few ways? I reckon we can get that done without breaking a sweat."

"We couldn't let you..."

"*Yes, we could*," Scully thunders. "Jesus, Forest. Accept the help. They'll earn...five percent or whatever, and we'll get this thing paid off in a couple of years. Nobody works harder than you. You're a safer bet than Fort Knox, at this point. And think of the viewing parties people could throw here."

My face flushes, because I know he's right. But it's still hard to ask other people to take a risk on my dream. "He's, uh, right. It would be pretty great to get that project going. I will, um, write up a plan and show it to you after the playoffs?"

"You do that," Hale says, his eyes on the shootout again.

Scully punches me in the arm. "That was really hard for you, wasn't it?" He laughs. "Hard to teach an old dog new tricks. Heads up, though. Somebody's hitting on your guy."

My chin snaps up, and I see Beck holding a beer and leaning against the wall. And there's another guy—a bar patron I've seen once or twice before—propping his own arm against the wall in a not-so-subtle way, casually boxing Beck in, as if staking a claim. "Oh, hell no." I throw down my sponge.

"Don't do it," Scully says. "Wait—I take it back. By all means do whatever toppy thing you're about to do. And then clock out, okay? Izzy and I can take it from here."

I'm already halfway across the bar.

FORTY-TWO

There's Mood Lighting

BECK

I'M KIND OF DRUNK, and I never get drunk, so I'd forgotten how it makes the world feel squishy. Rigsy's gone home already, and the Cougars have started leaving as well. They have morning skate tomorrow.

I'm almost too tired to peel myself off this wall and get a rideshare. Meanwhile, there's some hot guy from UC Boulder leaning over me, telling me about his favorite new gym routine. He's boring as hell, and I've already stopped listening. He's so close to me, I can see the flecks of gold in his hazel eyes.

And then suddenly he isn't there anymore.

"S'cuse me," says Forest's gruff voice. "But Beck already knows how to maximize his glute engagement, thanks."

Forest slides in beside me, his hand settling on the small of my back like it lives there. And I go from mildly buzzed to fully feral in under three seconds.

"Sweetheart," he purrs. "You about ready to get out of here?"

I'm so stunned that it takes me a second to organize my brain cells into speech. "Did you just..." *Call me sweetheart in public?* It's such an outrageous idea that I don't say it out loud. "Did you just *scare off* a guy who was chatting me up?"

"Yes, I did," he growls. "Something wrong with that?"

"No," I say immediately. Then I suddenly remember I'm supposed to be holding a grudge. "Actually, I'm still mad at you. Even if that was kinda hot. Never thought I'd live to see the day."

"Yeah, about that." He studies me with his dark eyes. "I'm sorry I've been such a dumbass. Meeting you is the best thing that happened to me in a long time. And from here on out, I'm going to make sure you always know that."

My mind is kind of blown, and the weird vodka Stoney poured me isn't helping. "So... All I had to do was get called up by the Cougars, and now I'm your favorite?"

Forest groans. "No, Beck. It's exactly the opposite. The fact that you have so much potential scares the hell out of me. I never wanted to feel like you settled for me, when you could have anyone."

I run the backs of my knuckles through his beard and think that over. "When did I ever give you the impression that I was settling? You've been, like, *goals* since the first time you ever poured me a beer. You're all I really need. Well, you, a lot of protein, and ten hours of sleep at night. But mostly you."

His brown eyes soften. He catches my hand in his and kisses my knuckles. "I've been a moron. How can I make it up to you?"

This requires some thought. "Well, sexually?"

He laughs. "That's not what I meant. But sure."

"Hmm." I lean in and whisper, "They let me keep the jersey. You could fuck me in it."

I get a warm chuckle and a kiss on my jaw. "Want to get out of here? I'll drive you home."

"Oh, definitely. Not home, though. The Cougars got me a Denver hotel room and it's... Okay, listen. It's at the Four Seasons, and it has a bed that takes up an entire zip code, and the shower has three heads and a bench. There's mood lighting I didn't even set. It just knew. So yeah. Take me there. Wreck me in a room with a really expensive mini bar."

His eyes flare. "You're on. Say goodnight to your coach, okay? And then meet me outside in my truck."

"Wow, this room," Forest says as we enter my plush lair at the Four Seasons.

"I know, right?" I slur. It's late, and I'm dead on my feet. But Forest is here, and my dick is suddenly very aware of that fact. I toss my suit jacket at a chair and lean over to untie my shoes.

As soon as they're off, I look around for Forest, hoping to find him naked. Sadly, he's still fully dressed. He's sitting on the side of the bed, strong forearms propped onto his knees, and he's watching me with a fond expression.

"What are you waiting for?" I demand, unbuttoning my shirt. "This bed must be tested. Explored. Put through its paces."

A slow grin overtakes his face, and it reminds me that I can't wait to feel his beard on my balls. "I missed you. The way you speak your mind. And your oddball commentary."

"What about this?" I turn around and drop my trouser pants and briefs in one go, showing him my ass. "Did you miss this?"

"You know I did. That was never my issue."

I feel pretty good about that as I stumble out of the rest of my clothes. Forest removes his own in about half the time, and peels back the covers on the aircraft-carrier-size bed. Then he lays down, the white bedding pulled up to his slim hips, all his ink on display. And that broad chest, with just the right amount of fur on it? Honestly, it's so distracting that I have trouble getting my last sock off. But I manage it and then dive into bed with him.

He rolls and pulls me in. I find his mouth like a heat-seeking missile.

The kiss I get is slower than I'm expecting. More thorough than urgent. His beard against my neck. His hands in my hair. The heat of his body against mine, and the scent of his skin.

I love it all. I'm hard and happy about it, but I also love these deep, slow kisses. Kisses that make a different kind of promise than I'm used to from Forest.

I lean into him and cling to his wide shoulders. A pair of sexy brown eyes studies me from close range. "You're exhausted," he whispers.

"No'm not."

He smiles, his thumb tracing my upper lip. "Sweetheart, it's three in the morning, and your eyes are barely open."

Sweetheart. "I'll rally."

"Yeah, you will." He reaches over and presses the glowing button on the wall. Darkness covers us like a blanket, and strong arms pull me close. "You'll rally in the morning."

"But..." I yawn so hard my jaw cracks. "I want you to bang me."

"Mmm," he says, stroking my face. "Sometimes the things we say we want aren't the things we really need. Ask me how I know."

That's kind of confusing, and I feel the need to ask a few clarifying questions.

I fall asleep instead.

***

In the morning, I wake up with my head on his chest, and his fingers combing gently through my hair.

My eyes spring open. I shift my body against his, running a hand down his taut stomach until I encounter the very thing I'm looking for. My fingers brush his erection, and he lets out a horny little sound.

"Oh, it's on," I say.

He chuckles and rubs my arm. "Do you need to get up and..."

"Nope." I kiss his chest. Twice.

"You didn't even hear what I was going to say."

I lick his slightly fuzzy nipple. "Doesn't matter. I let myself get talked out of sex last night. Not happening again."

"Okay," he says. "But just for the record, I was going to ask if you wanted to find your Cougars jersey for me to wear."

I stop midlick. "Really? You'd do that for me?"

"Beck, there's very little I wouldn't do for you. And, yeah, it's a little silly. But I'm okay with that."

I roll off the bed instantly.

***

Twenty minutes later, I'm groaning up at Forest while he fucks me on my back, sweating onto the official Cougars jersey.

If I never get called up again, I'll still have a *multitude* of positive memories of this blue piece of polyester.

"You're gonna have to come soon," he pants, the muscles straining in his powerful neck. "You look red-faced and properly fucked, and I can't take much more."

"Your fault," I pant back at him. "You tied up my hands, and now I can't get myself off." The bed is a four-poster style, and Forest wasted no time using my game-day tie to secure my wrists to one corner.

I fucking love it, but I can't stroke myself like this.

He stops thrusting and kisses me. "I don't want this to end."

"That's pretty impractical," I point out. "I thought the plan was that we're going to do this more often?"

He rubs his beard across my neck, and I shiver. "That's the plan, all right. So I guess I'll let you finish. How about now?"

He drops one of his broad hands to my cock, and my eyes practically roll back in my head. "Yes, fuck. *God*. I..." He starts thrusting again, and it happens. The words just tumble out. "I *love you*, Forest."

The moment the words are out of my mouth, I know I've fucked up again. He goes absolutely still above me.

"Oh hell. I just..."

"Beck," he whispers, his brown eyes warm. "I love you too. Kinda wish I'd said it first. I'm always a step behind you. I guess that's just the way it is between us. I'll just try to keep up with my super smart boyfriend."

I search my feeble mind for a reply that demonstrates my gratitude, but when Forest strokes me again, I come all over him instead.

FORTY-THREE

Lotta Wins This Week

FOREST

WE DON'T MOVE for a long time.

Lounging in a bed with Beck isn't *exactly* new. It's not like I've never lazed around reveling in post-sex endorphins with him before, drowsing with one hand on his washboard abs and the other one stroking his hair.

It's just that this time I feel no guilt. I don't think about my financial problems or the boiler or other places I need to be. I'm just living my life right now, one heartbeat at a time. The way I should have been before.

After a while, he shifts in my arms. "What if we shared a calendar?" he asks quietly. "I don't need to know where you are every minute of the day. But at least if you had a shift at work, I'd know better than to ask if you're free."

"Sure, no problem," I say. "But maybe I don't need to work so many nights. I deserve some fun, too."

He lifts his head off my chest and stares at me. "Who *are* you?"

I snort and pull his head back down. "Don't tease. The past year has been a real trial. But I can't keep up this pace. Our newest hires seem to be sticking around, and Izzy wants to take some shifts behind the bar. She never said so until last night."

"I like this for both of us," he says.

"Charlie is with me this weekend," I point out. "And I'm still not ready to have a lot of sex when he's on the other side of the wall. But if you're up for dinner and…"

"Video games?" Beck smirks against my chest.

"How do you know I wasn't going to say *math homework*? Maybe I'm just using you for your giant… brain."

He laughs. "Use me. I like it. What does Charlie like to eat? Maybe I should bring takeout again. I eat a lot, and I'm not much of a cook. But I know you hate it when I spend money…"

I let out a sigh, because he's right. I do hate it. "I'll cook—it's cheaper. But once in a while you can spoil us with burritos."

He nudges me with his heel. "How emasculating could it really be, when I give you my ass in return?"

I look up at the Four Seasons' ceiling and laugh. "You aren't like anybody else, Beck. You're really fucking smart, and you keep things in perspective."

He rolls, tucking a leg between mine. "Shame it took you so long to understand this. But I'm not mad about it. Tell Charlie I'm bringing over a new video game."

"You can tell him yourself." I skim a hand down his muscular back. "The Ice Cats play Friday and Saturday. So does Sunday work?"

"Look who has my game schedule memorized."

"It's almost the same every week, bud."

He bites my shoulder. "Let me take the win."

"Lotta wins this week."

He kisses my chest. "Don't I know it."

Beck decides to blow off the Ice Cats practice this morning, so we can order room service. "And the egg sandwiches will taste extra if we eat them in these," he says, tossing me a plush bathrobe.

I can't find it in me to argue. My ten hour stay at this five-star hotel is the closest thing I've had to a vacation in years. Besides, I don't have to pick up Charlie from school for another couple hours.

We're only two bites into our sandwiches when Beck's phone rings. He doesn't even glance at it.

"Aren't you going to get that?" I prod. "What if it's your agent?"

"My agent barely remembers my name."

I get up and grab the phone anyway, because a man doesn't unlearn all his clenched-up habits overnight.

It says, *Coach Powers Calling*.

FORTY-FOUR

Need a New Tie

BECK

HERE I STAND naked except for a bathrobe, feet sinking into the plush carpet, as Coach Powers says, "Hey, Beck. Don't make any dinner plans for the next eight weeks or so. After last night's performance, I'm calling you up to travel with us as one of our Black Aces."

Suddenly, I'm having an-out-of-body experience. I'm not even sure what I say to Coach. Hopefully, it's a stammered thanks and a promise to work hard. But I also might have said, "Cool. Yeah. I love poker metaphors, too. Always wanted to be a grim omen of playoff injuries. Total bucket-list moment."

Then I walk into a door. Not hard, but noticeably.

Forest, wincing, grabs me by the waist and turns me around again so I can pace the room unscathed while Coach spools out a bunch of details. They're putting me up in a residence hotel in Boulder. I'll be practicing with the Cougars every day and traveling with them for the duration of the playoffs.

"Which, hopefully, is all the way to the finals." Coach Powers chuckles. "We've done it before."

"Yessir," I say, my mind whirling.

When the call ends, Forest has to remove the phone from my hand, because all I can do is stand there, openmouthed.

He slaps me on the back. "Breathe, Beck. This is fantastic, and I'm not even surprised. I wondered if last night was sort of a tryout."

I sink into my chair and take a gulp of coffee. "They must be worried about Volkov."

Forest nods. "Or just cautious. Makes sense that Powers would choose a goalie as a Black Ace if they're rolling into the playoffs with, like, fewer than two healthy puck eaters."

"So I'm like...their new favorite spare tire. I love this for me."

Forest circles behind me, puts both hands on my shoulders, and squeezes. "You earned this. Ten bucks says you'll start another game before the playoffs, too. If I were Powers, I'd use you for one of the last couple games."

I take a deep breath and lean into Forest's firm grip. "This is going to be intense. You'll talk me down when I get rattled, right?"

Another sturdy squeeze from behind. "Yeah, I will. Promise."

My shoulders relax by a fraction. "Good. Because I so don't want to do this alone."

He runs a hand through my hair. "You don't have to. Now finish your breakfast. When do they want you in Boulder?"

"Tonight. Practice tomorrow morning, then we fly out to San Jose."

"Got it. So what errands do you need to knock out? Equipment? Laundry? New suit?"

I look over at where my Ice Cats tie is still tied to one of the bedposts. "A suit is a good idea. And I need a tie in Cougar blue."

He kisses me on top of the head. "Breakfast. Then a shower in that bathroom. Then Nordstrom or Suitsupply."

I tip my head back against his sturdy body. "Not gonna lie—I need all this dad energy right now."

"Just don't call me *daddy*, and we're good."

Two hours later, I've been fitted with three new shirts, a few new ties, and a sharp navy-blue suit. The store is going to rush the tailoring and deliver it to Boulder, too.

The bill comes to...a lot. I actually tense until the credit card screen says *approved*. "Feels like a big splurge," I say as the happy salesperson hands the shopping bag with my shirts and ties to Forest.

"It's not," he says. "You have a two-way contract, right? You're about to earn, what, three or four grand a night for a few weeks? You need the clothes, Beck. Dress for the job you want, not the one you have."

"Okay, yeah," I mutter.

"Besides, you look really fuckable in that suit. Just saying."

"You should've led with that."

He chuckles and squeezes my shoulder with his free hand. "Strap in. We've got more errands to run. Let's ditch one car and then I'll drive, okay? You'll open up the emails from Powers and read every word. Then you call your mom."

"Okay," I agree, happy to let him take charge. I'm at least as overwhelmed as I am excited. "I wonder how much I should pack to go with me. I only have the one suitcase."

He bleeps the locks on his truck. "We'll fix that too, Beck. Get in."

A while later I look up from the email I'm reading on my phone to see that we've pulled into the lot of Charlie's junior high school.

The kid himself comes running but pulls up short when he sees me. "Beck!" he screams. Then he yanks open the back door and climbs in. "I didn't finish my math homework last night because I was too busy screaming at the TV."

"Dude, really? And here I thought math was going well again."

"It's fine." He waves a hand, dismissing the problem. "The teacher will forgive me. I told her my tutor was playing for the Cougars last night, but I'm not sure she believed me."

"Not sure I believe it myself," I admit. "Now they've called me up today to practice with them throughout the playoffs."

Charlie's eyes practically bulge out. "Holy...! So what are we doing right now?"

"Shopping and helping Beck pack," Forest says. "Strap in. Next stop: Costco."

Forest pushes the cart while I play the role of anxious wreck in the aisles of Costco and then Whole Foods. It's a tag-team effort —protein powder, produce, toiletries, snacks that meet Charlie's approval. I don't even realize how much we're buying until my credit card gets hot enough to melt my wallet.

Forest drives me back to Loveland so I can pack, and then he and Charlie pop out to buy us some dinner. I'm left behind with the silence of my house and the realization that I leave for Boulder in, like, an hour.

It's fine. Everything is fine. Totally normal to be thirty percent packed and one hundred percent panicking.

Apparently, Charlie sees right through me, because I over- hear them in my kitchen while they're unpacking the Mexican food they bought.

"Beck seems nervous, Dad," he says in a voice that sounds

like he's trying to whisper. "He has that face—like a goalie trying to read the play when the puck is already in the net."

Ouch. Accurate, but ouch.

"He'll be fine," Forest says in a low, comforting voice. "It's hard to rearrange your entire life in a single day. He'll feel better when he puts his skates on tomorrow. All that hard work and all those hours of practice will pay off."

"Good thing he has us to help him," Charlie says, and my heart thaws a little more.

It's almost eight by the time we lug everything into the long-term hotel suite the Cougars set me up with. It's nicer than I expected—like they're trying to make me feel fancy, even though I know this is just temporary. There's a shopping bag on the coffee table full of Cougars workout gear in my size. And a Cougars puffer jacket, too.

"That's sick," Charlie says approvingly.

"Isn't it?" I can't resist pulling it on and walking over to the full-length mirror. "Look, Mom. They gave me the jacket. It has to be a sign."

Forest lets out a rumble of a laugh from the bedroom closet, where he's hanging the new shirts and ties we bought. Then he puts groceries in the kitchenette like this is normal, like he's just here to help and not breaking my brain with how competent and helpful he's being.

Like a real boyfriend.

Meanwhile, Charlie is supposed to be doing homework at the coffee table, but I'm ninety-nine percent sure he's assembling my gaming setup instead. When I'd wondered aloud if I should bring it with me, I felt like a teenager myself.

"Yes, if it helps you relax," Forest had said. "You're going to be in that hotel for at least three weeks, even if the Cougars stink it up in the first round."

"But they won't," Charlie had added, like it was the easiest thing in the world to believe in me.

So the console made it into the Jeep and into the hotel. Eventually the fridge is full, the gaming system is set up, and there's no more reason for Charlie to blow off his homework for my well-being.

They're going to leave any minute, and I'm not ready.

"Beck," Forest says softly from the bedroom doorway.

I follow him in there and shut the door behind me. He doesn't sit down or touch me or anything. He just gives me that look—the one where I feel like I'm under a microscope and also safe. "You good now? You need anything else?"

Gulp. "Well, no. Nothing except a good pounding."

He laughs, low and quiet. "Soon."

"I know. I'm not worried." Not about that, anyway.

"What time is morning skate?" he asks.

"Team breakfast at eight. Then video. Skating at ten."

He steps into my space and takes my face in his big hands. "You got this. You know this job. You know it here—" He taps my temple. "—and here." Then my chest. "You just have to relax enough to let your training take over."

"That's what all this was about?" I gesture vaguely toward the living room and the epic grocery haul.

"Exactly. Getting you ready so you can focus on what matters."

"You're what matters," I blurt, because it's the truth, and I'm not capable of pretending otherwise right now.

"I feel the same way about you. Promise." His hand curls around my wrist, thumb brushing my pulse. "But you need to slay some dragons before we can focus on us. I'll be waiting, okay?"

Something knotty unwinds inside my chest. I think I needed to hear that. "I hope you know how much I appreciate everything you did today."

His hand grazes my cheek affectionately. "I didn't do anything."

"Yeah, you did. You showed up, and that's all I ever needed from you."

He smiles. "That and a good pounding."

"Obviously."

Then they leave, and I get ready for bed. But I'm restless, bumping around the hotel suite alone. I text Rigsy with a couple of photos of my new Cougars gear. Mostly, I'm anxious and at odds with myself, and when I lie down in bed, sleep doesn't come. Even after I turn out the lights.

As I lie there, my phone vibrates with a text. It's Forest.

FOREST

Try to sleep.

BECK

How'd you know I wasn't?

Just a lucky guess. This is your goodnight text.

Goodnight, hunk.

Goodnight, sweetheart.

I like that a lot. So I put my phone down and close my eyes and somehow, I fall asleep.

It's Easier to Take Your Money

FOREST

BECK FLIES off for a week-long West Coast road trip. San Jose. L.A. Anaheim.

I set an alarm on my phone to remind me to text or call every single night. I need him to know that he matters. I'm not going to drop the ball again.

Except we only connect about half the time. He's been sucked into the vortex of a new team and their wild schedule. The tables have turned, and now *I'm* the guy who can't stop checking his phone, hoping that Beck has a minute to talk to me.

"Will you be playing your hand, Forest?" Kenji asks with a smirk in his voice. "Actually, we like you distracted. It's easier to take your money."

"Shit, sorry." I tuck my phone in my shirt pocket and pick up my cards. Pair of fours. Not much else to work with.

Denny chuckles. "Still no text from your guy?"

I shake my head.

CJ clears his throat. "Is there any chance he's sending you some kind of message? Must be a big ego boost to suddenly level up like this."

It takes me exactly half of a second to shake my head. "Beck doesn't play games like that."

"Sorry," CJ says quickly. "That was a dumb question. It's just that you look so fidgety."

"No, it's..." I pause for a moment as it sinks in how well I really do know Beck. He's not ghosting me. He's *busy*. "The thing is..." I let out a nervous chuckle. "The Cougars' coach will be fixing the starting lineup for tonight's game about now. And since Beck is too busy to get back to me..."

Kenji's eyebrows disappear under his hair. "You think they might put him in the net tonight?"

"You never know," I say, afraid to jinx Beck. "Middle game of a road trip, and back-to-back with tomorrow's game. They want their primaries rested for the playoffs." I take another glance at my phone, because I can't help myself. But the screen is dark.

"My dudes," Big Bob says. "We gotta play some poker now, so we can stop to watch the game if Beck is in the net." He kicks me under the table. "Focus, Forest. I need to take your money by... What time does the game start?"

"Eight, our time." It's six now.

Big Bob chuckles. "Let's wait to order dinner. I think we might have a hockey game to watch. Let's play, damn it."

So we do. I get terrible cards and I fold almost every hand. It doesn't matter. I'd happily give all my luck to Beck, if luck worked that way.

Kenji is dealing out another hand when my phone finally vibrates with a text.

BECK

Can't talk, but pls tune in to the game tonight.

My stomach lights up with fireworks, and I pump my fist.

"Is it happening?" Kenji demands.

"It's happening."

BECK

There is no good emoji for nerves. Except the green puke one. I hate that one.

FOREST

You got this. I believe in you.

Beck replies with the green puke emoji.

I'm a ball of nerves myself as the game begins. L.A. is two points behind the wild card line with two games left, which means they're hungry and desperate. The Cougars, on the other hand, are locked in for the playoffs, so this game isn't crucial for them.

It is for Beck, though. This is a big test of his abilities and his composure.

Denny orders Indian food, but I can hardly eat. I'm too busy shouting at his TV screen. Right from the first period, it's a weird, high-scoring game.

L.A. comes out flying—like hair-on-fire, playoff-or-bust energy. They throw pucks at the net from everywhere. Their forecheck is relentless. They pin our guys in their zone for long stretches, and Beck is just Jesus. He's everywhere. Glove, blocker, pad, repeat.

But the Cougars' skaters are loose. Too loose. They've already punched their ticket to the postseason, and it shows. Lazy backchecks. Fancy drop passes that don't connect. We're not winning puck battles, and Beck is getting hung out to dry.

"I'm so angry right now," I grumble, shoving a samosa in my mouth.

"He's doing it, though," CJ says. He's on the edge of his chair, too. We all are. "Your boy has moves."

By the end of the first, it's 2–2, and he's already stopped

sixteen shots. My stomach's in knots, and Denny's yelling, "This is the most stressed I've ever been watching a game that doesn't matter!"

Except it does matter. To Beck. And therefore to me. I hope he finds rage-texting romantic, because I keep firing off my thoughts to his phone.

FOREST

What are they doing tonight? Napping?

Ugh. That turnover is NOT your fault.

The rest of the game gets even more unhinged. We go up 3–2 off a fluke deflection that bounces like a pinball past their goalie. But then we take two dumb penalties in a row, and L.A. buries both power plays. One of them is a backdoor tap-in that Beck had zero chance on.

I'm pacing now, arms crossed over my chest, my food going cold on the coffee table. Denny's dog is hiding under the couch from all the yelling.

Then time runs out, and Coach Powers pulls Beck with ninety seconds left. The team rallies to give L.A. the same kind of barrage that Beck had faced all night.

But it's not enough. We've lost 3-4 when the buzzer sounds.

I text Beck.

This is not on you, and Powers knows it. You played really well tonight, and you kept your composure like a champ.

"We gotta take a selfie," Big Bob says. "Let Beck know we were pulling for him."

"Yes!" Kenji shouts. "Wait, Denny? Got a notepad? We need a message."

A few minutes later, after I've loaded up Denny's dishwasher with our dishes, I'm summoned to take a selfie with the guys in front of Denny's poker table. Kenji holds up the sign that says in Sharpie print, *YOU SLAYED TONIGHT!*

I laugh when I see it, and then Big Bob takes the pic, because he has the longest arms.

When I drive home, I feel strangely satisfied. The game didn't go how any of us wanted, but Beck can hold his head up high. And my friends are awesome.

After I get home, Beck responds.

BECK

I know, I know. That shit show wasn't my fault.
Hoarse from yelling at them from the crease.
Still kind of sucks though. I'll call you from the
bus if you're still up.

FOREST

I'll be up! This sucks the way ANY loss sucks.
But some smart guy told me you have to live by
goalie rules. So you're not allowed to think
about it tomorrow.

He hearts my text, and I discover that I like it a hell of a lot better than the thumbs up.

Too bad I fall asleep before he calls me. The next morning I wake up in an empty bed, a missed call on my phone.

Damn it all.

FORTY-SIX

Can I Ask You a Few Questions?

FOREST

THE NEXT NIGHT I'm working a shift, but Beck and I have arranged a call—six o'clock my time—when Beck is on his way to the arena for tonight's game. So I'm watching the clock like it owes me money.

Luckily, it's a quiet night in the bar so far. Izzy is behind the bar with me tonight, and I'm letting her mix all the cocktail orders for practice.

At 5:58, a customer takes the barstool right in front of me. He's wearing a navy-blue suit and glasses that are steamed up from the sudden change in temperature. He removes them as I set a coaster down on the bar. "What can I get you?"

"Just a Coke if you don't mind. Are you Seth Forrester?"

"Depends who's asking." I say it with a smile, so he knows I'm only half kidding. Then I grab a glass and fill it with ice.

He opens his wallet and shows me... Is that a badge? "Jay Callahan, FBI. Can I ask you a few questions?"

Wild. I push the Coke button on the soda gun and fill his glass. "Not gonna lie, that sounds serious."

He smiles. "It is, but not for you. I need to show you a few photographs and ask you if you recognize anyone."

"Sure thing. Lot of people come through here in a week, though."

"Just try, okay?"

"Sure."

He puts a leather folio on the bar and pulls out two glossy printouts with four photos on each one. He spins them around, and I give them a glance. All the men on the page are wearing army uniforms, and I don't know any of them. Then I turn to the second page and immediately lock eyes with an image of another army dude. The bottom falls out of my stomach.

It's *him*. The guy who drugged me in my own home. The guy who emptied my bank account as well as my self-esteem. Instinct causes me to reach out and cover his ugly smirk with my hand.

"Forest?" Izzy says, and her voice sounds like it's a mile away. "Remind me what's in a Moscow Mule?"

Vodka, ginger beer, and lime. The words don't come out of my mouth, because I'm drowning. I lift my hand and look again at the face I've been trying to forget.

"Forest." Izzy lays a hand on my arm.

The FBI agent comes to my rescue. "Miss, it's vodka, ginger beer, and lime. Can you give us a moment?"

"Of course. But Forest—your phone is ringing."

I glance down at my phone. Beck's face lights up the screen, and I answer like I'm grabbing a lifeline. "*Beck?*" It comes out as a gulp.

"Hi. You okay?"

"Hell no. There's an FBI agent here. He just showed me a photo of *him*."

There's a brief silence while Beck connects the dots. And then, "Holy shit! Really? That's fantastic."

"Is it, though? I might be sick."

"Aw, big man. Breathe, honey. Right now."

I exhale slowly.

"There you go. This is good news. They're going to nail his ass now. He isn't going to win. He never was."

"Okay, okay. You're right." *And it's so good to hear your voice. Like medicine.*

"So now you know his name?"

"Not yet. I'd better go and finish this conversation."

"Call me after. No matter what time."

"But you have—"

"Call me anyway. This is an emergency."

I close my eyes. "I love you. For real." The words roll off my tongue.

"I know," he says easily. "Talk soon."

We hang up and I turn back to the FBI agent, who's waiting patiently. I jab a finger into the perpetrator's face. "Okay, who *is* this asshole the cops told me they couldn't find?"

"Maybe they couldn't find him, but I did. The problem is that he gets around a lot. His MO never changes, though. I read your file, and it's the same story in every state—dating apps, drugs, and financial theft. His victims are always men. Usually near army bases. He's been at this for three or four years."

My chest tightens painfully. "Fuck. How many victims?"

"Six so far. You want to know how he finally got caught?"

"Of course I do."

"Bragging." Agent Callahan shakes his head in disgust. "Guy got wasted and told his best friend how he made a hundred grand last year, tax free."

"What's his real name?"

"Roger Antonio Porras."

"*Roger.* My life was turned upside down by a *Roger*?"

He gives me a stoic nod. "He's already in custody. But I'm going to need you to give me a formal statement that says you recognize the man in that particular photo."

My stomach twists. "Happy to do that. Is there any chance I'll recover some money?"

"Maybe?" He winces. "Hard to say, and it wouldn't happen fast. This is a federal case."

"Okay. I understand." Even though I've been stressing about my finances for over a year, the money suddenly matters less to me than it did ten minutes ago. I want him locked up more than I want my money back. "I'll testify, if it comes to that."

"Glad to hear that, Mr. Forrester. Some people aren't that eager to do so."

"I'm not embarrassed," I say, and suddenly, I realize that's completely true. "He's the one who should be."

"Agreed." He gives me a quick smile.

"How'd you find me?" I ask. "I didn't think the cops gave a shit about me."

"That's not true," he says. "Their investigation was pretty thorough. But this guy was slick, and he never targeted two people in the same metro area. So I had to make a lot of phone calls to figure out where he'd been. I called Denver PD on a hunch, because there are so many army bases nearby. I asked if they had any cases like this. And a smart detective said no, but he'd heard about one up in Erie..."

I force more oxygen into my lungs. "Wow. That seems fortuitous."

"It was. I'm sorry to make you relive all this, but he's going to be prosecuted. He's going to do time. I'll make sure you're kept in the loop."

"I really appreciate that."

"Before I go, I just need your statement," he says. "It'll only take a few minutes."

"Great," I say. *Leaves plenty of time for my breakdown.*

He pulls out a pad of paper and a pen.

Perfectly Understandable

I LEAVE the team's elimination soccer game to take Forest's call.

"Are you sure you're okay to talk?" is the first thing he asks.

"Totally sure." We're only ten seconds into this call, but I can already hear how rattled Forest is. "Talk to me."

"You're not playing tonight, are you?"

"Not a chance. Not even suiting up. Tell me what happened, Forest."

He takes a shaky breath and then gives me a disjointed data dump. The FBI agent. The photos. Army guys. A federal prosecution.

"That's a lot," I say quietly after he stumbles through the details. "You okay?"

"Of course I am," he says. "They *caught* him."

"I get that." *But you sound like a guy who just walked away from a car accident who doesn't realize he's going to have whiplash.* "It's about time."

We talk for another few minutes, and then he goes back to his shift, and I watch the seven p.m. game against Anaheim from the press box. Zack Walcott plays brilliantly and gets a shutout. Lucky bastard.

After, we fly back to Boulder, landing after one a.m. I get into my Jeep and start the engine. My suite in Boulder is only a ten-minute drive away on empty nighttime roads, but I'm picturing Forest in his darkened bedroom, alone with all his thoughts. I turn left out of the parking lot and head toward Erie.

———

BECK

You still up? You okay?

FOREST

Yes and yes. Just a lot on my mind.

Come open your front door.

Wait. Really?

I knock. Loudly.

The door flies open fifteen seconds later, and a half-naked lumberjack in flannel pajama pants pulls me into his brawny arms.

I gather his warm body against mine and let out a long sigh. This is already worth the pain I'm going to feel when my alarm goes off in a few hours. "You okay, really?"

"Mostly?" He laughs against my neck, and his beard tickles. "Won't lie—seeing that asshole's picture messed me up some."

"Perfectly understandable," I say, steering him inside and kicking the door shut behind us. "He's never coming back here, though. Never. I'd fuck him up if he tried."

Forest goes still in my arms. Did I say something wrong? "I mean... I know you can take care of yourself. I just... I'd like to get a few punches in."

"Beck." He sighs against my cheek. "I love hearing that you have my back."

My ego grows approximately two and a half sizes. Instantly. "Good. And he's going to *pay* for abusing your trust."

"Yeah," Forest says gruffly. "I might have to face him in court, though. I offered to testify."

"Of course you did. It won't be easy, but I think it'll help you heal. And maybe one of those other guys can't, you know? You'd be doing this for him, too."

Forest makes a warm noise and pulls back to look me up and down. "God, I'm happy you're here."

There's no way he could know how those words light me up inside. "Only place I want to be."

"Come to bed," he says, yawning. "Now that you're here, I think maybe I could finally sleep."

I strip off my jacket. "That's either a fantastic compliment, or an insult to my sexual skills."

"It's late, rookie," he says, pinching my hip. "Come to bed," he repeats.

Five minutes later, we're curled up under Forest's comforter. He's got an arm around me, and his fingertips are tracing the divot between my pecs. It's *outrageously* nice. And even if my erection disagrees (hello, down there!), this is exactly what both of us need right now.

"Thank you for coming," Forest says quietly. "It means a lot."

I roll in his arms and kiss his fuzzy jaw. "You show up for me. I'll show up for you. That's how this works now."

"Yeah, it is." He kisses me for real. Just once. "Let's get some rest. You must be tired, sweetheart."

"Mmm-hmm," I say, even though hearing that endearment only makes me want to fuck. But Forest's eyelids are so heavy. "Yeah, I'm exhausted."

He's asleep within seconds.

I, on the other hand, lie awake for a while, eyes closed, just appreciating him. The slack, trusting weight of his body against mine and the steady thump of his heartbeat.

And I realize this is *it*. I've peaked. There's a hot, fantastic man in my life who calls me sweetheart. So many people never have that, let alone the chance to play big-league hockey.

Maybe that should scare me—nowhere to go but down. It doesn't, though. All I feel is gratitude.

And then I sleep, too.

FORTY-EIGHT

A Heart Attack in Four Acts

FOREST

MAY

PLAYOFF HOCKEY IS BASICALLY a heart attack in four acts, and I'm willingly subjecting myself to it from row sixteen at the Denver arena, next to my thirteen-year-old son, who's busy bargaining with God. I think he just said he'd quit TikTok for a week if the Cougars could just kill this damn penalty.

I glance sideways. "A week? That's it?"

Charlie shoots me a glare. "I said a week *minimum.*"

I snort, but I'm feeling just as irrational as he is. The Cougars are one goal down as the clock ticks down on the second period. If we don't win tonight, L.A. wins the conference, which will sting. They shouldn't even be here—they snuck into the playoffs like a raccoon into a backyard wedding and have caused nothing but chaos ever since.

But here we are. Game six. Conference Finals. Backs against the wall.

Walcott's in net, standing tall so far. And by "tall" I mean slightly above average. He's letting rebounds spill like change out of a torn pocket, but the defense has bailed him out every time.

Beck is suited up on the bench, rostered as tonight's backup. Between plays, my gaze keeps traveling over there. With his helmet off, I can see every line of concentration on his handsome face. He keeps flexing his blocker hand like he's trying to keep it warm in case something goes sideways.

He'd called me at five p.m., asking, "Can you find backup at work tonight? I'm on the bench, which means I've got two tickets for you."

My answer, of course, was *hell yes*. Although I made Charlie show me his finished math homework before we walked out the door.

This is the Cougars' seventeenth playoff game, and Beck's fifth one on the bench. They didn't turn to him at all during the first round. But Volkov's old injury may be flaring, because Beck's been on the bench backing up Walcott several times in quick succession.

L.A. has the power play, and Charlie and I are eating our feelings. He's shoving popcorn into his mouth, and I have pretzel crumbs on my brand-new Cougars jersey that says *JAMES* on the back.

"They should put Beck in," Charlie grumbles as we fail on the forecheck. "This would be his grudge match against L.A."

"Yeah," I agree. *Especially if the hockey gods want me to throw up in public.*

"He'd get 'em this time," Charlie says confidently. "On his home turf."

"That's right." This *will* be Beck's home turf someday. I feel it in my bones.

We survive the power play, and I start to relax a little. But then there's a scramble behind the net. Our D-man gets tangled up and goes down, and an L.A. winger takes the opening to crash the crease like a goddamn wrecking ball.

Walcott gets bowled over.

Hard.

Time slows down. The whole Cougars bench stands up for a better look at their teammate. The crowd downshifts from a roar to that eerie playoff silence when something goes sideways.

Walcott's helmet is off, which is scary.

Players swarm the crease, blocking my view of the situation. But I note that Walcott's feet aren't moving.

Charlie whispers, "Oh fuck."

I don't even reprimand him.

Trainers hit the ice. The arena holds its collective breath.

Like everyone else, I'm praying for Walcott to get right up and shake it off. But I have the feeling Beck—our Beck—is about to get the nod.

FORTY-NINE

Here He Comes

EVERYTHING STARTS HAPPENING in fast forward. They cut to a media timeout. The officials huddle up to chat about a potential penalty. And now the trainers have Zack sitting up. Talking. Hooray for that.

The referee booms, "L.A. number 17, five-minute major penalty for goaltender interference." The fans cheer, and the bench relaxes a fraction of a degree.

Meanwhile, Coach Powers, one of the assistant coaches, and DiCosta, who witnessed the play, are huddled behind me, having a fast-moving conversation about next steps.

"He was *out*, right?" Coach asks. "You're sure?"

"Yeah," DiCosta responds. "For maybe ten seconds. Unresponsive. Then he opened his eyes and said *oh shit*."

"Here he comes," the assistant coach says, and we all watch as Zack skates with the team captain toward the bench, his helmet under his arm, while the stadium applauds him.

"I'm fine, really," is the first thing Walcott says to Powers. "I'm good."

"You blacked out," Powers says tersely. "That means—"

"It was only for a sec," he argues, but his gaze is squinty.

"Doesn't matter," Coach insists. "You're coming off for the rest of the period. Start the concussion protocol."

"Coach—"

Powers cuts off the objection with a slash of his hand. "No. I'm not willing to risk your *brain*, no matter how much is riding on this game."

Then he turns to me and says what everyone is thinking. "Becker James, you're going in for the rest of the period."

Holy, holy shit. My eyes cut to the clock, which reads 5:32.

"Boys, keep the pressure up! We've got a power play, so let's use it. Don't give them a minute's rest. Clean passes. Keep up the momentum. And *communicate*."

Yanking my glove on, I step onto the ice, stretching furiously and listening to Powers wrap up his comments. "Pressure, guys. We're not missing a step, here. Show me a goal in the next five minutes."

I skate to the crease and try to settle in. Going in late in the game has its own weird energy.

Then the announcer says, "In the net for the Cougars, goaltender Becker James!" And the crowd lets out a roar of support.

"James," DiCosta says, skating by me. "You got this."

"You so do!" Stoney says, gliding by.

"Talk to us. We got you. You're not alone down here," Kapski says.

You're not alone. Good thing, because this is one of the highest-pressure moments in my entire life. Unbidden, my eyes dart toward the section where Forest's seats should be, and I find him like a heat-seeking missile. He's on his feet, cheering frantically, with Charlie bouncing beside him.

Seeing him up there does something to me. No matter what happens in the next five minutes of play, I can still call Forest after the game and hear the rumble of his voice in my ear. Or drive to the bar and see his smile when I walk in the door. That's not going to change.

Even so, I might as well show off a little for him.

"Let's fucking *go*," I whisper, dropping into my stance. I narrow my focus to the face-off circle.

The ref flicks his wrist, and I'm locked in. Stoney wins the puck and passes to DiCosta. Who passes again. *Zip. Zap. Smack.* I'm tracking the action like I was born for it, even as the speed of play ramps up to a dizzying pace.

After a few false starts, Stoney finally gets a shot on net. But it bounces off the post, and we don't get the rebound. L.A. has sent out their PK team, with fresh instructions to rattle my cage. And now that they've got the puck, they do their damnedest.

Like a tidal wave, the action rolls toward my end of the rink. L.A. is doing its best to sow confusion, with lots of faked shots and quick passes. But my skaters are dialed in and ready to defend their turf.

During a line change, I sneak a glance at the penalty clock. We're running out of time to capitalize, and now the puck is changing hands like this is a speed-dating mixer. As the power play ticks toward its inevitable end, the game gets fast and chippy. Lots of elbows and cursing, while I try to track the puck through the scrum.

Newgate and L.A.'s center battle it out for the puck at the boards. L.A. gets the puck, but the guy flubs it, sending it dribbling in my direction. Newgate trips him, sending the guy sprawling, and doesn't get called for it.

Thank you. I move up, take it on my stick, and look up for the pass.

"Take your time," I hear someone yell—might be Stoney, might be God. Either way, I hunt for my best option. I notice that L.A.'s line change is a hot mess. Their forwards are tangled up like a phone charger in my gym bag.

My guys are resetting, so I could wait another breath until one of them is open.

But there's a wide, clear lane in front of me. Just ice. Glorious, empty ice.

I've done this a hundred times in practice. Not seriously, not under the lights, but—

Screw it.

I'm not thinking, just reacting, like my body has turned into a slingshot, and the puck is the stone. I tap the puck to the blade of my stick, and then I fire.

The puck soars. David sailing toward Goliath.

Somebody gasps as it sails past center ice. Possibly me.

Then I clock the moment when L.A.'s goalie realizes what I've done, and he dives forward. He's a millisecond too late, and the puck sails past his catcher—so close that he probably felt the breeze.

Then it finds the net.

The fucking net. Top corner.

The lamp lights, and I just blink. This isn't the kind of thing that happens to me. Or to most people. Goalie goals happen only a few times a decade.

But the whole arena is screaming, so I think maybe this actually happened.

I might have just scored a goal.

Me, of all people.

The ref points at center ice. *Goal.*

Stoney and Kapski and DiCosta rush the net at warp speed, laughing and screaming. They mob me, and I'm laughing, too. Not too loudly to miss the announcer's voice, though. "Goal scored by number 90, Becker James. Unassisted!"

"Jaysus Christ, rookie!" Kapski hoots. "Why the hell are you not a forward?"

My skates leave the ice. They've hoisted me in the air. "Because I'm too weird to be a forward," I holler.

"Then how do we account for Stoney?" someone yells from below me.

Good question. But I can't answer it because everything is chaos. The fans are still screaming, and the game stops for a media break, so I skate over to the bench where Powers is red-faced from yelling and laughing. "Never a dull moment with you!" He slaps me on my shoulder pads. "Now shake it off, reset, and show me another forty-seven seconds of brilliant goal-tending before the period ends."

I skate back to the crease, still grinning behind my mask. I treat myself to another glance toward Forest and see that he and Charlie are clutching each other and waving frantically at me with their free hands.

I lift my catcher and wave right back at them.

You are not alone, my teammate said a few minutes ago.

For the first time this season, I truly believe him.

FIFTY

Denver Daily Sports Report

A WILD NIGHT IN DENVER

BACKUP GOALIE BECKER *James Scores Once-in-a-Lifetime Goal as Colorado Tops L.A.*

By Marla Knox

The Cougars' most promising rookie will be dining out on this for years.

In what started as a tense, series-defining battle against L.A., the Colorado Cougars clawed their way to a 4–3 win Wednesday night in Denver, preventing their exit from the playoffs.

But it wasn't the score that will go down in history—it was how they got there. Late in the second period, with starting goalie Zack Walcott temporarily sidelined after a brutal collision in the crease, backup netminder Becker James stepped in under the spotlight and stole the show.

Fending off a slippery L.A. counterattack, James shocked the league and the 18,000+ fans in attendance by scoring a goalie goal, a full-ice shot that soared past L.A.'s scrambling defense and past the glove of goaltender Kaspar Andersson to tie up the game.

"I saw the opening and figured, why the hell not," James said postgame, still visibly in disbelief. "Not like I practice those. Except... okay. I maybe practice those."

The goal, scored with 0:47 left in the second period, lit up the arena—literally and figuratively—as teammates mobbed the young goaltender while the building shook with cheers. It was the first goalie goal in Colorado Cougars history, and only the twenty-first ever recorded in NHL play.

"Kid's got ice in his veins," said Coach Clay Powers. "And apparently, a cannon for a stick."

James's Cinderella moment was made possible by Walcott's temporary exit after a crease scramble. After concussion protocol testing during the second intermission, the Cougars cleared Walcott to return, and he took the net again to start the third.

Walcott made eight saves in the third, including a critical blocker stop on a shorthanded 2-on-1 that kept the Cougars in control. Defenseman Hudson Newgate added a late goal at 14:27 of the third, sealing the game and sending the hometown crowd into another round of celebratory chaos.

The win gives Colorado another shot at sewing up the conference title tomorrow night.

Meanwhile, all eyes remain on Becker James, whose post-game locker stall was surrounded by cameras, teammates, and a reporter who handed him a Sharpie and asked, "Can you sign my stat sheet?"

Sources say that reporter might have been me.

When I asked James for his takeaway from last night's wild ride, he hesitated. Then he said, "Nobody expected this tonight. Didn't know I'd be playing. Didn't know I was about to become the answer to a pub trivia question. That's so extra. I just wanted to stop some pucks and impress my favorite bartender."

Sources say it probably worked.

— End Copy —

Epilogue: The Shining

Six Months Later

PRACTICE IS OVER, and my body is loose and tired in a good way. I tie my shoes and then check the time. One thirty. Plenty of time to meet Forest for my two o'clock appointment. The place is only a fifteen-minute drive from the Cougars' Boulder headquarters, where I've been spending a lot of time this season.

Since August—when Zack Walcott took a trade to a team who wants to make him their starter—I've more or less become a Cougar. I have a new one-way contract, which makes my status as Coach Powers's number-two goalie less precarious.

Tending goal for *another* of our winning playoffs games in the fourth round didn't hurt either. We didn't win the Cup, but we got damn close. I feel good about our chances this season, too.

I pull on my coat against the winter chill and grab my wet towel off the bench. Before I walk out, I take a quick glance around the room in a moment of silent appreciation. This is my life now. It's demanding as hell, but I feel a lot of gratitude for all the new people in my life. Working hard for them is worth it.

"Want to grab lunch?" Volkov asks me as we both toss our towels into the laundry bin by the exit. "Still thinking about that sandwich place you found. The menu is super weird, but I can't argue with that pastrami."

"Isn't it great?" He's not wrong about the menu—all the sandwiches are named after horror films. The Shining, for example, is rare roast beef, camembert, and pickled onions. Plus horseradish, with a creeping heat that sneaks up on you while you eat it. Just like the film. "I could really go for a Soylent Green right now, if I had the time. But I'm meeting my boyfriend first."

He frowns. "What's in the Soylent Green?"

"Grilled zucchini, goat cheese, and pesto."

"Where you off to?" Stoney asks, gripping my shoulder.

"Going to look at an apartment. But Volkov wants a lunch date."

"Ooh! Looking at anywhere good? Lotta guys live at Red Rocks. You know that development? Nice place. Plenty of room. Plus, there's usually good leftovers in Newgate's fridge."

"You mooch," Newgate grumbles. "Last night I went home and found this dude sitting at my place at the table. He thinks he can just show up with a good bottle of red and invite himself to dinner."

"Works every time." Stoney shrugs. "His husband thinks I'm funny."

"Funny *looking*," whispers another player, and there's laughter in the corridor as we trudge toward the parking lot.

"I'm not ready for Red Rocks, sadly," I point out. "That's way too much house for me." Translation: too much money and commitment. My position on the team isn't secure enough for me to sign a lease on a three-bedroom rowhouse. I need at least a solid year of NHL play under my belt before that would start to make sense.

"Then find a place with a hot tub." Stoney squeezes my shoulder. "Nobody has one of those yet. We could have parties."

"If you find a place and need furniture, I have a guy," DiCosta says.

"Let 'im find the apartment first," Kapski says, cuffing him on the arm. "I hear it's a tight market out there."

"You're not wrong." I peel off from the pack. "Better see this place before someone snaps it up."

"Go get it, rookie!" Kapski says.

I give him an awkward salute and head toward my Jeep. There's an extra spring in my step because Forest is meeting me. I asked him to time the driving distance from his place in Erie to this place on the east side of Boulder.

My life is awesome but it's also a logistical nightmare. I live in Loveland but effectively work in Boulder now. That's a forty-two minute drive. And Forest's place is also a forty-minute drive from Loveland.

So I've been spending a *lot* of time behind the wheel of my Jeep—but all for good reasons. The Cougars are starting me in the net once a week, and my performance has been almost as rock solid as my relationship with Forest.

For all these reasons, I'd like to rent something more convenient. The distance from Forest to this new apartment on the edge of Boulder should be like twenty minutes. If I move, I'd be closer to both Forest's place and the Cougars. My two favorite places in the world.

I warm up the Jeep and text Forest.

BECK

On my way. Lunch after this?

FOREST

You know it. Mexican food or horror movie sandwiches?

We'll make it a game time decision.

FOREST

"Units in this development are going FAST!" shouts Jean, the agent who's showing Beck around. "I signed three leases today!"

I resist the urge to cover my ears. Jean is a tiny human, reaching only to my collar bone. But what she lacks in stature, she makes up for in volume.

"I'll bear that in mind," Beck says, taking a step back, trying to save his hearing. "Give me a minute to look around."

"Absolutely! Take twenty of them, actually! That's when my next showing is. My calendar is stacked with interested couples!"

Beck winces, but I can't tell if it's because of Jean, or because of the apartment. On the one hand, it's roomy, and I like the open-plan layout. But I saw the price, and it costs a mint, probably because it's brand new and sparkling.

Literally sparkling, in the case of the white marble countertop. In fact, *everything* is white. The walls, the surfaces, the sofa and the throw pillows. It's blinding.

Beck heads into the spacious bedroom, and I follow him. "What do you think?"

I hesitate. I don't like it, but it's not my decision. "It's very attractive in... a clinical sort of way."

He turns to give me a sideways glance. "Yeah, especially if you've ever dreamed of living on the international space station."

I snicker. "There's a view of the mountains," I say, still trying to be supportive. But even the landscaping has the barren feel of new construction.

"The price, though," he grumbles. "Ouch."

"Yeah." I sigh. "It's a little steamy for this end of Boulder. Maybe you'd rather live closer to the rink."

"Would I?" He bites his lip. "This place is closer to you. You do realize that matters, right? I drive to Erie a lot."

"Yeah, you do, and I'm grateful. It's just that this place is a little... soulless."

"Whatever. I'm never home." But then he shrugs. "I dunno. Maybe I'm not ready to pull the trigger. It almost feels like a jinx. Like—if I sign an expensive lease, I'll get sent back to Loveland."

"You won't," I say, and it's not just loyalty talking. Beck's future with the Cougars is bright.

"But Rigsy doesn't care that I'm month to month. He told me to take my time."

"Careful!" Jean yells from the next room. "Units are going fast!"

We both ignore her. I step into Beck's personal space and wrap my arms around him. "What does your gut say?"

He rests his head on my shoulder. "My gut wants lunch. And my gut says this place isn't the one. Even if the commute is pretty great."

"Fifteen minutes to the practice facility?"

He hugs me a little tighter. "And nineteen minutes to you and Charlie."

My heart skips a beat. The last six months have been the best of my life. I'd forgotten what companionship feels like, but that's what we have together. Even when our schedules don't align, we're still there for each other in all the ways that count.

Which is why I take a deep breath. "I have another idea."

"Hmm?" He releases me. "About apartments? Or lunch?"

"Neither. What if you moved to Erie?"

Beck's blue eyes widen. "Wait. What are you suggesting?"

"Move in with *me*." I lean in and kiss him on the jaw.

He freezes. "Really? You mean that?"

"Do I say things I don't mean? This is not a drill. You'd have a better commute, free rent. We could try it out."

He steps back and stares at me, and the look I see on his face isn't the one I was hoping for. "Forest, I don't think it can work like that."

My heart drops. "Why not?"

"You want to *try* it." His blue eyes look sad. "But I'm like a dog at the pound who wants a forever home. I can't be casual about moving in with you. I can't just *try it out*."

Oh, shit. I've really fucked up now. "Honey, no." I caress his jaw. "*You're* not the experiment. I already know I love you. When I said *try it out*, I meant the house. The commute. Not the relationship."

"Oh," he says, and looks away.

"...Because you're a keeper, and I'd like to keep you close to me. I wouldn't ask you to move in if I thought it wouldn't work between us."

He takes a deep breath. "In that case, I accept. I like your house. I *love* you. And you're shaving a lot of drive time off my week."

I step closer and pull him against my chest. "The booty calls will be a lot more frequent."

He kisses me on the jaw. "Do you want to sleep on this idea? Maybe you need to think it through. It's a big change."

"For you?"

His gaze snaps back to mine. "Well, no. Easy as rolling off a log. But all I'd have to do is pack up my snow-globe collection and take down my posters. I don't have a mortgage or a kid to take care of."

I put a hand on the center of his chest. "This isn't the first time I had this thought. I promise you that I've already had a chance to overthink it."

He grins. "Aw, you sexy beast."

"So I don't need to sleep on it. All I need to sleep on is *you*." Then I grab the front of his jacket and kiss him. I make it a good one.

"Gentlemen?" Jean the loud realtor strides into the room, and we break our kiss. "Ooh! Does this mean good news?"

"It does, but not for you," Beck says, stepping back. "This isn't the right place to call home, but thank you for your time."

She frowns. "Are you sure? Because if you change your mind..."

"I won't ever change my mind," I say.

Beck throws me a hot smile over his shoulder, and I already know I made the right decision.

The
End

THE HOCKEY GUYS

The New Guy

I'm Your Guy

The Last Guy on Earth

IN THE WORLD OF *TRUE NORTH*

Roommate

HELLO GOODBYE

Goodbye Paradise

Hello Forever

FROM THE *IVY YEARS* SERIES

The Understatement of the Year

WITH ELLE KENNEDY

Him (Him #1)

Us (Him #2)

Epic (Him #2.5)

Top Secret

WITH LAUREN BLAKELY

The Best Men

For more hockey check out:

THE BROOKLYN BRUISERS & BROOKLYN HOCKEY SERIES (MF)

Rookie Move

Hard Hitter

Pipe Dreams

Brooklynaire

Overnight Sensation

Superfan

Sure Shot

Bombshells

Must Love Hockey

Shenanigans

Love Lessons

NEW YORK LEGENDS (MF)

Thrown for a Loop

Big Stick Energy

THE IVY YEARS

The Year We Fell Down (MF)

The Year We Hid Away (MF)

The Understatement of the Year (MM)

The Shameless Hour (MF)

The Fifteenth Minute (MF)

Extra Credit (Mixed)